SUSPICIOUS BEHAVIOR

"Tell Abraham about the boat that does not fish," Carlos urged.

Yulanov seemed only too happy to have the opportunity to continue to vent. "One morning I go back same place where I have been fishing many days but Chinese are anchored right over place Yulanov marked with flag. When Yulanov tell them they are poaching, they tell him to go away."

Acosta confirmed Yulanov's story. "Big boat," he repeated, ". . . like Viktor says, like a trawler." Then he looked at Carlos. "Viktor is right when he says it looks like a fishing boat, but it does not act like one."

"Tell him about the net they put out," Carlos pushed.

The light was such that it was hard to tell exactly what Viktor Yulanov looked like. The veranda's half-moon shadows conspired to conceal his features, but the smoldering resentment was evident in his voice. "When Yulanov get close to Chinese boat, they use loudspeaker. They tell Yulanov to go away. They tell Yulanov they have nets and longlines out, but Yulanov not see a longline reel on deck. That net, it's not like any net Yulanov see before. It is made of some kind of metal wire material. Radio beacons attached to it . . ."

eulogy. "So, what about him?" I asked.

Arnold seemed a tad more than slightly dismayed that I hadn't kept up with the news of my classmates. "You haven't heard?"

"Heard about what?" Arnold can be a bit irritating at times.

"Tyler's yacht, the *Baja Lady*, disappeared off the coast of Baja California Sur somewhere near Bahia Magdalena a couple of weeks ago," he said.

Given the nature of the information Love Handles was passing along, is it necessary to mention that at that point in our conversation he was rasping every word? It made me wonder what he would have sounded like if he had been passing along news of the *Titanic*.

While Arnold rambled on, I listened politely and attentively. I'm rather good at both. Being a good listener allows me to drink while I'm listening. The aforementioned attributes are gentlemanly qualities which have nothing to do with all too many days spent at Forest Academy in Biloxi in my youth. Good ole FA is the same rather stodgy prep school attended by my stepfather and his father before him. Those qualities, if in fact I still possess them, are solely the result of many years spent living in the Furnace family abode and abiding by Furnace family standards.

During my reflections on days gone by, Arnold was elaborating at length on what he knew about Tyler Rowland's misfortune and where he had obtained his information. I don't know why I was taking notes—but I was. Most of his information, he said, came from one or two obscure news items in San Diego and Los Angeles newspapers, plus a phone call from some of his "friends."

While Arnold plodded on, I was quietly resolving to do my own research, perform my own analysis, and draw my own conclusions about Rowland's final hours. Caveat: If and when I found the time and if and when I was inclined to do so.

Reflecting back on that conversation, I have no way of knowing whether Love Handles finally ran out of things to talk about or his mouth was exhausted. He concluded our little palaver by thanking me again for my help and hanging up. Moments later I had put through another call, this time to my own office at Furnace Station. Dara snatched up the phone before the second ring.

Let me explain a bit about Dara Crawford. Dara is a genuine treasure. I have had her insured as such. She can solve any problem, anywhere, anytime, under any circumstances, with or without my assistance. I would propose marriage if she did not already have a live-in weight-lifter boyfriend on steroids. In any takeover attempt, it would not be his mass of muscles that would concern me, it would be his emotional stability after years of ingesting all those pharmaceuticals.

"Furnace Station Oceanic Research Center," she announced. "Abraham Furnace's office."

"You forgot to mention the Abraham Furnace the Third part," I reminded her.

R. KARL LARGENT

THE
BAJA
CONSPIRACY

LEISURE BOOKS NEW YORK CITY

A LEISURE BOOK®

May 2002

Published by

Dorchester Publishing Co., Inc.
276 Fifth Avenue
New York, NY 10001

ISBN 0-8439-5015-3

The name "Leisure Books" and the stylized "L" with design are trademarks of Dorchester Publishing Co., Inc.

Printed in the United States of America.

Visit us on the web at www.dorchesterpub.com.

THE
BAJA
CONSPIRACY

Journal No. 1

Friday, May 29

It was Friday and I was doing a friend a favor. For the record, I like to do friends favors, especially when it gets me out of the office on a picture-perfect May day. William Taft Arnold, better known as "Love Handles Bill" in our days at Stanford, had called the previous afternoon and asked for help. He needed, he said, a down and dirty appraisal of three fifties-vintage fishing trawlers moored at a run-down set of docks near Seal Point, north of Los Padres National Forest.

According to my former roomie, the aging vessels had been proffered as collateral by one of his oldest customers and he hated to say no without knowing just how bad the floaters really were. And, since

R. Karl Largent

Seal Point was a long way from Los Angeles and much closer to my native San Francisco, it was both easier and faster for me to drive down the coast, make a few notes, take a few snapshots, and fax the results to Bill at his office. It was the kind of assignment a man likes to have on a Friday—a great way to get away from the flurry of Friday meetings.

Let me back up here. The truth is, I figure I owe Bill a favor or two. I was the one who hung him with the nickname Love Handles. Parts of him tended then, and probably still do, to hang out over his belt. Consequently, the name stuck.

I found the rust buckets just exactly where Love Handles said they would be. I looked them over, took a few pictures, talked to a couple of the locals hanging around the docks, eventually worked my way back to Moss Beach, and found a place that charged three dollars a page to relay what I had learned. It was only after I was back in the car, grumbling about the ways the locals hosed the tourists, that I decided to call L. H. at his office and add a verbal postscript. I had forgotten to pass along the comments of the locals.

The woman answering his phone announced that her name was Shane. She hissed the "Ms." part of it. I had a mental picture of someone with the mind-set of a U.S. marshal in the witness protection program. Obviously, Ms. Shane was a woman determined not to let anyone or anything interfere with her pet bank officer. But after I dutifully revealed my name, rank, and reason for calling, she

2

informed me she would "see if Mr. Arnold was available." I didn't tell Love Handles, but Ms. Shane wasn't doing his bank's community relations program justice. She sounded like an annoyed shareholder who had just discovered that one of the officers of the institution was wasting time on matters other than business.

William Taft Arnold came on the line affable, effusive, and thanking me for my quick response. He had already read and digested my fax. "I take it you weren't impressed?" he concluded.

"Rust held together by rivets," I assessed. "I didn't even bother to fax you the photos of the worst one."

Apparently, the eight pages of fax had been enough. Before I had even finished my clipped condemnation of the tendered collateral, he was on to other things. He glided through the two or three years since the last time we had exchanged pleasantries, updating me on a list of fraternity brothers who had either gone on to their last big bonus payout or had somehow managed to grab other headlines. "I suppose you heard about Tyler Rowland?" he finally asked.

I had to admit that I hadn't. I did not confess that a quick flip through my mental card index yielded *nada*—no recollection of who or what Rowland was. The name meant nothing to me. Love Handle's cadre of college-gleaned friends and acquaintances embraced a far bigger circle on the Stanford campus than mine ever did.

Would I sound like I was whining if I said I had

studied while Love Handles partied? In other words, it was no surprise that I had no idea who he was talking about. "Tyler who?" I asked.

"Surely you remember Tyler Rowland," Love Handles chided. "He married the right girl. His brother-in-law appointed him president of Unitrieve a couple of years ago. CEO's can do that sort of thing, you know."

"Unitrieve," I repeated. The name sounded vaguely familiar but I couldn't say why. Maybe I had read something about it. Maybe I had heard the name at one of Roger's meetings. Or maybe it just sounded like something that I, as Director of Operations at Furnace Station Oceanic Research Center, was supposed to be familiar with. "Doesn't ring a bell."

"Supersecret, high-tech stuff," Arnold guaranteed me. I was suddenly remembering that William Taft Arnold, boy bank executive, was the one who always seemed to rasp his words when he thought he had something important enough to rasp about. "Our boy Tyler has become a certified high roller," he confided. Then he added, "Obviously not the first in our class to do so, but he has certainly become a staple in the San Diego gossip columns, and every now and then he even gets a mention in *The Wall Street Journal*."

Whether he knew it or not, Love Handles was flipping back and forth between the present and past tense. There were several "hads" sprinkled into what was fast beginning to sound like a banker's

Dara gave me her patented rock-opera laugh and waited. She knew that silence was an effective way of forcing me to get down to business. "Any calls?" I finally asked.

"Nothing that can't wait until Monday. You're blowing your cover, though. I've been telling everyone you were already gone for the weekend."

"Good. I shall maintain the appropriate low profile. Before you go, however, see what you can find out about an old classmate of mine by the name of Tyler Rowland. Also look up a company by the name of Unitrieve. It's located in San Diego. Put anything you find in a file folder and leave it on my desk. I'll stop by the office on my way home and pick it up."

There was silence on the other end. I think Dara was holding her breath, no doubt concerned that I might be so end-of-the-day insensitive as to tack an even more time-consuming task onto my initial request. When I had nothing further to offer, she gave me her standard "ta ta," wished me a pleasant weekend, and hung up.

By the time I had nestled the receiver back in its cradle, I finally remembered where I had heard the name Unitrieve. Unitrieve was the firm that had recently been approved by the DOD as an alternate software supplier on the new Pony submersible we were under contract to design for the navy. Concurrent with that announcement, my younger brother Roger was appointed to Unitrieve's board of directors. You don't suppose that has anything to do with the fact that he and Rowland were both in the same class at Harvard? Nawwww.

Back in the car again and headed for the city, the names Tyler Rowland and Unitrieve kept muscling their way back into my thoughts. Missing yacht. *Baja*. Intriguing stuff.

Even though I am a bona fide, reasonably healthy, marginally intelligent forty-year-old bachelor living in good old Baghdad by the Bay, I have an assortment of bohemian friends who will vouch for the fact that I don't exactly live a life of bacchanalian revelry. Most nights, this particular Friday being no exception, I escape from the city and head for my Sausalito sanctuary with its view of the bay. On a clear night the view doesn't get any better.

My abode happens to be constructed on the side of a hill (as is most everything else in Sausalito), a circumstance which prompted one young lady I occasionally escort to observe that I am seldom on the level. Note that I have dated her less frequently since she said that.

At any rate, I had stopped by my office at the Research Center, gathered up the papers Dara had left on my desk, paid a brief visit to the Venice Delicatessen on Bridgeway for a carryout, and headed home. I had, as I frequently do, rewarded myself with a corn beef on rye liberally slathered with bourbon mustard. I have learned that, coupled with an ice-cold Dos Equis, it is a perfect way to bid *adieu* to the workweek.

After checking my answering machine, I sat down with Dara's reports and proceeded to make myself a little more familiar with the life and times of one Tyler Rowland. Why was I interested? Was it because he was an alum of The Farm? Was it because I vaguely recalled that Rowland's firm was an approved supplier to the Center? Was it because Roger was on the board at Unitrieve? Who knows? I tend to get overly involved or carried away sometimes. I once sat down with little more than a mild curiosity about road racing and ended up purchasing and having a race-ready 427 Shelby Cobra shipped up from Long Beach.

As it turned out, Dara had rounded up reading matter from the *San Francisco Examiner*, *The Wall Street Journal*, and the *Los Angeles Times*. Plus she had pasted one of those little yellow sticky notes to the outside of the folder. (If Dara had been a man she would have used a paperclip.) The note informed me she wasn't through. She promised to comb the Internet to see what else she could find and fax me anything that looked interesting. As Benny, the bartender at Ruby's Diner on Bay Street would say, "Ain't technology wonderful?"

A quick scan of what Dara had dug up corroborated much of what Love Handles had told me. According to the *WSJ*, Tyler Rowland was president of Unitrieve. His brother-in-law, Jacob Hake, was CEO, and Unitrieve was a San Diego-based DOD supplier with cyber world connections. The article went on to say that Unitrieve had become a heavy hitter in the world of Defense Department contractors when it was awarded a mucho-million-dollar contract back in the mid-nineties.

That contract called for them to message archival but highly sensitive military info into something the folks at the Pentagon could use on their new computers. Apparently, Rowland's firm had performed admirably. Since then the company had been the recipient of numerous bigger and better DOD contracts. Sales for the current year were expected to hit several billion dollars.

At that point I made a mental note to talk to Roger, my brother, about the degree of our involvement with Unitrieve and promptly forgot about work. I had turned my attention to the Dos Equis.

Saturday

Furnace Standard, I admit somewhat modestly, is, even by today's fast-track standards, a rather successful business endeavor. It was founded in 1855 by Abraham Furnace. Whatever it did in those days it doesn't do now. Today its efforts are related to shipbuilding, real estate holdings, undersea mining, and my little niche of the company, designing and building a variety of submersibles, primarily for the United States Navy, a few academic institutions, and an occasional salvage contractor.

My younger brother, also adopted, who goes by the name of Roger, is the CEO of this money-generating sprawl. We were adopted because Galen and Leslie Furnace were unable to have children and the Furnace clan was insistent that the company's leadership lineage be continued. All of which is real swell by me because I was a poverty-stricken four-year-old orphan haunting the halls of Saint Vincent's Villa when Galen and Leslie discovered me and made me a faux Furnace.

However, that is the end of what might have been a first-rate fairy tale. Somewhere along the line, between prep school days in Biloxi and undergraduate years at Stanford, someone in Stepfather Galen's empire recognized my shortcomings and limitations. My star, they decided, was destined to twinkle in some other capacity than leading the corporate fortunes of the fifth-generation Furnace domain.

Little A. J., it seems, had developed an interest not in becoming an industrial giant, but in submarines. In time, submarines became more clearly defined as submersibles and Stepelder Galen, with brother Roger's help, formed Furnace Station Oceanic Research Center. I had a home.

When that happened, I was told in no uncertain terms to go play in the water. I have been doing so ever since.

Like I said, FSORC (the F is silent), as it is known to those who have exhibited even a modest interest in what we do, now embraces deep-sea salvage work for both our and other governments and private interests as well. When we aren't occupied with those endeavors, we design, build, and test a line of deep-sea salvage vehicles and recovery vehicles.

11

At any rate, you now have some idea why I don't exactly feel compelled to jump up on Saturday morning and make a political appearance at the office. I view Bro Roger's indulgence of my lax behavior as one of the many benefits of owning nearly twenty percent of the outstanding stock of the parent company and being the head muckety-muck of the FSORC division.

I rolled over in bed, clicked on the television, and surfed to CNN. Before I could become absorbed in what was happening on other world stages, my phone was ringing.

"Hello," I grunted. Sometimes I find it difficult to hide my annoyances, petty or otherwise.

"Are you alone?" Roger asked.

"Would I have answered the telephone if I wasn't?"

After saying, "Just wanted to be certain I wasn't interrupting anything," Roger injected his usual Saturday morning conversational pause. I have always assumed he does so in order to allow me time to shoosh a bevy of lusting lovelies out of my bedroom. As I have pointed out to supersecretary Dara many times, it is my observation that married men usually entertain highly erroneous concepts of the comings and goings in a bachelor's bedroom.

Even so, Roger and I understand each other. More important, we understand each other's priorities. And if that isn't enough, we genuinely like each other. Roger, Dara likes to point out, has his fecal material together (honest, that's the way she says it). He is married, has two sons, the older of which will no doubt someday be the ringmaster of the ongoing Furnace circus, but even more important in this familial scheme of things, Roger allows me to be me. In return, I vote my shares the way he tells me to vote at the annual stockholders' meeting. The system works; the value of my holdings improves each year, and for the most part, Roger leaves me to my own devices. He does, however, expect me to answer my telephone. Which only proves there is no such thing as a perfect world.

"What's on your mind?" I inquired.

"What's on your schedule today?" This is standard Saturday morning repartee. Roger, I have learned, answers questions with questions. I think that must be a Harvard MBA thing.

"Little A. J. is planning to play with his Cobra. Why?"

Roger also tends to pause before he tells me something he knows I don't want to hear. I waited. Finally he said, "How about meeting me at my office at one o'clock." Before I could complain, he was telling me why. "Late yesterday afternoon I received a telephone call from a man by the name of George Templeton. Templeton is the chief financial officer and senior vice president of Unitrieve."

"Not to mention the fact that you are on the board at Unitrieve," I said. I say those kind of things to Bro Roger because I like to needle him. It also shows that I read the memos he sends me.

I heard Roger sigh on his end of the line. Oh,

what a burden it must be to have to tolerate a less than respectful relative who owns twenty percent of the company.

"Unitrieve?" I repeated. It was one of those names that has NASDAQ written all over it. "Did he say what he wanted to talk about?"

"He did, but I would rather not go into it over the telephone," Roger said. "It's much too convoluted. Besides, I want you to hear it cold. If you have as much trouble making sense of it as I did, then I don't think we're going to be able to do Mr. Templeton much good."

"Then why have a meeting?"

"Be a good brother and do as I say, damn it."

Roger hung up and I got up. Only because I knew I could spend the rest of the morning cavorting around my garage, casting frequent covetous glances at the 427. Until I stepped outside and managed an agonizing appraisal of what looked like a sky in mourning, I had actually considered taking the body glove off and driving the Cobra to my one-o'clock meeting. By noon, however, my fears and suspicions had been confirmed; it was raining in Sausalito and it was even darker over the city.

Actually, it wasn't raining all that hard. But even a minor drizzle can curtail all thought of taking the Cobra out of its environmentally controlled sanctuary. I will admit that it did get wet once. I washed the beast. However, I have since discovered a waterless cleaning method and have vowed it will never be wet again.

14

All above aside, the morning did pass and at ten minutes to one I was whipping my wallet out of my pocket and flashing my ID at the security officer in the lobby of the Furnace Building. A large painting of a scowling octogenarian is hung as the focal point of that lobby. It is a portrait of Abraham Galen Furnace II, the man who would have been my great-grandfather if I had really been born a Furnace.

Perhaps I should also mention that Great-grand-stepsire Abraham is also the man who constructed the office monument to Furnace family immortality on Sutter Street in the SFO financial district. The building is both tall enough and situated in such a fashion that you can see over the Embarcadero to San Francisco Bay from Roger's office. I like that. I'm never very comfortable if I can't see water.

I took the elevator up to Roger's office and even though I was a few minutes early, discovered that George Templeton had already arrived. Templeton may have been the CFO of Unitrieve but he looked like the loser on *Divorce Court*. He was appropriately attired, clean-shaven, hair slicked down, but behind his designer glasses he was falling apart. He could have been the poster boy for hypertension. His eyes were mouse nervous, his voice was edgy, and I decided then and there that I didn't want this guy for a dive buddy.

Roger seated us at his burled walnut conference table, handled the introductions, smiled somewhat disapprovingly at my attire of Dockers, deck shoes, and a cardinal red sweatshirt with (what else?)

Stanford emblazoned across the chest. One of my former girlfriends gave me the shirt.

When I shook hands with Templeton, his hand was damp. Nothing profuse, mind you, but the kind of thing you notice when you exchange greetings with someone you know who worries a lot.

Templeton didn't need any prodding to get started. He apologized lavishly for intruding on our weekend and thanked us for finding the time to meet with him.

"A mutual friend, Sebastian Frank, suggested that I contact you," Templeton began. At the mention of Frank's name Roger was nodding knowingly. The name meant nothing to me. (I am terrible with names. I forgot the name of my date once.) Still, I had the feeling that the mere fact Frank was lateraling Templeton and his problem to the Furnace brothers was corporate recognition that this was a problem we could handle. "It seems," Templeton explained, "that our president, Tyler Rowland, is missing."

What was it Yogi Berra said, something about it being déjà vu all over again? Tyler Rowland's name was like one of those dolls you knock over and it pops right up again. At the moment I wasn't quite sure I knew what to do. I was (a) reluctant to mention my conversation with Love Handles and (b) equally reluctant to admit I had been reading the file on Unitrieve the night before. Neither of which presented me with a problem, because there were a host of obvious questions I could ask him, starting with, had he reported his president's disappearance to the police? Who, how hard, and how long had they already searched for him? And even the question, did Rowland have a history of hiding from his CFO? What I really wanted to ask him was why was he screwing up my Saturday with a problem that there were numerous agencies better trained than Roger and I to handle?

Instead I listened while Roger went through a litany of questions to determine if Sebastian Frank had sent Templeton to the right place. "What makes you think my brother can help you?" Roger finally asked. It had suddenly gone from Roger and me to plain old me.

"Because," Templeton explained, "we have every reason to believe Mr. Rowland was aboard his yacht, the *Baja Lady*, when he disappeared. And your brother has a reputation for . . ."

Roger looked at me, and because we grew up together and got in trouble together, I had little trouble detecting the nearly imperceptible questioning shrug. That shrug meant, *It's your turn, A. J., say something intelligent.*

I rose to the occasion. "If that's the case," I said, "have you informed the Coast Guard of your suspicions?"

Templeton hemmed and hawed. "It would be better," he finally admitted, "if the disappearance of Mr. Rowland was not confirmed at this time."

Roger said he understood. I don't know why he said it unless it was one of those corporate things only presidents of large corporations can understand. I certainly didn't. If the president of Furnace Standard (that would be Roger) were missing and the last time anyone saw him he was in his boat, never mind what kind, I would not be concerned about public knowledge and confirmation of his status. I would be looking for all the "find Roger" help I could get. Besides, weren't the papers already reporting the Rowland yacht incident?

"Maybe we better go back and start at the beginning," I suggested.

Templeton asked if he could smoke, obtained Roger's approval, lit up, and began. I had the feeling he wished he did not have to tell us what was troubling him. If Roger had just agreed that we would help him look for his boss without a display of corporate laundry, Templeton would doubtless have been happier. I think he was concerned about a Unitrieve board member knowing something that presidents and CEO's usually don't tell the board.

"As you no doubt already know, two years ago, Unitrieve was awarded the multibillion-dollar CARTO contract," Templeton said.

Roger was doing his *I know* nod again and I had to interrupt. "Bad assumption, Mr. Templeton," I said. "Suppose you explain a little bit about this CARTO contract."

George Templeton, still edgy, still apprehensive, swallowed hard and explained that CARTO was a Pentagon contract that vaulted Unitrieve into the realm of big-league cyber stuff. "We agreed to design a whole new language based on the concept of random numerical syllabification. Part of that contract stipulated that Unitrieve would convert certain ultrasensitive archival documents to the new language, as well as author field sensitive software that would be known only to the DOD."

"In other words, you agreed to do some programming for the government," I said.

Templeton appeared to be somewhat dismayed that I wasn't more impressed than I was. Maybe I would have been more impressed if I had understood what he meant by random numerical syllabification. When he got around to continuing, he said, "The magnitude of the program is such that, in terms of both manpower and capital, it has taxed Unitrieve's resources. And it did it from the day we were awarded the contract. The Pentagon knew we had the brainpower. But in the final analysis it was Tyler Rowland's reputation for getting the job done that was the deciding factor in Unitrieve getting the contract."

"So where does the project stand now?" I asked.

"We have delivered the base text and unveiled the completed random numerical syllabification concept for Pentagon officials," Templeton said, "... and we have initiated the first phase of the translation and conversion of the ultrasensitive archival material."

"Which I assume means Unitrieve is due a modest progress payment. Correct?" For some reason I felt compelled to show Senor Templeton I was not just another corporate pretty boy. I couldn't let Roger do all the impressive stuff.

"A sizable one," he admitted; "over two hundred and fifty million dollars. That brings the CARTO total paid to Unitrieve to date the sum of one point one billion."

"The coffers are bulging, then," I observed. "Must be a good feeling."

"Not really," Templeton said. "In the process of making certain we were complying, we incurred a great deal of unanticipated debt. Our suppliers, hands outstretched, were lined up the day the Pentagon transferred the money to our account."

"I assume there was some left over for all the good and faithful servants," I said.

Templeton had a rueful look on his face. Then he made a surprising admission. "Not as much as we had hoped. There was enough of a shortfall that Mr. Rowland went to Washington and asked the Pentagon to renegotiate the contract. They refused."

I looked at Roger. We were in agreement. George Templeton wasn't acting or talking like the chief financial officer of a firm reporting sales in the neighborhood of two billion dollars for the previous year. Every chief financial officer has to go through basic money management classes when they start their climb up the corporate ladder. It's there that they receive an age-old cosmetic surgery: the lips are removed and a mouth zipper is installed. Templeton was either a poor CFO who talked too much or he really was as nervous and upset about the disappearance of his leader as his demeanor indicated.

"Back to what it is you think we can do for you," Roger reminded him.

"A number of us want you to find Mr. Rowland," Templeton repeated.

"I still don't understand why you don't go to the police or the Coast Guard or some agency that is geared to take on this kind of assignment," Roger said. "Explain that this is the kind of thing that makes investors nervous. They'll understand and they'll be discreet."

I was frowning, wondering if Roger really believed what he was saying.

Templeton lowered his voice. "Sebastian Frank said that you and your staff"—he was looking straight at me—"had been able to recover certain very important items for his firm on two different occasions."

Suddenly I remembered who Sebastian Frank was. Well, not exactly Frank himself; I never met him. But I did remember his firm, Depth Finder. Depth Finder had paid FSORC a handsome sum of money to locate a couple of sunken vessels on which his firm had purchased salvage rights. It was SOP—the insurance firms were simply trying to recover some of their loss. In other words, Sebastian Frank was a big-time risk taker. The way he saw it, an unlikely long shot could pay big dividends. He was betting he could recover and salvage the contents of a downed ship and in the process show a tidy profit.

I like people who think like that, I just don't like to pay for their habit. On the two instances he had contracted FSORC for assistance, it had paid off. The odds against three in a row were high.

"Those were ships," I reminded Templeton, "not individuals. It's been my experience that ships are easier to find. They are bigger and they don't move around as easily."

Templeton gave me one of those looks accountants are prone to exhibit when they don't understand. I felt compelled to explain. "It's like this: After a ship sinks, the vagaries of the ocean bottom can move it around. But not as much," I quickly added, "as a man who doesn't want to be found. I get the feeling your president doesn't want to be found."

Templeton scowled, shrugged, stole a glance at Roger, and ventured on, obviously unimpressed by my meager attempt at homilizing. "The last time I saw Tyler Rowland," he said, "he was on his boat or yacht or whatever you call vessels of that size."

I'm not usually paranoid, but from the way Templeton was curling his lip when he was looking at me, I was getting the distinct impression that he didn't care for the little obstacles I kept throwing out. When I asked if he could describe Rowland's yacht, he admitted he did not know the difference between a cutter and a scow—or care. All he knew, he said, was that two weeks ago he was standing on the pier at the marina and Rowland was standing on the deck of the *Baja Lady*, telling him he was going to "take her out." Then Templeton added, "No one has seen him since."

"No one?" I repeated. The first thing I think of when someone says something like "no one has seen him," it could well mean "no one is willing to admit they have seen him."

Templeton was adamant. "No one."

An hour later Templeton was gone and Roger and I retired to the small but well-appointed apartment adjacent to his office. On several occasions Bro Roger has felt obliged to confide that the lavishly furnished four rooms plus bath are nothing more than signs of his position. As a brother I can accept that. Somewhat. As a stockholder, it seems ostentatious and uncalled for.

Observations: One: It does not seem to matter if the day runs too long or the meeting the following morning starts too early, Roger does not enjoy staying at the aforementioned apartment. Two: I am not married but I have stayed at the apartment on several occasions. I recall the time my Sausalito plumbing had to be replumbed, and another when I wanted to impress a young lady with the view of the bay from Roger's office. As I recall, she said, "Gee. Look, A. J., is that the water?" Amorous intentions squelched.

The post-Templeton powwow revolved around two questions. In both cases Roger did the problematic articulation. I did the prodigious pondering.

Question number one. Was there any reason for Furnace Standard, its subsidiaries, or resources (in this case, me) to become involved in the search for Unitrieve's president, one Tyler Rowland? The answer seemed fairly obvious to me. A little less so to Roger. He was, after all, on the board at Unitrieve.

Question number two: What did George Templeton, boy accountant, have up his sleeve? Quite obviously, either Templeton had not been totally honest with us or he had approached the dynamic duo of Roger and Abraham without knowing the full story. The former could be branded shameful. The latter, shamefully foolish. Conclusion? There had to be a reason why Unitrieve people were unwilling to go to the proper authorities to help them find their leader. Put a big fat X under the "why" column.

The conclusions we had summarily reached (sort of) in dispatching the first two questions made the answer to the third and final one fairly obvious. There was no reason for Furnace Standard, FSORC, or any of its personnel to become involved. Roger, in his finest presidential fashion, instructed me to call Templeton the following morning and inform him of our decision.

"Aye, aye, sir," I said. Roger doesn't like it when I salute.

Monday

I feel certain my adopted father loved me. Nevertheless, it is not easy to forget the night I overheard him tell my adopted grandfather that there were times when the best way to describe me was "not quite what we had hoped for." That frequently comes to mind when I am doing what someone tells me to do.

Templeton had left several phone numbers where he could be reached. I had chosen not to call him the day prior for the simple reason I seldom conduct company business on Sundays. Sundays are mine.

The number I chose, however, was that of his home in Menlo Park. Understand my reasoning. It was Monday morning. It was early. No one is prepared for Monday mornings. So, what better way to get even with someone for ruining a Saturday than calling them early Monday morning and delivering the response they are least prepared to handle?

It was early enough when I called that I figured boy George would still be getting ready for the workday. My reasoning was predicated on the fact that if Unitrieve's chief financial officer was the animal I had him made out to be, he would get my "no further interest" response just about the time he was sitting down to his oatmeal. Well-conceived plan. Poor timing.

Someone picked up the phone on the third ring. Whoever or whatever it was that was handling the phone chores at the Templeton digs had an unpleasant voice wrapped around a one-word greeting, "Yeah?"

I had just turned onto Lincoln Boulevard after

successfully negotiating morning rush hour traffic on the bridge. Buoyed with my first success of the day, I was tempted to tell the person on the other end of the line that a more appropriate response might be "Templeton residence," followed by "to whom did you wish to speak?"

Instead I kept it simple. "George Templeton, please."

"Who is this?" the voice growled. What else was there for me to think? I must have misdialed the devil's instrument and was now in direct contact with Grunts Anonymous.

Even so, I decided to wait and see what would happen. I was still waiting for Templeton to come on the line when suddenly the voice showed signs of marginal intelligence; it added two new words to its vocabulary. "Who's calling?"

I was tempted to hang up on Mr. Surly, but good manners and honesty are compulsions with us Furnace boys. "A. J. Furnace," I replied.

"This is Captain Powers, San Francisco Police." Then he added the word "homicide." "What did you say your name was again?" he grunted.

"Furnace," I repeated. "Abraham Furnace. I was calling Mr. Templeton to inform him—"

Powers cut me off. "How come your name is on a piece of paper I found beside the phone next to Templeton's bed?"

"He was probably expecting me to call him first thing this morning," I volunteered.

"About what?"

I was about to reveal the purpose of George's visit to the Furnace Standard building the previous Saturday when I recalled what Templeton had said about low profiling the subject of Tyler Rowland's disappearance. I had nothing invested in Unitrieve, but there is an old saying, "A loose lip can sink a corporate ship." "He asked me to call him," I said.

Note: I live by the truth. But one needs to understand, truth is elastic. It's not always what you say. Many times it is what you leave out that is most important.

Powers wasn't that easy to put off. "Call him about what?" he insisted.

I told Powers my call was related to the fact that Unitrieve was a supplier to FSORC, something he could check and verify, and that my call was related to business.

Despite the fact that I was dancing with the truth when I told Powers the reason for my call, the tone of my voice must have lacked a certain veracity. Why do I say that? Simple—he didn't believe me. At precisely nine minutes after nine o'clock, my office phone rang. It was Dara. She was informing me that the receptionist at the desk in the FSORC lobby was being confronted by one Captain Leland Powers of the San Francisco Police, homicide division. Then, as only Dara can, she added, "They finally caught up with you, huh?"

I hung up, but only after telling Dara to have Pow-

ers sent up and reminding her that I Was Tarzan
and this was my jungle.

Captain Leland Powers looked like you would expect a homicide officer to look. The moment he
walked (in reality it was more of a belligerent me-
ander) into my office, two things were blatantly obvious. One, his wife picked out his clothes; obvious
because trousers, sport coat, shirt, and tie were co-
ordinated. Men don't know how to do that. Second,
he could sense it when someone or something he
was investigating didn't smell right.

"Have a seat, Captain," I said. I was eager to avoid
giving him the impression that I did not wish to talk
to him. There was a brief exchange of what for a
homicide officer must pass for pleasantries, followed by his inquiring into just exactly what it was
that FSORC did. I informed him that the F was silent
and that we designed, built, and tested submersibles. Presumably, that was all he needed or wanted
to know because he quickly skated from FSORC's
purpose to the untimely demise of George Templeton.

"Just exactly how well did you know him?" Powers grunted.

"One meeting," I said, "that's all, last Saturday at
my brother's office in the city. My brother was there;
he can vouch for everything I'm telling you."

Powers was a minimalist when it came to communication. Still, he managed to ask three questions in one. "What is your brother's name, why did

Templeton want to talk to you, and what was the conversation about?"

He had presented me with a challenge. Three in one. I attempted to answer it in the same fashion. "Roger," I said, "a business acquaintance suggested he contact us, and I'm afraid the reason he wanted to talk to us was never made quite clear."

Concerning that last point, perhaps I should mention that I do not lie well. On the other hand, there are times when no more than mediocre prevarication skills are necessary to achieve one's objectives. Apparently, this was one of those times. Powers appeared to be eager to get on with whatever homicide officers get on with.

"I assume, then, that conversation was business related," he finally said.

All of a sudden it seemed too easy. Powers was nodding, agreeing, and smiling. I watch a lot of detective movies; homicide officers don't do that. At that point I had to wonder how much Powers knew and how much he was trying to see how much I knew.

"Business," I nodded. It was my best confirming nod.

"Did it have anything to do with the fact that Tyler Rowland, Unitrieve's president, hasn't been seen by anyone in his company for a couple of weeks?"

Would you think it terribly trite if at this point I said I was beginning to hear things that made me think the legendary cat was out of the proverbial bag? When Templeton talked to Bro Roger and me, he expressed concern about the ramifications if word of Unitrieve's disappearing prexy became common knowledge.

Powers already knew that. Was it conceivable that several folk already knew where Skippy had skipped and Templeton wasn't in on the joke? Or were folk simply pretending not to know when they really did? If so, why?

For the moment, though, I decided not to discuss Templeton's concern over Rowland's dematerialization. Why? Because one never knows what's behind these disappearing deals; maybe it's a simple matter of a guy going out on a two-week toot. Presidents of even bigger things than Unitrieve have pulled the old evaporation routine only to pop up later with a story that stockholders were willing to buy.

Powers was no doubt thinking about what else he wanted to ask me when I saw an opening. "My turn," I said. "Suppose you tell me how Templeton was murdered," I said.

"How did you know he was murdered?"

"A natural assumption since you're with homicide."

Powers scowled. "Somebody shot him. When, with what, and why, we don't know yet. We're just beginning our investigation."

Following Powers's proclamation concerning Templeton's untimely departure from planet Earth, he asked a few final questions. None of them were terribly penetrating, and I was able to respond without seeking Roger's counsel. Ostensibly, the good captain was satisfied; he thanked me and got up to take his leave. As he did I inquired whether or not I could leave town without telling him.

Powers looked at me as though he thought one of my spark plugs had misfired. I always feel foolish when I have to explain my ill-conceived little attempts at humor. "Isn't that what the police always say when they are through interrogating someone?"

Powers continued to scowl. "What the hell are you talking about?"

"Never mind," I said.

Considering what had happened earlier in the day, the rest of that particular Monday was uneventful until quitting time rolled around. It was at that point when Dara was endearing herself to me by regaling me with the recipe for broiled grouper marinated in lime juice. We had just reached the erotic stage where we were adding a clove of garlic when the phone rang. It was Roger.

Corporate presidents always call late in the day. If you are still in your office, it pleases them. So many green stamps or whatever go into your personnel file. If you are not, you may be next on the RIF list.

"Did you call Templeton?" he asked.

"I did," I said.

31

"We're not committed?"

"Perhaps we should be, but I think we've heard the last from Templeton," I said.

Roger seemed satisfied. Don't you just love it when you know something your boss doesn't?

Journal No. 2

Monday, June 1

The first Monday of each month is poker night. Despite the fact that my gambling skills usually allow at least two of my card-playing friends to view me as an annuity, I enjoy these sessions. Plus I knew that I would enjoy this one even more since I was no longer preoccupied with lingering doubts about the misfortunes of one George Templeton. After all, the entire event was behind me. Wasn't it?

I had driven home from my office through one traffic snarl after another with my thoughts seldom straying from the freaky scenario being played out at Unitrieve. "Forget it," that little voice was telling me; "close the book."

By the time I had digested the closing numbers

on Wall Street and rustled up a delightful meal of eggs scrambled in cream and butter, subsequently enriched with chunks of crabmeat, I was ready to trundle off to Ruben's digs. As I reached for the door to the garage, the phone rang.

There are times when I fervently wish that Alexander Graham Bell had never invented his invention. This was one of them. Nevertheless, I released my death grip on my bag of nickels, set my bottle of spirits with a French name on the telephone stand, and picked up the receiver.

"Hello," I said.

The voice on the other end of the line was feminine. Really, really feminine. She made "hello" sound like an invitation to happenings wicked and wanton. When I curtailed my fantasizing and started listening, I realized she was continuing. "My name is Amy Reed," she said. "I am a field representative with California Maritime—"

"I don't care who you are or who you work for," I interrupted, "I'll go anywhere you want to go. Do anything you want to do. Spend any amount it takes."

Amy Reed had a nice laugh. "I'm trying to reach one Abraham Furnace. You wouldn't happen to be him, would you?"

"If I wasn't I would have my name changed," I said. Then it occurred to me that she might think me even more appealing if I presented myself as serious. "What can I do for you?" I said. Hey, I was trying.

"You can look at your schedule," she said, "and tell me when you would have time for you and I to sit down for a chat." Then she added, "Preferably not at your office. Does that sound a bit arcane?"

"Not at all. Just tell me where and when."

She laughed again. "Aren't you the least bit curious what this is all about, Mr. Furnace?"

"Should I be?"

"It's customary. Suppose I tell you this concerns a Mr. Tyler Rowland. Are you familiar with Mr. Rowland?"

I was tempted to tell Amy Reed I knew everything there was to know about the man. If she wanted to talk about Tyler Rowland, she could find no better source. On the other hand, if she discovered that my introduction to Rowland 101 had occurred as recently as seventy-two hours ago, there was a chance she would disappear into the night. I couldn't take the chance. "What do you want to know about him?"

"Would you think me unprofessional if I told you I would rather not discuss this matter over the phone, Mr. Furnace?"

It was the second time I had heard that line in the last three days. "Not at all," I heard myself saying.

"Well, then, could I impose upon you to meet me somewhere? I'm not exactly familiar with the area, but I have a car and I can find my way around. Do you have a suggestion?"

I did, but I had the feeling it would kill a budding

35

relationship. I asked her if she was familiar with the Marina District. Amy said she could find it, so I suggested Turk's on Chestnut Street. We agreed on nine-thirty. I hung up, sprinted up the stairs to grab a quick shower, but will admit to being decidedly more intent on applying a liberal measure of my new aftershave.

How do I describe Amy Reed? Amy Reed turned out to be the mirror image of Lorrie Morgan, short, close-cropped blond hair and all. When I say "all" I mean "ALL." She had a Tiffany smile, a voice that sounded like she had borrowed it from Lauren Bacall, and the rigging of an expensive submersible.

She entered the room wearing a tweedy-looking ensemble that consisted of coat, skirt, and ivory-colored blouse. She had held the jewelry to a minimum, and there was nothing on the third finger left hand to indicate she had any enduring commitments. If there was a flaw in this fantasy, it was that she was carrying a laptop computer. She gave me an "aren't you glad you decided to meet me?" smile and sat down. I could tell she had practiced the smile and entrance routine; she was far too good at it for it to be a casual happening.

Before she had even straightened her skirt, she had further defused my amorous intents by whipping out a pair of horn-rim glasses. Damn. This lady really intended to work. For some reason, I was remembering that old aphorism, "Men seldom make passes at girls who wear glasses."

"It was very nice of you to meet me on such short notice, Mr. Furnace," she began. "You must be a very busy man. I called your office three times today. Each time you were in a meeting. Your secretary indicated you didn't even have time to take calls."

I made a mental note to have Dara shot at dawn and motioned for the waiter. Amy ordered a Manhattan, no special instructions, and I opted for a Black and White over shaved ice. By the time the man returned with the drinks we were into the subject of Tyler Rowland and Ms. Reed was informing me why Rowland was the topic *du jour*.

"You'll have to forgive me if some of this doesn't make sense to you, Mr. Furnace—"

"Call me A. J."

She smiled. The minute she did I found myself trying to think of other equally witty tidbits I could throw into our conversation. "All right A. J., what do you know about Unitrieve, Rowland, Templeton, and crew?"

"Probably not as much as you think I do," I admitted.

"Good, I like honesty. It saves time," she said. "But let's find out exactly what you do know." In the space of less than ten seconds Amy Reed had gone from sounding like Wonder Woman to an IRS auditor. The Manhattan was ignored, the glasses were on, the notebook computer was activated, and her fingers were poised to record everything I said.

R. Karl Largent

I held up my hand. "One moment." I took a sip of my scotch and leaned back in my chair a bit concerned. I had the sudden feeling that when you got on the discourse track with Amy Reed there was great wisdom in buckling your seat belt. "Suppose we start by you telling me why California Maritime is interested in Unitrieve," I said.

To my surprise, she seemed inclined to do so. "Are you familiar with the CARTO Project, Mr. Furnace?"

Small quandary. I wanted to remind Ms. Reed that she had agreed to call me A. J. That concern, however, was secondary to why we were even having this meeting. "As I recall, the CARTO Project involved something called random numerical syllabification." I purposely mumbled the project's purpose for two reasons. One, I wasn't certain I knew how to pronounce it. Two, I wanted Amy Reed to think I was cool. It must have worked, because at that point she took over.

"What I am about to tell you must be held in the strictest confidence," she began. (You hear that a lot in government work and places like Turk's Bistro.) The disarmingly attractive Ms. Reed was choosing her words carefully. "In the life cycle of corporate performance, Unitrieve's annual execution of its business plan over the last several years can best be described as erratic. This alarms us."

Eyes the color of Amy Reed's orbs are distracting. I was finding it difficult to concentrate. Nevertheless, I urged her to continue. "Suppose you explain

38

two things, one, who is 'us,' and two, the reason for your concern."

"Let's start with concerns. Plural. More than one," she corrected. "First and foremost, money. Unitrieve, as you no doubt know, is highly leveraged. If any one of their principal backers decided to call in their markers, Unitrieve could find itself in its death throes."

I did not know whether to say "No kidding" or "It's that serious, huh?" I decided on the latter. I thought it sounded more professional.

"Some of it, quite obviously, is our own fault. We were not careful enough in our original assessment of their performance capabilities or their staying power. In the latter, I am referring to their financial stability. The fact of the matter is, we did not dig deep enough."

I was suddenly beset with the disturbing feeling that this entire scenario was getting away from me. The enchanting Ms. Reed was working hard at elevating our budding relationship (at least in the business sense) to the second level, and I knew nothing about her. I only knew what she wanted me to know about her, her company, and how her company viewed Unitrieve. A less smitten man would probably have taken a step back and asked himself what in the name of the Federal Reserve was going on?

Instead I decide to barge in. "Would you think me terrible if I asked you what all of this has to do with me, Ms. Reed?"

Apparently, she didn't because she began to explain. "When we contacted Mr. Templeton and relayed our concerns, he advised us of Mr. Rowland's disappearance. I in turn advised my superiors, and they instructed me to have Mr. Templeton hire you to find Mr. Rowland."

I feel certain that at this juncture I must have been wearing the pained expression of a puppy not quite in tune with the concept of paper training. "Ah," I said, "that's where the confusion comes in. You think Templeton hired me. Is that what you think?"

Amy Reed was nodding.

"After he left your office Saturday, Mr. Templeton called me, just as he was instructed to do. He said you had agreed to help him look for Rowland."

"Let's go back to square one," I suggested. "This time I'll tell the story the way I understand it."

The lady pushed herself away from the table and studied her drink as I started. "Unitrieve is heavily leveraged. Your firm, California Maritime, holds one or more of those levers. Right?"

Another nod.

"Unitrieve's performance in the marketplace has your people concerned about their money. That concern was heightened when Rowland disappeared several weeks ago. You contacted Templeton and told him to hire me to find Rowland. He called you after he talked to us and said it was a *fait accompli*. Did I leave anything out?"

"Only why are you acting as if this is all news to you."

"I'm acting that way because it *is* news to me," I said. "At the conclusion of Saturday's tête-à-tête between Templeton, my brother Roger, and me, we told George boy we would get back to him on Monday morning to let him know if we had decided to help him in the hunt for Tyler Rowland. True to my word, I made that call, from my car phone, on my way to work. Said call was intercepted by Captain Leland Powers of the San Francisco Police. When he informed me he was with the homicide division, I had a sneaking suspicion it had something to do with Templeton's health. A subsequent visit from Powers at my office later in the day confirmed my suspicions. And you, although you will never be reduced to second place in my heart, have, by virtue of sequence, just become part two of this rather convoluted farce." I could not help but wonder if the lady would see fit to correct me and call it a "tragedy."

"You're telling me you did not agree to look into Rowland's disappearance?" Right off the bat she knew it would be perfectly pointless to be aggravated with Templeton for lying to her. What can you do to a dead man? "Well, if that's the case," she said, drawing herself up, "I'll just have to hire you myself. When can you get started?"

Sometimes two ships passing in the night run smack into each other. An evening that had started out with a goodly bit of promise was atrophying with each passing word. That was obvious when one by one I enumerated the reasons why I would be unable to accommodate California Maritime, Ms. Reed, Unitrieve, or whomever. One, I had a division of a company to run. Two, I had prior commitments, both institutional and social. Three, the state of Unitrieve's financial condition was really no concern of ours. (*Ours* in this case being Furnace Standard.) And finally, I just plain did not want to do it. The good people at FSORC had been working feverishly to complete the Pony Project on schedule, and I was looking forward to scheduled Pony tests in the Caribbean late in the May/June time frame.

"Sorry," I said, concluding. "No can possibly do. A. J. has a very full plate for the next several weeks."

She simply smiled. "We'll see," she trilled. We finished our drinks, made a few attempts at small talk, and within another fifteen minutes she was gone. There was an instant emptiness in the room and my life.

It was ten-thirty, and even at this late hour I was still a good thirty to forty minutes from A. J. Central in Sausalito. But not too late, I figured, even if I waited until I made it home, to call my younger, check-writing kinsman and tell him about my day. Organized wretch that he is, I hoped my call would wake him up.

One of my nephews, Hiram (nine and nasty), answered the phone, and I assumed the role of Uncle Abe for a few moments until Roger came on the line. Before he could protest at the hour, I launched into a detailed description of my session with Ms. Amy Reed of California Maritime.

"You told her no?" Roger asked. I believe I noticed an element of incredulity in his voice.

"Indeed I did."

"Call her back and ask her where and when she wants you to start," Roger said. There was a bit of a twit and snoot in his voice.

I was beside myself. "Why?"

"Because, dear brother, if you had bothered to read the interoffice memo I sent you well over a month ago, you would know that California Maritime now has a ton of money invested in Furnace Standard. Let me rephrase that; it is an entity with a very large block of common stock which has considerable clout when it comes to the annual stockholders' meeting. I find a certain wisdom in acknowledging their strength and cooperating wherever and whenever possible. My advice is—"

"Call her and cooperate?"

"Exactly."

"I was hoping you'd say that," I said.

Tuesday

Whenever I find myself baffled, bewildered, mystified, and otherwise perplexed by the machinations of big business, I seek serious counsel. In other words, I turn to the Bay Area's own Percy Culpepper. Around the Cannery District he is known as "Buck-a-Minute Culpepper." Consultations are

dispensed by the great man for the going rate of
one dollar a minute. All business is conducted at
the counter of Ruby's Diner on Bay Street. Buck-a-
Minute sets his wrist alarm when the seeker of wisdom sits down beside him.

"Good morning, Abraham," he wheezed. Buck-a-
Minute wheezes a lot. He is an octogenarian. He
knows me. I'm on Buck-a-Minute's "A" list by virtue
of my surname and my habit of slipping him Giants
tickets whenever the Dodgers are in town. "What's
going on under the surface these days?" he inquired.

"Buck," I began, "what do you know about an
outfit named Unitrieve?"

I deftly slipped a twenty-dollar bill under his coffee cup and revealed that I had more at the ready.

"It depends on whether you are really referring
to Unitrieve or to its president, Tyler Rowland. The
company has a few problems—nothing that four or
five hundred million wouldn't solve. From what I
hear, Rowland has even bigger problems; some of
them might not be solvable . . . even with money."

"Someone told me that his yacht, *Baja Lady*, went
down off the coast of Baja Sur. Fact or fiction?" This
was info I had obtained from Love Handles during
our phone conversation the previous Friday. Neither Templeton nor Powers had said anything
about Rowland's broken boat or that it might have
deep-sixed. The fact that they hadn't mentioned it
could be construed in a number of ways. One, they
didn't know. Two, they did know and didn't men-

tion it because they wanted to know what I knew. Three, Love Handles was guessing.

Buck-a-Minute took a sip of his coffee and studied my reflection in the long, greasy mirror behind Ruby's counter. When a client, acquaintance, or friend engages in discourse with Buck-a-Minute, that person does not actually look at the great man. Instead, one talks to his reflection in the mirror behind the counter. Just a Buck-a-Minute idiosyncrasy.

As Stepmother Leslie has often pointed out, when you don't look directly at someone you are very close to, you tend not to see all those disturbing little flaws in them. Perhaps this is why lovers close their eyes when they are kissing.

When Buck-a-Minute isn't too sure of his information, he mumbles. "My sources tell me it exploded, burned down to the water line, and went to the bottom."

"Rowland was on it?"

Buck-a-Minute was nodding. He is the only man I know who can nod and sip coffee at the same time. "Let me put it like this, he was on it when the fire broke out. Whether he was on it when it went under is up for debate."

I began musing. "If Rowland was able to get off his fancy floater before it went down, he would have surely contacted his company to let them know he was all right. Right?"

Buck-a-Minute furrowed his considerable brow, took out a Camel, tapped it on the counter, lit it, and eventually exhaled. The gesture was theatrical. Its meaning obscure.

"But since he hasn't called . . ." I suddenly realized how imperious I sounded and how much assuming I was doing.

"The fact that he hasn't contacted anyone in his company doesn't prove anything," Buck-a-Minute was saying. "Maybe he doesn't want anyone to know he's alive."

I found myself thinking that anything was a possibility. Someday I hope to be able to reason things out just like the sage of Ruby's Diner.

"Thank you, Buck," I said and started to get up from the counter.

Buck-a-Minute put his hand on my arm, glanced at the twenty-dollar bill, and checked his watch. "You still got seven minutes left. Wanta talk about the Giants? The upcoming Dodger series—"

"Some other time," I said. Buck-a-Minute's ruttish face mirrored disappointment. From that I assumed his day was not going well. Apparently, none of his clients, acquaintances, or friends had wanted to talk about the Giants bad enough to plunk down the required greenbacks.

By the time I managed to push my way through the crowd at Ruby's, got my car out of the parking lot, and crawled behind the wheel, my wireless was ringing. "A. J. here."

"Have you called Amy Reed?" Roger growled. When supersibling does not bother to extend a civil greeting before he launches into what's on his mind, it is safe to assume that Clara burned his toast at breakfast.

"Just about to do so," I said. "I was just putting the key in the ignition when you called." That part was true. "Calling Ms. Reed was next on my agenda." That part was false. "I'll call you as soon as I'm back in our stockholders' good graces."

"Be sure you do," Roger said. As usual, he managed to hang up first. Someday I plan to hang up when he starts to talk just so I can say I beat him.

I did not inform Roger that there were several things I wanted to know before I called the ravishing Ms. Reed and caved in to her demands. Besides, I figured there was a good chance that California Maritime would have no need for my services if I knew the answers to the following questions. First, had anyone heard from Tyler Rowland in the last four weeks? Second, did the Coast Guard have any information on the *Baja Lady*? Third, just exactly what was the *Baja Lady*?

Before I called the ravishing Ms. Reed, I called Dara. "Mr. Furnace's office," she snarled. A bit snappish, I would say.

"It's me," I announced.

"Where have you been?" I was detecting petulance. "I've been glued to this phone for the last hour. Your brother called. A Captain Leland Powers of San Francisco Homicide wants to talk to you. Sebastian Frank called to thank you for helping someone by the name of George Templeton, and"— Dara's voice turned icy—"you also had a call from some vamp by the name of Amy Reed. She sounded like a fugitive from the Romance Channel."

Bro Roger has permitted me to play leader of FSORC just long enough to feel comfortable with the charade. Dara's frequent insistence that I act like a grown-up boss type no longer chafes me. "Priority number one," I said, "see what you can find out about the *Baja Lady*."

"And exactly what is the *Baja Lady*?" Dara sniffed.

When I explained that it was, in all probability, a somewhat expensive yacht, Dara showed a modicum of respect. Dara likes money. She once said she would like it even more if she had more of it to like.

By the time I glided into the parking lot at FSORC and searched out a parking space, I had called Sebastian Frank (he wasn't in) and Captain Leland Powers (away from his desk). In both cases, however, monotone, disembodied voices had answered their phones and promised to have them get back to me. I left the phone number of my office.

Despite Roger's poking and prodding, I did not call Amy Reed as I said I would. Before I called her I was determined to determine that there really was a "for sure" problem with Tyler Rowland. I was not eager to take time off from the Pony Project. The way I see it, anyone who has fought the wet winter battle in San Francisco is entitled to sun time in the

Caribbean. A month of Pony testing fit in nicely with my tanning planning.

The last thing I did before I crawled out of my car was phone Tyler Rowland's office. Stepfather Furnace, better known as Galen the Wise, taught me that when you have questions you can save a great deal of time by going straight to the man with the answers. In this case a woman. The Unitrieve receptionist put me through to Rowland's secretary, who put me through to Rowland's administrative assistant, a woman by the name of Elizabeth Carter. I was being passed around more than a football in the West Coast offense.

I also had the feeling I was talking to a machine until I told Ms. Carter I was an old friend of Tyler Rowland's, passing through town with only a few minutes between planes.

When the lady was convinced she was going to be able to get rid of me by simply passing along a few words of greeting, some of the Siberian permafrost started to melt. I knew she was all poised to hang up when I hit her with one final question. "How is the old boy?"

"We assume he is quite well," she replied. "He has been out of the country for several weeks now."

This filly was good, real good. Who was going to question her? She sounded like sincerity dot com, and I had to admire her. If she knew something, she was without peer in the hiding game. If she didn't, Unitrieve had what they needed, someone who sounded totally believable.

R. Karl Largent

"Well, little lady," I drawled, "you tell old Tyler that Charlie Mason from Houston was in town." I hoped my voice had taken on the appropriate sober dimension. "You may also want to pass along that Cynthia passed on last summer."

Rowland's administrative assistant conveyed her heartfelt condolences, said she would relay our conversation, and hung up. I reached for the notebook I always carry in the glove compartment, jotted down her name, Elizabeth Carter, and put a couple of exclamation points behind it. Why? Because I had the curious feeling my association with Ms. Carter had just begun.

For some reason, my brief conversation with Elizabeth Carter gave me momentary cause to reflect on the women in my life. There were currently, at the center of my mad social whirl, Georgina, Lenora, Ashley, and Bambi. In the wings there was Amy Reed. That was enough. I decided to forget about Elizabeth Carter. When you see a similarity between your love life and the *Titanic*, one iceberg is quite enough.

Tuesday

The day Roger appointed me to head up the fortunes of FSORC for the Furnace clan, he had his Human Resources people transfer Dara Crawford over to the newly acquired division as my administrative accomplice. That was eight years ago. In those eight years I have learned that I could not possibly have survived without her. By the same token, she has expressed her conviction that no one else could do the job quite as well as she does. Her reasoning, of course, is predicated on her unshakable belief that no other human being could get along with me for eight years.

She may be right. I have been on the verge of proposing to fair young damsels on no less than two occasions since Dara came to work at FSORC. However, I have never been quite enthused enough to try to close the sale. It seems that I am always comparing them to some standard that no one could attain. Dara?

When I returned from a quick visit to the roach coach, croissant and coffee in hand, I discovered that Dara had managed to round up some very pertinent info on the *Baja Lady*. She had located the ship's architect (San Diego), talked to the builder (also a firm in San Diego), and obtained, via electronic data transfer, original drawings and schematics of the vessel. The latter were acquired from the California VHSC registry and the insurance company that had covered the vessel from the time the keel was laid up until the time Tyler Rowland took delivery. First factoid: The *Baja Lady* was leased.

"Some boat, huh?" Dara assessed. Dara has a curious habit; at five foot three inches in height, she never stands in front of or beside me when she is looking at something. She always peeks around from behind me.

"When they get as big, as opulent, and as expensive as this one, Dara my dear, they no longer call

51

them boats, they refer to them as pleasure craft, cruising vessels, yachts, or anything else that sounds very, very expensive."

"High-priced, huh?"

"Enough so to make the IRS nervous."

Dara paid me no heed; she was busy studying the drawings. "Does that number right there mean it is forty-eight feet long?" she asked.

I was nodding my head. At the same time I was pointing out that the *Baja Lady* was powered by two 1,350-hp Detroit diesel engines and she sported a 16-foot diesel-powered tender aft.

"Oh," Dara cooed, "isn't that sweet. The big boat has a baby boat."

The observation was intended to be as it was received, caustic.

"So what else have you learned?" I pushed.

Dara was eager to show me how much she had accomplished while I was dawdling my life away checking on progress in the engineering labs. She elaborated on her conversation with the Coast Guard and the *Baja Lady*'s insurer. "First of all, our Coast Guard says they have not received any reports of a ship being lost near Bahia Magdalena— at least not in the last thirty days. Same from the Mexican Coast Guard. In fact, they wanted to know where I had heard about the *Baja Lady* sinking."

"Don't they read the papers? What did you tell them?"

"I told them I had heard it from my boss but that you tended to become confused rather easily.

Don't worry, I hung up before they could pry your name out of me."

"You said, 'first of all.' What's second?"

"Well, if I wanted to know where someone was, I'd probably call their home to see if their spouse knew of their whereabouts. So I called Mrs. Rowland."

"Clever girl."

"It doesn't require much," she admitted. "I looked the number up in the phone book." She proceeded to hold the first digit on her right hand up where I could see it and blew on the tip like a smoking gun.

"Did she tell you where her husband was?"

"Negative; she doesn't know. At least that's what she told me. Now ask me your next question."

"Which is what?"

"Do I believe her? The answer is . . . yes."

"Why do you believe her?"

"A woman knows when another woman is lying."

Mama Leslie used to say, "Sufficient unto the day is the evil thereof." This means different things to me on different days. Today it meant, find out what Mrs. Tyler Rowland knows before caving in to the demands of California Maritime in the person of Amy Reed.

So what did I do? I picked up the phone and called Mrs. Tyler Rowland. When I began to inquire about her husband's whereabouts, I was surprised by her reaction. She seemed relieved that someone besides herself was concerned about what had happened to the old boy. As relieved as she claimed to be, the lady still displayed a certain amount of reticence when I began asking questions.

"Would you feel more comfortable if we would talk face to face?" I asked her.

She surprised me when she indicated she would be happy to meet me and even suggested a time and place. "Would you think me terribly forward if I suggested we meet somewhere? Perhaps for lunch?"

I said I thought that would be a fine idea.

"Do you like Thai food?" she asked.

I indicated that those who knew me from the time I was a mere swaddler (that being the time when Galen and Leslie were introducing me to Furnace land) claimed I was born hungry. That being the case, I had not yet discovered anything I did not like except sushi and cooked carrots.

"How about Khan Toke on Geary Boulevard?" she suggested.

"Splendid," I said, and we agreed to meet after the lunch-hour crush.

I hung around the office, tried to phone Leland Powers, (unavailable), called Bro Roger (in a meeting), and when nothing else seemed to pan out, considered calling Bambi to see what kind of plans she had for the weekend. (Women must find men painfully obvious.)

* * *

Rita Rowland would have been worth the trip even if I didn't like Thai food. She was bright, quite attractive, and sufficiently perplexed by her husband's disappearance. She carried one of those little flowered calendars with a matching pen. She rummaged through the pages until she found the precise date that Tyler Rowland had vanished. Why she had to check the date, I don't know. I would have thought that a disappearing husband would be an event of such magnitude that the date, if not the exact time, would have been etched into the memory. "May 11, it was a Sunday afternoon," she said with some degree of certainty. "He said he was going down to the marina to do some tidying up. He had just had the engines worked on, something about the injectors."

"And that is the last time you saw him or talked to him?"

Rita Rowland confirmed it with a bob of her more than pretty head. She had short coal-black hair and eyes of similar color and intensity. She was wearing an obviously expensive, tailored black cashmere blazer with a complementing gray wool skirt. On her lapel she wore a diamond-studded broach in the shape of a scorpion. The earrings matched the broach. The lipstick matched the nails. I believe the current appellation for such pageant and dash is "trophy wife."

"Now comes the obvious question, Mrs. Rowland. Is there some reason why you did not report the fact that your husband was missing to the police?"

Rita Rowland never flinched. "I was told not to," she said.

I was in the middle of one of Khan Toke's specialties, tom yam gong lemongrass shrimp with mushroom, tomato, and cilantro soup. "You were told not to?" I repeated. "Who told you that?"

"My brother."

Before contacting Rita Rowland I had noodled out that Tyler Rowland, erstwhile president of Unitrieve, had married Rita Hake, the only other surviving Hake except Jacob, her brother. Convoluted? Not really. Jacob, according to what Dara dug up, is currently the CEO of Unitrieve, thus making him number one and Tyler Rowland number two in the decision-making hierarchy. "Would you mind explaining why he advised you to stay away from the police?"

Rita Rowland hesitated, fumbled with her cigarette lighter, and finally lit her cigarette. She was one of those smokers who prop their elbow on the table and seem to strike a pose between each puff. "First you should know that Jacob said he would hire a private investigator to find Tyler for me. You should also know that Jacob said he is not yet alarmed over the fact that Tyler has come up missing. Then he reminded me, Tyler has a history of disappearing for a week or so every now and then."

"You still haven't answered my question," I reminded her. "Did he say why he did not want you to go to the police?"

Another puff. Another pose. "Jacob said the company simply cannot stand the negative publicity if Tyler is nothing more than out on another one of his toots."

"Toots?"

Rita Rowland nodded her pretty head again. "I'm afraid Tyler has a drinking problem," she admitted. "Jacob says he has known about it for some time."

"But you didn't?"

She shook her pretty head yet again and lapsed back into more of what wasn't making a whole lot of sense to me. "I suppose I knew about it, Mr. Furnace. I guess I chose to ignore it. At any rate, Jacob said negative publicity at this point could seriously jeopardize negotiations for an add-on clause to a major DOD contract. He says if they can get the funding they need, it will means a very large sum of money to the company."

I was nodding like I understood. I didn't. "Back to this private investigator your brother said he was going to hire," I said. "Have you received any progress reports?"

"Maybe Jacob hasn't hired him yet."

"Have you asked?"

"No."

At this point I was beginning to draw some very different conclusions about Tyler Rowland's wife. No doubt about it, Rita Rowland was one fine-looking woman, but she was a long way from a high

R. Karl Largent

level of mental agility. An hour into our luncheon she was coming across like one of those folks who had missed their connection on the brain train. Neither mental agility nor assertiveness appeared to be in Rita Rowland's arsenal.

Through it all I was trying to envisage daring Dara caught up in the same set of circumstances. If her weight-lifter live-in had disappeared for a like period of time, she would have seen to it that the local sheriff, the FBI, and the National Guard had been called out by now. I recall Dara describing a similarly attractive woman like Rita Rowland with, "She had advanced to the 'see Jane run' level."

By the time we finished our pompano topped with assorted goodies and yellow bean sauce, I had asked most of the questions I had in mind when I called Rowland's wife. If I hadn't asked any one specific question, it was because she had already indicated she was unable to answer that particular question's predecessor. As Stepfather Galen used to say, "If you are unfamiliar with two, it is highly unlikely you will be conversant with three."

We each said our "have a good day" line and parted with promises to contact each other if either of us learned anything new. And since Rita Rowland did not seem to be the overly inquisitive type, I was convinced that it would be I who would be getting in touch with her.

I dashed back to my office and devoted some long-overdue time to doing what it was that Bro Roger

58

was paying me my handsome salary to do.

As I continually remind myself, testing time in the Caribbean will soon beckon. Resolution of small irritants such as those revolving around stockholder obligations associated with the disappearance of the *Baja Lady* and Tyler Rowland are not, I repeat, *are not* going to interfere.

Later that day I quit thinking about FSORC business and returned to my office determined to order my thinking on the matter of the missing Unitrieve prexy. I took out a pad of paper and began to make notes.

One: Tyler Rowland had not been seen by wife, wife's brother, or corporate associates for a period now in excess of two weeks. I went to the calendar and counted the days. Total days disappeared, eighteen.

Two: According to Rita Rowland, brother Jacob, Tyler's boss and Unitrieve CEO, did not want her to report her husband's disappearance. Why? Because he believed it was entirely possible that Rowland had done nothing more then "go out on another toot." To wit, I made a note in the margin. "Eighteen days constitutes a significant toot."

Three: The *Baja Lady* had slipped her slip at the marina. Like her skipper, she too had disappeared. Where?

Four: Several of those involved apparently knew that Tyler Rowland had a drinking problem.

I did not list other items except to record a few key words to ensure that I would not forget them.

Among them were Jacob Hake's concern over negative publicity, California Maritime's financial involvement with both Unitrieve and Furnace Standard (curious coincidence), Percy Culpepper's none-too-veiled insinuation that Rowland had more problems than Unitrieve (what did he know that it was going to cost me more than a couple of Giants tickets to find out?), and finally, Love Handles' gossipy news bit that the *Baja Lady* had sunk somewhere off the coast of Bahia Magdalena. Fact or fiction? The papers reported it. The Coast Guard knew nothing about it.

With all that in mind, I decided to add one more item to my growing list of thought provokers. Two words, seven letters. Amy Reed.

Journal No. 3

Wednesday, June 4

It was nearly midnight before I finally wound up the day's affairs and crawled between sheets previously consecrated by one Patricia Palmer (brief pause while I savor a reminiscence). Prior to retiring, however, I encountered still another puzzling dimension to the riddle of Tyler Rowland and his missing yacht. Sad to say, it was at the same time and approaching nine o'clock when I realized that I had once again been derelict in my assigned domestic duties; I had forgotten my Tuesday night obligation to Agatha Alden, my slightly bohemian next door neighbor.

On Tuesday nights, when I am in town, I am responsible for seeing that her cat, Sex Pistol (a cu-

rious name because the beast has been neutered),
is both fed and exercised. To fulfill my obligation,
it is necessary to trundle next door, open a small
can of whatever cat delicacy Agatha has selected
for the day, and when the overweight brute is finished dining, take it for a walk. Since I consider the
latter a chore, I usually wear a hat with the brim
pulled down and a light jacket with the collar
pulled up so that none of my sports-car friends or
business associates will recognize me.

It was while walking the cat, however, that I was
reminded I had not completed still another one of
my duties for the day. I still had not called Ms. Amy
Reed of California Maritime to inform her that my
brother had changed my mind. What did I intend
to tell her? Well, that I was and would henceforth
be available to help her search for the missing Tyler
Rowland. If she asked me why I had changed my
mind, I would be less than honest and say it was
because the matter intrigued me.

So, after completing my obligation to Ms. Alden's
gib, I hurried back to my home on the hill and
rushed a call through to California Maritime in the
hope of obtaining a phone number for Ms. Reed.
As you might suspect, my attempt at that time of
night was intercepted by a gravel-voiced security
officer charged with, in addition to his other duties,
the responsibility of answering incoming calls.

"Who?" he said when I inquired as to whether he
was permitted to give out Ms. Reed phone number.

I repeated the woman's name and attempted to

defuse any suspicions Security Man might be entertaining of a stalker or depraved deviate by informing him I was with Furnace Standard and that Ms. Reed was expecting my call.

That's when Security Man informed me that there was no listing for an Amy Reed in the California Maritime corporate directory. At first I considered the information to be just a bit odd, but then I reasoned there was probably a good reason for it. Ms. Reed could have been the victim of a recent intercompany transfer (there were five convenient California Maritime locations in the Bay Area alone) or, for that matter, a recent hire. The alternative to patrolling the streets throughout the night and calling out her name was to wait until the following morning. Easily done, because I suddenly remembered where I had put the lady's calling card—in my office.

Now, as day three of the Unitrieve affair was unfolding, I found myself sitting in my office, completely shorn of reasons why I should further delay my call to Amy Reed.

I called California Maritime. This time the response was completely different. I asked. I received. Different operator. Suspicions defused. Amy Reed was on the line.

"How long have you been employed there?" I blurted. (As Galen repeatedly reminded me when I was a puppy, there is no excuse for rudeness.) I was therefore much chagrined when Ms. Reed was forced to ask me who was calling.

It was grovel time. I do it well. I am, after all, a bachelor. "Sorry," I said. "I was trying to do two things at once, talking and thinking."

Amy Reed authored a girlish and completely charming musical chuckle. "I recognize the voice. Is that you, A. J.?"

"I said I'd call you if I thought we could help."

"That's what you said all right. But it was your brother that was the motivating factor. Correct?"

I decided to mumble. Mumbling works best early in relationships. Later on, the woman knows the man is either lost for words or stalling. "He did point out that cooperating could be to our mutual advantage."

"Well, then, let's get started," Amy Reed said.

At precisely two o'clock Amy Reed, with bulging briefcase, laptop computer, cell phone, and horn-rimmed glasses, situated herself across from me in the small conference room adjacent to my office. An envious FSORC receptionist had earlier informed me that an entire battalion of FSORC engineers had spotted Ms. Reed in the lobby and followed her to my office. Was I upset? On the contrary, I was pleased. Even though they are engineers, their conduct proves that their libido sometimes gets exercised over something other than a bridge, bus, or boat.

"So you have decided to join us in the search for Tyler Rowland," Amy began.

"Because of my ongoing commitment to integrity and forthrightness, I feel compelled to admit you are right, my brother is making me do this."

Amy Reed laughed. Sweet music. When she did, I found myself racking my brain trying to think of a whole bunch of other things I could say that would elicit the same response.

"So where do we start?" I said.

Amy Reed was frowning. "Well, do you think you have pretty well exhausted your sources of information around here?"

I did my best Groucho Marx impression. "They may not be exhausted, but I think they're ready to sit down."

Amy Reed completely disregarded my attempt at humor.

One thing I do have is a good sense of timing, and I had the feeling it was time to play serious. "I am curious," I said. "Now that we're a team, where do you think we should go? Better yet, where do we start?"

Amy Reed was one of those women who bring their hands into the conversation. She petted her pretty lower lip with forefinger and thumb as she considered my question. "Who haven't you had an opportunity to talk to that you feel might be able to shed light on Tyler Rowland's disappearance?"

"At least two people," I admitted. "Jacob Hake and Elizabeth Carter. But I get the feeling that neither would be willing to share what they know even if they could."

"And why is that?"

"Well, to start with, Rowland's wife, Rita, is Jacob Hake's sister. Jacob Hake, as you already know, is Unitrieve's CEO. But when Rita Rowland called her brother to express concern over her husband's extended respite from his usual bed and board, Brother Jacob did not respond like she hoped he would. He told her to lie low, keep quiet, and whatever else she did, under no circumstance should she consider contacting the police."

To my surprise, Amy didn't look surprised. "What about Elizabeth Carter?"

"Phone conversation only. Assessment: cold, calm, and collected. Every word is measured. My guess is Jacob Hake has issued some sort of corporate dictum instructing people inside Unitrieve to clam up when people outside Unitrieve begin asking questions about Tyler Rowland."

"Think that's why Templeton was killed?"

I shrugged. "Well, if Jacob Hake has issued such a dictum, Templeton was certainly ignoring it."

I wonder if Amy Reed was listening as intently as she was staring. "Do you have a theory as to why Hake doesn't want his people to cooperate?"

I did, but I wasn't ready to try to articulate it. There were too many pieces missing. I shook my head. "Not one I'm ready to talk about."

"Then let me suggest a course of action," Amy said. Her fingers were dancing over the keyboard to her computer. "You handle one phase of the investigation; I'll handle the other. That way we won't be getting in each other's way and we won't be covering the same ground. How does that sound?"

I didn't tell Amy I disliked her plan for the simple reason that if I was being forced to become involved in this seemingly tawdry affair, I felt there should be fringe benefits. The best fringe benefit I could think of was Amy Reed. Under her plan I would see very little of her. "You will have to be more specific," I finally said.

"I think I might be able to dig around at Unitrieve and find out why Rowland's disappearance is being handled like it is," she said. "While I'm doing that, you can trundle down to the Baja Sur and look for Rowland's yacht. If it did sink, someone, somewhere, knows something about it. If it's tied up at some marina somewhere like the Cabo San Lucas area, someone has seen it. A yacht that size is hard to hide."

The minute Amy Reed said that, I knew my Meg Ryan look-alike was not familiar with the Baja. South of Ensenada there were literally thousands of bays, inlets, harbors, and basins where a person so inclined could hide darn near anything . . . including a gaudy forty-eight-foot pleasure craft.

"Did anyone ever tell you that you look like Meg Ryan?" I asked.

Amy Reed furrowed her pretty brow and gave me one of those inquisitorial stares that people usually summon up when they find something wholly unexpected in their soup. "No," she finally admitted, and promptly returned to the subject of the investigation. "How will we stay in touch with each other? We should have a plan."

I suggested a nightly call at a specific time and went on to inquire how and where I could contact her. Pretty Amy promptly reached into the darker recesses of her briefcase and produced a business card, this one very much different from the one she had given me when she introduced herself as a California Maritime employee. Her name was on one side. On the reverse were her office phone, home phone, e-mail address, fax number, and cell phone.

"Every evening at ten?" she suggested.

Amy and I concluded our meeting shortly thereafter with a firm, formal, and exceedingly businesslike handshake. No hugs. No winks. No girl-encouraging-boy glances.

Shortly after, I wrapped up my day at the office by taking the backstairs down to the engineering lab to see what, if any, progress FSORC's stalwart engineers and technicians had made that day. Progress was apparent. The Pony Project was moving forward indeed. Hopefully, in a few days it would also be moving down.

One of my former infatuates once complained that I made an exceedingly poor Lothario because, based on everything the young lady had observed, I appeared to have far too many irons in the fire. As I recall, she was rather emphatic. "If it isn't your damn poker club, it's the damn sports car club. If you aren't walking your neighbor's cat, you're having dinner with your mother." The young lady concluded her tirade by asking, "Where do I fit in?" My answer to her question must have been wholly inadequate. That was the last time I saw her.

But, getting back to the subject of Wednesday nights, at least twice a month I have dinner with the current matriarch of the Furnace clan, Leslie Martin Scot Furnace. We conduct our little gastronomic rituals at the family abode on Vallejo Street on the first and third Wednesday of each month. We do not dine out, because the great lady has a standing appointment to have her hair done first thing Thursday mornings. She has repeatedly stated that she is wholly averse to being seen at any of the more up-scale restaurants where a woman of her stature might choose to dine . . . in a coiffure a full week past its prime.

I arrived at the usual six-thirty hour and was greeted with my stepmother's questions. "How are you, dear? You look as though you have lost weight. Have you been to the doctor? Are you still dating that wretched (fill in the blank)?" Note: Stepmum has never approved of any female I have ever dated. Typical of the youth of my generation, Stepmum's disapproval did nothing more than spur me on to a more intense relationship with each of them.

Suffice to say that while I was presenting the grand dame with a parade of unacceptables, younger brother Roger took a bride, sired two stalwart sons, and that was the last time I heard the "When are you getting married?" question. Leslie had her two grandchildren to dote on.

On this particular night, there was the standard fare of small talk prior to dinner. I was brought up to speed on the accomplishments of my two nephews, heard about the latest from her bridge club, and was regaled with the details from her Internet adventures. Mama Leslie, a term she despises, has, as she teeters on the cusp of her seventieth year, become a slave to cyber master.

At dinner I informed her I would be out of the country for a few days. This inspired her to inquire whether I was going somewhere to "play with one of my water things." Stepfather Galen, may he rest in peace, obviously did a rather poor job of informing his wife where the money for her hairdresser was coming from.

"No," I explained, "I'm taking care of a little matter for the company."

"That's nice," Stepmum assessed. I know the woman well enough to know that in that one statement I said more about business than she wanted to hear at the dinner table. She smiled benignly and signaled Louise, Stepmum's constant companion since Steppater Galen played his last hole, for another wedge of caramel cheesecake. "Is there anything else on your mind, dear?"

"Yes," I admitted. "When, or where if you will, did the family develop the habit of describing people they encounter by comparing them to movie stars?"

"Do we do that?" she asked.

"Frequently."

"I'm afraid I don't understand, dear."

"Well, I met a young lady who I think looks a great deal like Meg Ryan," I admitted.

"And who is Meg Ryan, dear?" Stepmum sniffed.

An evening with Leslie usually concludes somewhere around nine o'clock, an early hour to be sure, but one that offers one the advantage of engaging in other social activities, if one is so inclined. A waste. My social life, if one can bring oneself to call it that, usually consists of little more than paying bills, sorting through junk mail, making telephone calls, or returning the ones on my answering machine.

My first call on this particular Wednesday evening was to Love Handles, Mr. William Arnold, boy banking executive. On this occasion I was not in the mood to dilly-dally. I got straight to the point. Where, when, and how, I wanted to know, had he heard about Tyler Rowland's misfortunes at Bahia Magdalena? Love Handles took a while to gather himself and order his thoughts. Finally he informed me that Tinker Bowman, also a fraternity brother from Farm days, had heard about the mishap through connections he had with other equally obscure sources I had no knowledge of.

"But you're pretty sure Bowman is giving you the straight skinny?" I pressed.

Love Handles assured me he had the utmost faith in Bowman's veracity, and we concluded our chit-chat.

Following my conversation with Love Handles, I decided to close the loop with Bro Roger. I dialed. He answered. "Remember Amy Reed?" I asked. Younger sib indicated he did, as well as recalling why he did. It was not the same reason I did. "Ms. Reed and I have developed a plan that in the long run may satisfy California Maritime's curiosity about the disappearance of Tyler Rowland," I said. Before Roger could ask his questions, I explained. "Ms. Reed is going to snoop around the Unitrieve head-quarters in San Diego, and I'm headed down to the Baja to see what I can learn."

"Stay in touch," Roger said. That was all? A cryptic "Stay in touch." No "Have a good trip," or "Good luck down there." Just "Stay in touch."

After my confab with Roger, I dialed Margo Christman's number to inform her that our Friday night date was off. She sounded somewhat disappointed, but with Margo it's difficult to tell. She studied method acting at some studio in New York, and I'm never quite sure what her real sentiments are.

Lastly I called Dara to tell her that I was on my way to Bahia Magdalena and would not be coming into the office the following morning. Like Roger, she did not see fit to wish me well, or even to have a pleasant journey. She instructed me to call in at least once a day and then asked, "Is that Ms. Red or Ms. Ready or whatever her name is going with you?"

I told Daring Dara that it was none of her business and hung up. Amy Reed going to the Baja with me? In my dreams.

Thursday

The alarm went off at the ungodly hour of six-thirty in the morning. Perhaps savages have need to get up and "go at it," as they like to say, but I find the practice of getting up before the sun profoundly bestial. Nevertheless, I crawled out of my comfortable cocoon and attended to the morning rituals. Before packing for what I expected to be no more than a three-day trip, I turned on the Weather Channel and tried to get a handle on current climatological conditions in Baja Sur. Following my attention to that little detail, I called Bro Roger to find out if one of Furnace Standard's planes was available.

"Is that how you intend to get there?" he asked.

"Well," I said, "I could walk, ride a bike, drive a company car, rent a boat, book myself on a commercial flight, or borrow one of the jets you and your board of directors seem to feel are so important. However, all but the last option would appear to have certain undesirable dimensions. Also, there is this to consider: Borrowing one of the company planes would allow me to do my poking around and return in a timely fashion."

"Are you quite through?"

"I am," I said.

"Take your time and do it right," Roger grunted. From the surly attitude he was exhibiting, I had no choice but to assume I had awakened him from a sound sleep. If I did, good for me.

After I hung up, I went to the window that affords me the best view of the bay and was rewarded with the spectacle of a slate-gray world devoid of color and texture. A thick fog had rolled in. It was obvious I wasn't going to fly anywhere until the fog lifted.

Of all the aircraft Furnace Standard has accumulated over the years, my favorite by far is the Brazilian-built EMBRAER EMB-110 Bandeirante. Stripped of armament and outfitted in suitably corporate opulence, this stylish little craft can cruise along at 240 miles per hour and has a range more than adequate to hustle me down to La Paz in minimal time. I say La Paz because it is the closest airport to Bahia Magdalena that is able to accommodate the Bandeirante.

With instructions for the plane to return to SFO as soon as I had been deposited in La Paz, I was on the ground, suitcase in hand, watching the plane take off and head north. In five hours time I had been transported into another world: temperature in the mid-eighties and ultradry wind blowing across the Baja Sur peninsula.

I rented a car from Budget International at the La Paz airport, picked up a packet of maps, and headed north on Highway 1, also known as the

74

Transpeninsular Highway. I had in mind getting as far as the northern end of Magdalena Bay before it became too dark to avoid the inevitable potholes. In Mexico, even the major roads don't often get all the attention they deserve.

When I pulled into Las Cuevas, I was where I wanted to be and the sun was getting ready to fold its tent for the day. A sign proclaimed that the pueblo's primary tourist attraction was a number of off-shore spearfishing caves. There appeared to be a definite shortage of tourist types. Thus far I had counted none. In addition, my rented two-year-old blue Taurus, sadly in need of a wash job, was drawing more than its share of attention from the locals. It did not take me long to decide it was not exactly a tourist hot spot.

I had entered Las Cuevas from the south, and when I turned left onto the main street (no pavement, compacted hardpan), I was looking directly west at a colorful Bahia Magdalena sunset. That was a real tourist attraction.

How do I describe the rest of Las Cuevas? Well, the street was flanked on both sides by a string of monotonous gray clapboard buildings. Some were built out over the wharf. Crude, hand-lettered signs above the door to several buildings indicated their purpose for being there. Even so, my limited knowledge of Spanish left me pretty much in the dark. Most of the structures were small and sadly in need of paint. Weathered gray appeared to be the dominant color.

At the end of the street there were several fishing boats tied up at the wharf. A couple of them were in the thirty-five- or forty-foot range. The rest were smaller. Fishing nets were hung out like a series of armatures for yet-to-be-determined artwork.

A second, more in-depth survey of Las Cuevas' nearly empty streets left me with the impression that mine might be the only *tourista* car in the village. The village appeared to consist of four or five blocks (more or less) with *la iglesia* at the head of the main street. In our small towns in the States there would have been a courthouse in that location instead of a church. Across the street from the church was *el hotel*. I knew that was what it was because that what what the sign above the door said. It was a two-story wooden and adobe affair with a covered porch that extended the length of the building. I parked the car and went in.

Inside there was a bar at one end of a large open room. Over the bar was a sign, *fondas*. Behind the bar was a row of amber, green, and clear bottles. I recognized the tequila and the dos gusanos. Everything else on the shelf was a mystery.

Behind the bar stood a clone of Anthony Quinn. He had thick, close-cropped black hair, an even blacker moustache, and intense same-colored eyes. He was smiling. At least I think it was a smile. I know people who have mastered the art of both smiling and sneering at the same time.

Whatever the intent of his expression, it did not actually come across as malevolent or sinister; it was more along the lines of what one might expect of the sergeant at arms at a bikers' convention.

He sized me up, stepped out of the shadows, and leaned forward with both huge hands on the bar.

"Habitaciones?" I tried.

The man behind the bar began to laugh. When he did, he displayed bone-white teeth in vivid contrast to his saddle-leather complexion and dark features. "Where the hell did you learn to speak Spanish? Off the back of a mescal bottle?"

"That bad, huh?"

He was still laughing. "I had a German couple in here back in January. They were worse . . . but not by much. Stick to English, okay?"

I was grateful. Same question, this time in English. "How about a room?"

"Cash or credit card?"

"What's the difference?"

"If you've got one of them damn American credit cards, I have to pay them a percentage and it's six months before I get my money. Credit card, I charge you more. Cash, I charge you less. Those card people think they can screw us over down here."

I peeled off a crisp, new fifty-dollar bill, and his smile continued to broaden. He not only could see that I was unlikely to card my way through my stay, he could also see that there were a few more where the first came from.

"How long do you intend to stay?"

"Three, four days max. I'm looking for someone. If I can't find them in that time, they aren't here."

"Well, then, let's celebrate your arrival. How about something to drink?" he said. When he said that, it was my turn to smile. I like people who cut straight to the chase.

"How about a cold Dos Equis?"

He shook his head and stared at me. "Appears to me you don't get down here much, do you?" he said. I was still shaking my head when my host went on. It was more gruff than growl. "Around here Dos Equis is just too damned expensive. Besides, everyone in Las Cuevas drinks Budweiser. And as for the ice, not in your wildest dream." Then he added, "Keep in mind, this is Las Cuevas."

My room as the locals would describe it was *casa de huespedes*, which translates into something like "room above the bar." At any rate, it is small, there is a bed, a hook on the back of the door, a ceiling fan, and the air conditioning consists of a window that opens to the breeze (when there is one) off the water. The bathroom is down the hall—nothing more than a minor inconvenience because, as my host pointed out, I am at present the only guest.

Speaking of my host, he had managed to tell me a great deal about himself in the few short minutes we talked. His name was Carlos Martinenez. He was the son of a doctor. He was born in Cabo San Lucas, moved to the States with his parents on his fifteenth birthday, eventually attended UCLA, and dropped out after completing his second year. Why? His grandfather, based in Las Cuevas when he passed away, left him two fifties-vintage fishing trawlers, both tied up at docks which gave him access to Bahia Magdalena.

I sat down in my room, made the appropriate set of notes, and, although it was far too early to conclude the day, went downstairs to find the nearest phone. Amy was due a report, never mind the hour, and Carlos was due another laugh.

"There's a phone here but it doesn't work," Carlos informed me. "There's a phone that works back at the place where you turned off the main highway."

"How far is that?"

"Eighteen kilometers."

The thought of crawling back into the Taurus and driving back out to the highway in the darkness held minimal if any appeal. I therefore decided to invest my evening in a good meal and began probing Carlos about the evening's fare.

"*Gambas*," he said, "*la sopa, verduras*." When he saw my inquisitive frown, he explained. "Today's catch—prawns—plus soup and vegetables. Marie will fix whatever and however you want it. Providing of course we have it."

I ordered and waited. An hour later I had savored a plate of prawns and assorted other local goodies the woman called Marie had prepared, seemingly on a moment's notice and without much fanfare. Marie, I should report, somewhat resembles a bowling ball. A buoyant soul with a light-hearted attitude, she is indeed an excellent cook. She stands less than five foot tall and is nearly the same in

79

circumference. She, Carlos informed me, "came with the hotel." He then described how she had worked for his grandfather when he bought the hotel and had even logged a few years with the owner previous to that.

After dinner, served on a tin plate and accompanied by a tin cup full of tea with milk, I invited Carlos out on the veranda. I wanted to know what he knew about sunken yachts. We found ourselves a place where we could detect a light breeze, and Carlos lit a cigar. It looked like a piece of rolled hemp, and by the third puff it smelled that way as well.

I saw no reason to refrain or hold back. Had he, I wanted to know, seen or talked to anyone who had seen an oversized American yacht tied up at the wharf in the last thirty or so days? Carlos gave the question considerable thought and after some deliberation shook his head. "Nothing near that big," he assessed. "Some smaller ones maybe. Sometimes they pull in to fuel up. Other times they stop because they are curious about the caves. Generally speaking, they don't stay long."

Then I asked him if he had seen anything in the neighborhood of a fifty-footer pass him on the way south while he was tending his nets. That also elicited a negative response. He didn't even have to think about it.

When I started to ask him my next question, Carlos held up his hand. "Wait a minute," he said.

"What are you, some kind of insurance investigator?"

"No," I said, "I'm just trying to find out what may have happened to a former business associate." Admittedly, it was a vague, not wholly truthful answer. But there was reason for my duplicity. It was altogether possible that Carlos might come up with questions I couldn't or did not want to answer. As Stepmum Leslie would have sniffed, "You just don't know the man that well."

"Something happen to this guy you're talkin' about?"

"We're not certain," I admitted. I then launched into several abbreviated versions of what had already been pieced together, concluding with Love Handles' report that the *Baja Lady* had sunk somewhere off the coast of Bahia Magdalena.

"Wouldn't surprise me none," Carlos said. "We lose one or two of 'em down here each winter. Appears to me some of your American friends up there don't know much about handling big water."

"Have you lost any this winter?"

"Sure have. Two that I know of. But there could have been more."

"Tell me about them."

Carlos took a deep drag on his cigar and stared up at what had become a sailor's delight. The stars were out in abundance and there was a modest breeze. "No need to tell you about 'em; stick around a couple of days and I'll show 'em to you."

"You know where these wrecks are?"

"Sure do. Everybody does. I'd take you tomorrow, but I already promised Bo Bo and Viktor we're fishin' a shoal south of here. The wrecks I'm talking about are north, seven, maybe eight miles out, but still inside the reef."

"What about the Coast Guard?" I asked.

"Yours or ours? If you're talkin' about ours, they keep themselves busy elsewhere. You could call 'em today but you aren't likely to see 'em for a month or more. As for your Coast Guard, they don't come down this far unless it's one of yours that's involved."

"This was one of ours," I reminded him.

"Bet they didn't know that."

Carlos and I sat on the steps talking until almost one o'clock in the morning. I was the proverbial happy camper. I had found myself a good source of local info and tapped into it. Marie, bless her heart, came out twice to check on us before she retired. The second time she brought out shooters of Dos Gusanos. I managed to get a good look at the two-inch-long worms floating at the bottom of the attendant bottle and begged off. Carlos found the whole thing terribly amusing, but I consoled myself with the thought that it seemed unlikely there was any future in drinking something that had already brought about the death of two worms.

Before Carlos trundled off to bed, he gave me some advice. "Poke around some tomorrow. Ask questions. If that boat belongin' to your friend is as big and fancy as you say it is, someone around these parts may have seen it. Just keep diggin' until they get to know you. Somethin' you should know: Fishermen tend to be kinda secretive about a lot of things, especially if they think someone is gonna cut in on 'em."

Later, when I sat down in my room to organize my notes, I realized that despite all the hurly-burly of the day, I hadn't accomplished a great deal. For all intents and purposes, Wednesday, June 4, was a wash. True, I was in Las Cuevas. And if my old fraternity brother was right, I was at least in the area where someone named Tinker Bowman claimed Tyler Rowland and his yacht had last been seen and possibly sank. Secondly, there was one clear plus to the day's activities. If this was the area where the *Baja Lady* went down, it appeared I had stumbled across a reasonably reliable source of information in Captain Carlos Martinenez. He seemed open and knowledgeable—good qualities in a source.

On the negative side of the ledger was the fact that I had not closed the day by reporting to Ms. Amy Reed as previously agreed. The late hour, the distance, and the condition of the road back to Highway 1 precluded it.

Thursday

Upon retiring I found my room to be too warm and stuffy. Opening the window was not the solution. Turning on the overhead fan (which made an abominable noise) and peeling back what was intended to serve as bed clothing worked only briefly.

Then the breeze shifted around to the west and the room seemed a bit coolish. I would have complained, but I could envision Captain Martinenez handing me a book of matches and instructing me to stand close to the fire for warmth.

At any rate, I was up early, intending to attend to my morning rituals, only to find there was no hot water. No hot water, no shower, no shave. I consoled myself by thinking I could take a refreshing dip in the Pacific later that day.

In the hotel dining room (I'm being kind), I found Maria. "Would Senor Furnace like some *café con hielo?*" she asked. She was smiling. A lesson relearned: Stepfather Galen was right, there is no reason for anyone to smile before the ungodly hour of seven o'clock in the morning. As he was fond of saying, "Anyone who does should be given a urine test."

"Café con hielo?" I repeated.

Maria had to work at it but she finally managed to convey that she meant strong black coffee, sugar, and ice. The former sounded great, but I told her to forget the sugar and the ice.

Later, with heavy china mug in hand and coffee that was strong and thick enough that I really wouldn't have needed a cup, I stepped out on the veranda to greet the new day. The streets of Las Cuevas, with the exception of a few scruffy dogs, a cat, and three chickens, were deserted. I attributed this to the fact that everyone in the village was still sleeping. Maria, however, was quick to inform me that the streets were empty because folks were already at work. I liked my scenario better.

I remember once studying a map of the climatological conditions in the Baja and noting that there were few if any storms of any significance during the winter months. June in San Francisco is one thing; in the Baja it is apparently quite another. I had expected warm to hot. It was real hot. I expected sunshine and I got it. But out over the big water and to the south where Carlos had indicated he would be for the day, it appeared to be raining.

As I think about it, stormy would be much more accurate.

I finished my coffee, sat the cup on the railing, and proceeded down the street to the dock area. There wasn't that much to see—a few neglected prams and an equal number of tenders of questionable serviceability. There was no such thing as individual slips; the Las Cuevas mooring pattern seemed completely random, bordering on chaotic. I did notice a motorboat of more recent vintage, but it was powered by an ancient Johnson outboard. The motor looked tired.

No one was around, so I decided to trudge north along the beach. Las Cuevas itself seemed to end a few hundred yards north with the last row of houses and a few chicken coops. After no more than another three or four hundred yards of trudging, I was at least that far from civilization.

I found myself walking along the shoreline look-

R. Karl Largent

ing for whatever it is people who walk along sandy beaches look for. As always, the sea had washed up those things it couldn't decide what to do with or its creatures couldn't eat. I found a number of items of curiosity, none of any value, and nothing that might indicate it was wreckage from the *Baja Lady*. It was all pretty unexciting until I saw someone walking toward me.

From a distance, the only thing that was apparent was that whoever was approaching was female. She possessed a decidedly feminine walk, and there was something refined in the way she carried herself. What she was doing, men can't do. To my surprise, though, the closer she came, the less feminine she looked. Up close, her skin was coarse-grained, her hair, once blond, was now yellow-white, and her eyes were hollow. The lady had quite obviously spent too much time and too many days in the Baja sun. It had taken an unkindly toll.

She was less than twenty feet from me when she saw me bend over, pluck a small metal object out of the brown sand, and hold it up for closer examination.

"If you're going to scavenge this beach, you better get yourself one of those metal detectors," she said. "The pickin's are probably pretty slim by now. The few tourists we get around here snap up everything of value that's even semi-close to the surface. About the only things you're likely to find now are the items that washed up on the beach in the last couple of days, or the stuff that's buried five or six inches down in the sand."

I didn't know who she was, but she had summarized the entire experience of beach scouring in one paragraph and left me with nothing to say. That being the case, I smiled. She stepped forward and we shook hands.

"The name is Jean Jean," she said. "I own that little eating place you see up the beach there."

It must have been little, because I was squinting in the direction she was pointing and there was nothing to see but more beach. "Furnace," I countered. "Abraham Joseph Furnace. Most folks call me A. J."

"Then that's what I'll call you," she said. "Where are you from, A. J.?"

"Frisco; good old Baghdad by the Bay."

"Down here for a vacation?"

I shook my head. "Nope. Looking for something."

"From the way you were scouring that sand, I take it you haven't found what you're lookin' for yet."

"Not yet."

Jean Jean turned away from me and looked out over the water. The cloud deck that had earlier seemed so threatening had drifted south, and the sun was prominent. I could tell from the latticework of wrinkles around her blanched gray eyes that she had spent more than her share of time squinting into that sun.

"Well, good luck," she sighed. She sounded like

she meant it. "This Baja is a strange place. People tend to disappear when they come down here." Then she added, "If they want to, that is. But if they spend any time at all around Las Cuevas, they eventually end up at my place. So who you lookin' for?"

"It isn't a who, it's an it. Actually, I'm looking for a yacht. If I find the yacht, chances are I'll find the who."

Jean Jean seemed to lose a little interest in whatever it was I was searching for. She shuffled her feet in the sand and changed the subject. "Well, if you tire of that search and decide to start searchin' for the best tequila on Bahia Magdalena, stop by. I make it myself."

Jean Jean and I lolled away a few more minutes in idle chatter before she decided she had strayed far enough from "that little eating place" and decided she should head back up the beach. In however long it had taken us to get through the introductory stages of getting to know someone, I had learned quite a bit about her.

Jean Jean Baybone was from Philadelphia. Forty years ago she had married a young man and come to the Baja with him on her honeymoon. During the two weeks that followed, she claimed she had learned two very important things. One, she had married the wrong man. Two, she had discovered where she really belonged, Baja Sur. Bottom line, Jean Jean's husband came with a young bride and left without one.

Now, with the early June sun shimmering off the

sand and the day warming, I was watching Jean
Jean disappear in the distance. During our brief
conversation I had made it a point to keep one eye
on the water. Easy to do, because we had been
standing on the far west side of a small natural jetty
that afforded me a clear view of passing vessels inside the barrier. Carlos had explained that there
were barrier reefs approximately eight to nine miles
out from the bay, and those reefs, he claimed, tra-
versed the Baja coastline for close to fifty miles. If
that was the case, mariners had two choices: sail
inside the reef or sail outside the reef. I did not
know the level of Rowland's nautical expertise, but
it seemed natural to assume it was fairly extensive
if he thought himself capable of skippering a craft
nearly fifty feet long.

At any rate, in that brief period of time I had spotted no less than two vessels headed south and two
headed north, all inside the reef. My conclusion
was that most captains thought it prudent to sail the
safer waters inside the reef.

At the same time, I reached another conclusion:
If someone made a habit of watching ships, the
passing (or sinking) of such an oversized vessel as
the *Baja Lady* would probably be noticed. The challenge, of course, would be to locate that individual.

At this juncture, Stepdaddy Galen would have
counseled me to seek the assistance of a professional. "Hire someone who knows what they're doing, Abraham."

The problem, of course, was that I did not know

R. Karl Largent

anyone who fit that bill. Bahia Magdalena did not appear to be a hotbed of professional services. I marched on up the beach to continue my search.

Moments later, with hunger pangs evident, I realized I had worked my way north several hundred meters and saw Jean Jean's "little eating place" in the distance. Score one for the rookie investigator. I was now in position to right two wrongs. I had skipped breakfast. I still owed Amy a call. Within minutes, I was convinced, both would be rectified.

Journal: No. 4

Wrong again, or at least partially so. The complaining stomach as the result of skipping breakfast could be fixed. The fare listed on the broken piece of slate blackboard above Jean Jean's counter didn't exactly indicate fine cuisine. Fortunately, however, most of it was at least food I had heard of before.

The phone, on the other hand, was a definite "absolutely not." Jean Jean elaborated where Carlos did not. The phones around Las Cuevas had been out for over a month. Apparently, the good folk of Las Cuevas had suffered through a rather nasty storm in early May. That was when the phones went out. The repair crews hadn't gotten as far as Bahia Magdalena yet.

The fish *du jour* for Friday, June 6, was yellow-jack. Jean Jean had chalked it in under the word "fish." There was also an offering of chowder, and something called Jean Jean's gumbo. I opted for the gumbo.

Jean Jean's "little eating place," as it turned out, was not a misnomer. The building was, as were many in the Las Cuevas area, made of wood, bereft of paint and no more than 12' by 20'. In one half, Jean Jean cooked and served the food. She had a two-burner gas stove, an assortment of pie tins which served as plates, a collection of mismatched knives, spoons, forks, and miscellaneous cooking utensils, tin cups, china cups, and glasses.

The area where Jean Jean's customer's ate was equipped with hurricane shutters that hinged out from the roof to reveal a counter. Customers sat on stools (there were four), and depending on the time of day and the location of the Baja sun, the shutters could conceivably provide the customer with shade.

The other half of the building appeared to be Jean Jean's home. She had left the door between the two sections open, and I could see a bed, a small chest, a lamp, and little else. Jean Jean's digs weren't exactly a study in opulence.

I took a seat, requested a menu, Jean Jean pointed at the blackboard, and I pointed at the gumbo selection. She turned around, grabbed a bowl, spooned ample amounts of a thick brew of assorted fish parts, peppers, vegetables, and local spices out of a bucket on the back burner and put the bowl on the counter in front of me. Then she stood with her hands on her hips, waiting. When I didn't say anything, Jean Jean sighed and reached under the counter for the tequila. "It won't make it taste any different, but in twenty minutes or so you won't care how it tasted."

I glanced at my watch, noted the time and the fact I was the only customer in the house. "Lunch rush over?" I asked.

Jean Jean's expression did not change. "You're it," she said. "When the weather's nasty, I sometimes have three or four customers this time of day. When it's nice, I frequently dine alone. That's how I learned about the tequila. Sometimes Admiral doesn't catch anything. When that happens, it isn't fish du jour, it's fish du yesterday or fish du the day before that."

"Admiral?"

Jean Jean's eyebrows had a way of knitting themselves into an expression of puzzlement and apology. "You're a newcomer to these parts. You haven't even met Admiral, have you?"

"Admiral who?" I asked.

The lady's frown became a half grin. She rolled her eyes up and around. "Gee, I guess I don't really know what his real name is. Everyone was calling him Admiral when I got here. I've been calling him Admiral ever since."

I finished the gumbo, shoved the bowl away, and made a *boy, was that filling* gesture. That seemed to please Jean Jean, and we lapsed into another conversation. She confessed that she did not miss life back in the good old United States and that she had come to love both the land and the people in Baja Sur. "There isn't much pretense down here," she said. "Everyone takes everyone at face value. We all kinda know what we're getting." Then she added, "I figure I'll die here. They can bury me out just past the reef."

The comment was a tad too maudlin for my tastes and I said, "Tell me about Carlos Martinenez."

Jean Jean studied me for several moments before she said, "Why do you ask? I mean, you aren't a cop or something, are you?"

"Nothing like that. Remember that yacht I was telling you I was looking for? Well, I was thinking about hiring Captain Martinenez to help me find it. What I really want to know is how well he knows the waters around here and how dependable he is."

"Around here? You sound like maybe you think this yacht you're looking for went down in the waters somewhere around Bahia Magdalena."

"One of my source's claims it did," I said.

"You don't volunteer a whole lot, do you?" Jean Jean appraised. "When do I get the whole story, or do you *tell* whole stories?"

I was in the process of trying to decide whether to regale Jean Jean Baybone with the whole story. If I did, I would still see no reason to get into such

potentially confusing things as corporate identities,
defining defense contracts, or the divergence in reports of Rowland's whereabouts.

All of this was still rattling around in my head
when I realized that Jean Jean was looking past me
and out at a figure approaching in the distance.

"You're in luck," Jean Jean said. "Here comes the
Admiral now."

It would not have mattered whether Ms. Baybone
had given me ten minutes or ten days to conjure
up a vision of Admiral; I would still have been
wrong. Never would I have envisioned an emaci-
ated caricature of a bony little man who made Mo-
handas Gandhi look like a study in muscle
development.

The Admiral was walking toward me, a bald,
chicken-chested aberration more or less materializing out of the sea mist on a day when there was
no sea mist. He was walking along the beach,
dressed in a pair of dirty, cut-off khakis held up by
a piece of clothesline. That was the sum total of his
clothes. His skin was the color and texture of burnt
parchment, he wore no top, no shoes, and he was
carrying a string of banjo fish.

Jean Jean greeted him with a toothy smile and
began the introductions while he was still a good
ten feet away. "I found us a new friend, Admiral. I
don't know how long he'll be staying here in Las
Cuevas, but I want you to meet Mr. Furnace. He says
his friends call him A. J."

The Admiral stood looking at me, blinking like a

sand lizard in the glare of the hot Baja sun. When
he managed to work all those sun-baked wrinkles
into what passed for a smile, it revealed the fact that
he had no teeth. I've been in, on, and around the
water ever since I discovered my interest in submarines, but never have I encountered a man who
more deserved to be called an "old salt."

The way his mouth moved when he greeted me
reminded me of a fish mouthing oxygen, but the
sound was more like the screaks of a dolphin. I was
still trying to figure out how I was going to communicate with the man when I realized that Jean
Jean had already launched into a detailed description of why I was in Las Cuevas.

"A. J. here is looking for a friend and his yacht,"
Jean Jean said.

Under most circumstances I would have expected someone in the Admiral's position to ask a
bevy of questions, whether feigning interest or being genuinely inquisitive. The Admiral did neither.
Instead, he sat there, slightly slack-jawed, and
waited for the woman to continue. As far as I could
tell, thus far Las Cuevas's Admiral had exhibited all
the life signs of the two dead worms in that bottle
of Dos Gusanos.

On the other hand, Jean Jean Baybone was less
daunted. Apparently, she knew what it took to get
through to the little man, because she promptly
went into more detail about my search for Tyler
Rowland. "A. J. says he has it from a reliable source
that his friend's yacht went down somewhere

around here. It was a rather large yacht, a forty-eight-footer. Did you happen to see it, or remember it?"

I wanted to add, "Or see it sink?"

The Admiral displayed his keen grasp of the magnitude of the Rowland/*Baja Lady* situation by yawning, looking past me, and gesturing in a fashion I could only interpret as a secret signal. Jean Jean reached under the counter, brought out the bottle of tequila, filled an eight-ounce glass, and pushed it in the Admiral's direction. At that point he handed over the string of banjo fish. I was witnessing commerce, Baja Sur style.

The Admiral gulped down the tequila and wiped his mouth with the back of his hand. I now had perhaps the most vital clue in working my way through the puzzle of the Admiral's lack of communication skills. There was reason to believe that bolting eight ounces of tequila every time he handed fish over to Jean Jean had seriously diminished his communication skills. Either that or it was too early in the day to do any talking. I would later learn it was both.

"Or do you know anything about it?" Jean Jean finally asked.

The Admiral began grunting, wheezing, and gesturing. Slow at first, I could tell he was building up a head of steam. His face was shaped like he had a whole mouthful of things to say but was having trouble spitting the words out. " 'Bout two—two—

97

three weeks ago," he finally stuttered, "Rainbow say he saw one go down."

Jean Jean's eyes darted from the Admiral's tormented face back to me and finally back to the dollop-sized Admiral. "Rainbow said he saw a boat sink?"

The Admiral's head continued to bob up and down like it was on a spring.

"A big one?" I asked.

The Admiral held up his hands with the palms facing each other. They were a good two feet apart to indicate the immensity of the vanished vessel.

Jean Jean and the Admiral appeared to be communicating in some kind of cryptic language that consisted of very few words but lost of gestures and grunts. Finally she hit him with the sixty-four-dollar question. "Do you think Rainbow could show Mr. A. J. here where he saw it happen?"

The Admiral grunted, clapped his hands together in glee, signaled for a refill on the tequila, and managed to get his head bobbing again. I took that to mean "yes."

The Baja lunch club ended with Jean Jean eliciting a promise from the Admiral to bring Rainbow by the "little eating place" the following day. Purpose, as Jean Jean explained, to inform both her and me where he saw the yacht go down.

I wasn't sure how I felt about Jean Jean suddenly inserting herself into the search for Rowland without my invitation . . . but there she was. And since

I did not know the territory all that well, maybe that wasn't all bad.

Following the Admiral's departure, I had the opportunity to ask a few more questions, like just how reliable was this Rainbow character?

Jean Jean admitted that she did not know him all that well but had heard nothing negative about him. Then she added that she had heard nothing negative about the Admiral either. That's when I began to worry.

I took my time meandering back toward Las Cuevas. Along the way I had time to figure out what I wanted to do next. It involved finding out what Carlos knew about the Admiral and Rainbow.

I was still waiting for Carlos on the steps of the Las Cuevas *el hotel* when the Baja sun began playing hide-and-seek with a deck of stratus clouds hugging the western horizon. It was cooling off fast.

Marie was waiting as well. She sat in a rocking chair dutifully calling off the names of each of the fishermen as they returned to port and hung out their nets. As she did, she explained how the Las Cuevas economy worked. A man by the name of Raymond Acobar would come by with his "icebox" truck and buy many of the fish the locals had caught that day. He in turn would sell his catch in La Paz, Todos Santos, Cabo San Lucas, and San Jose del Cabo. "And maybe some other places," Marie said with a shrug.

"What about the rest of the fish?" I asked.

It occurred to me that if the good folks of Las Cuevas ever decided to build a Chamber of Commerce, Marie would be the ideal person to run it. She had an answer for everything, and her answer always seemed to put her village in the best possible light. "We eat some, the rest go to the fertilizer plant." Marie pinched her nose and made a face. "Not a good place to work."

I mused for the next several minutes trying to imagine just how foul a fish fertilizer plant would smell. Then I threw into the equation such factors as *no wind* and *June midday Baja sun*. A small voice inside my head told me to speculate no further.

Meanwhile, Marie was pointing out that she could see Carlos and his crew tying up at the dock.

Two hours later, after Marie had worked her grilling magic on a sea bass with mustard sauce, Carlos and I again retired to the hotel's veranda where I struggled with tequila and rose water, but no ice. Smell: good. Taste: marginal. Carlos nursed a warm Bud. Carlos was adamant that he had no intention of cranking up the ice machine unless there was surplus fish to keep iced.

Our after-dinner conversation had tiptoed through Jean Jean and her dining establishment (Carlos knew her and had nice things to say about her), to the Admiral (Carlos had heard some things about him but had met him only once or twice), to the one called Rainbow (Carlos offered no comment—he just shook his head).

"You say this Rainbow fella claims he saw where

a fairly good-sized vessel sank?" Carlos asked.

"That's according to the Admiral," I reminded him. "Think we can put any stock in the report?"

"Did he report it to the Coast Guard?"

I didn't know the answer to that one so I did what everyone else in Las Cuevas seemed to do under similar circumstances: I shrugged.

I was aware that Carlos still had not answered my question about the wisdom of accepting Rainbow's report at face value. "Think it's worth the time it takes to check it out?" I persisted.

Before he answered, Carlos hauled a very big, very black cigar out of his shirt pocket, scratched a match on the porch flooring, lit the cigar, and made life lamentable for sand fleas, flies, and a bevy of other night creatures. Even the old dog sleeping at the end of the porch got up and moved. Carlos was shaking his shaggy-haired head through the entire ritual. "What better lead have you got?"

Theoretical questions seldom have answers. It was time for me to shrug again and take a swig of my tequila and rose water.

"Heard somethin' on the ship-to-shore radio today," Carlos volunteered. "I like to do a little eavesdroppin' every now and then. Heard two of your American friends speculatin' on what that big Chinese commercial fishin' trawler was doin' in these waters."

"Is that something out of the ordinary?" I asked.

Carlos paused, took a drag on his cigar, started shaking his head, and exhaled. The cloud of purple smoke along with its distressing aroma hung heavy over our heads. "We don't see many of them commercial fishin' boats down here," he said. "We used to get some Japanese fishin' boats hangin' around in the winter months a few years ago, but we ain't seen more than one or two of them in the last three or four years. Everyone around here figures the pickin's musta got too slim for them to justify comin' all the way over here."

"Then why would the Chinese?"

It was Carlos's turn to shrug again. "Maybe the Chinese think the Japanese just got a little too picky. Maybe they think there's is enough here for them to justify the trip. Or maybe they think a bunch of dumb, damn Mexicans are just too poor and too ignorant to complain."

It was at this juncture that Carlos sighed and allowed his voice to trail off. He had said enough. People who have a legitimate complaint seldom find it necessary to elaborate on why a wrong is a wrong. To Carlos, the Chinese bringing a commercial fishing vessel into their already overfished waters was wrong. Nor was it necessary for him to further articulate his displeasure at the way the waters were being overfished by the Mexican commercial fishing fleet, at the hordes of charter and so-called "sport fishing boats," and the unending invasion by posturing Yankee pleasure craft. "Sometimes it just gets a little too crowded out there," he said.

"I know this sounds like an impertinent question," I began, "but how much money do you make on a really good day?"

The Anthony Quinn look-alike and captain of a brace of nearly fifty-year-old fishing vessels stared at me for several moments. I think he was trying to decide whether he was going to answer my question or slug me. He was glowering, and I realized I had laid the groundwork for a sudden freeze in our burgeoning friendship. When he finally answered, his response was surprisingly civilized. "I assume there's a good reason for you wanting to know?"

"There is," I said. "I would like to hire you and one of your vessels to help me find the *Baja Lady*. And I would like to know how much it's going to cost me."

"You or your company?" he probed.

"What difference does it make?"

"If *you* want to hire me, it's one price. If your company wants to hire me, it'll cost you more."

I knew Bro Roger would find fault with my negotiating skills (remember, I am the Furnace sent forth into battle without benefit of an MBA), but I took a certain delight in instructing Carlos to bill me at the going corporate rate. "Send the bill to Furnace Standard, care of my brother, Roger," I said. Was it the right thing to do? After all, it was Bro Roger's decision to cave into veiled threats by Amy Reed and her California Maritime cohorts.

It was at that moment I realized I had once again been derelict in my obligations to the fair Ms. Reed. Two days had passed without me calling her. An hour or so later, after negotiating price, departure time, and who and what would be included, I decided the eighteen-mile drive to the phone booth and the subsequent call would be an unnecessary expense as well as vastly inopportune. After all, at the moment I really didn't know any more than I did when I landed in La Paz. I reasoned that if I called tomorrow, that would be soon enough.

Saturday

By the time mid-morning rolled around I had accomplished a surprising amount. Surprising indeed after a night of tosses and turns sandwiched in between puzzling dreams populated by the likes of Jean Jean, the Admiral, Marie, and the dog on the hotel porch. I bounced out of bed, suffered through my second blood-congealing cold shower in as many days, and trundled down the stairs to see what Marie had cooked up. Then, after a feast of *jamon de York* and *los huevos* topped off with Marie's version of *sun café solo*, I yielded to feelings of guilt. I had been remiss in fulfilling my daily exercise regime. To assuage my guilt, I jogged all the way to Jean Jean's place. When I got there, she was making gumbo out of day-old banjo fish.

As usual, she was affable. "Good morning," she chirped.

"Good morning," I said. It's too bad Galen didn't live long enough to see how well I had developed my social skills.

"Learn anything else about your friend's boat?"

she asked. Where had I given the impression that Rowland was a friend? And when had a forty-eight-foot yacht become a mere "boat"?

"That's why I'm here. I need some info. I need to round up the Admiral and his friend, Rainbow. I've chartered one of Captain Martinenez's boats to go take a look at that spot where Rainbow told the Admiral he saw the yacht go down."

"About a mile up the beach you'll see a jetty," she said. "They live on the hill behind it—maybe another five hundred yards. If they aren't out fishing, there will be a couple of dinghies tied up at the pier." Jean Jean glanced at her watch. It was an old Timex, bent and battered but still working. It reminded me of the old black-and-white TV ads when I was a pup, "It takes a licking and keeps on ticking." I thanked her for her directions and headed north along the beach. The last thing I heard her say was, "Don't be surprised at what you find when you get there."

After the Admiral, I thought to myself, what could be all that surprising?

Okay, I was surprised. Maybe caught off guard would be a better way of expressing it. The Admiral in some fashion or other had managed to lay claim to a prime but desolate piece of Baja Sur real estate, and promptly plunked a road-weary old semitrailer down right in the middle of it. A number of square holes had been cut in the side walls of the trailer. They were the windows. There was a large hole in the center section. That was the doorway. The porch and other wooden appointments had been fashioned out of driftwood and assorted pieces of construction material that had washed up on the beach.

Both dinghies were tied up at the pier, and an assortment of fishing gear was scattered about. I positioned myself in the middle of the small patch of Baja clutter and started calling out, "Admiral, are you in there?"

It took a while, but finally the Admiral appeared in the doorway. Thankfully, he was facing me full on. Had he not been, I might not have seen him. As dear Dara would have phrased it, "He was one skinny cat." Behind him was a huge black man with a barrel chest, massive arms, a bald head, and eyes bitterly opposed to the concept of working in unison.

"You—you—want something?" the Admiral asked. I was impressed. Jean Jean's reticent fish supplier had tied three words together in one sentence and they came out in the right order. At the same time, he had emerged from the shadows of his trailer-made house to stand in the middle of the compound. He was carrying a revolver of some vintage and eyeing me like a bounty hunter.

"Is that Rainbow?" I asked, pointing at the hulking figure in the shadows behind him.

The Admiral nodded.

"Ask him if he's willing to show me where he claims he saw that yacht go down."

The Admiral turned around, slowly backtracked his way into his steel shanty, and engaged Rainbow in a semianimated conversation. It continued for several minutes. When he emerged the second time, he was holding a slip of paper.

"Got—got—two questions," he said. He began reading from the paper. "One, Rainbow wants—wants to know—how we're going to get—get—out—out there? Two, he wants to know how much—much you'll be—be payin' him for goin'—out—out there."

There was a certain irony in that the younger man, who most would say had most of his wits about him, was being exploited by a certifiably enfeebled older man. I was a good foot taller than the Admiral and outweighed him by at least 125 pounds. It was one of those rare instances when size really doesn't matter. He was calling the shots.

"Tell Rainbow I chartered a boat from Carlos Martinenez. Then tell him I'll pay him twenty-five dollars, American, for going out there with us and pointing out the spot where he thinks he saw the yacht go down. You can also tell him I'll pay him another twenty-five dollars if it's the yacht I'm looking for."

This time there was no need for the Admiral to trundle back for a second confab with his portly pal. Rainbow, it seems, was capable of making up his own mind when it came to money matters. He lumbered out of the shadows, held out a ham-sized hand, and waited for me to peel off two tens and a five. He was buck naked.

"When?" Rainbow grunted.

"How about leaving now?" I said.

"Now?" he repeated. The urgency must have hit him hard. His expression when he looked back at his skinny friend reminded me of a child who had just been informed there was no time to finish his Jell-O. "Admiral go where Rainbow go," he announced.

"How—how about it?" the Admiral asked. "Is—is there room for—me—me in that boat?"

"Sure." I grinned. "I'm easy to get along with. But if we take you out there and we need an extra pair of hands when we locate that yacht, you're part of the crew. Got it?"

I could tell from the Admiral's expression that he wasn't overly thrilled with my offer, but neither did he hesitate. If there was action, he wanted to be a part of it. "Got—got to protect my—friend," he said. "Me and—and—Rainbow, we shares."

I mulled the word "shares" over in my mind several times and then forgot about it.

The morning was pretty well shot, the sun was high in the sky, the noon hour had come and gone, and it was getting hotter by the *minuto* when everything was finally ready. I wouldn't exactly call it yacht-search fever, but it didn't take a whole lot of effort to get everyone headed in the same direction. Money motivates.

I, of course, was last in line as the village's main man led his scruffy entourage of intrepid *Baja Lady* hunters down to the community pier. When we got there, we bypassed the two antiquated trawlers Carlos had inherited from his grandfather and moved on to an equally elderly twenty-three-foot-long inboard runabout. Somewhere in its past it had served a master of higher station. There were Mexican Coast Guard numerals and insignias on the side to vouch for that fact.

I watched Carlos stow his gear. Actually, he just threw it in the boat. Despite its advanced years, the craft still appeared to be seaworthy. As a matter of fact, the make and model of the vessel looked familiar. I vaguely recalled the time Bro Roger sent me east to work with the boys and girls at Woods Hole. It was there I learned that back in Massachusetts they called a craft of similar construction a "yard boat."

Constructed of wood, the vessel had a center-mounted engine, a towing post at the stern, and the bow was enclosed back to the helm. Despite its apparent age and the scars of a multitude of summers, it still managed to look decidedly more serviceable than the twenty-one-foot dory tied up alongside it.

Lastly, there was the matter of the vessel's name. Someone with more wit and aplomb than I had christened the vessel the *Mezcal*—a shot of which should have been passed out along with every boarding pass.

As it turned out, even getting the engine started was an achievement of considerable merit. It took Carlos a good ten minutes of tweaking and carping before the brute coughed to life. I suspect that even that would not have been enough had he not unleashed a stream of profanity and threatened to put a bullet in the beast's carburetor.

Then, just moments before two o'clock, with a crew consisting of Carlos, the Admiral, Rainbow, and I, we pulled away from the pier and chugged toward the mouth of the inlet. Carlos was at the helm, I was beside him, and both the Admiral and Rainbow had assumed seats in the stern. From time to time one or the other muttered something that to me was either inaudible or impossible to decipher. On the other hand, each time they did, Carlos checked his compass and altered his course slightly.

Now there were two-foot swells in the channel to contend with. As we trudged laboriously from the sanctuary of the inlet into the open water inside the reef, Carlos launched into a lengthy dissertation on the waters of Bahia Magdalena. According to Carlos, Las Cuevas had been settled and named by fishermen sometime back around the 1850s. The name of the village, of course, meant *the caves*. The area encompassed a nearly fifty-mile-long and seven-to-nine-mile-wide expanse just inside the Magdalena barrier reef. It was dotted and interlaced, he informed me, by a series of holes or caves that went down up to forty or fifty feet before tunneling horizontally.

The surface was dotted with occasional rocky outcroppings, a few pinnacles, and the inevitable ocean rocks.

We had motored about five miles out when Carlos lit one of his cigars, squinted out over the sunbathed waters, and started talking about the caves. "Some of them have names," he said. "Some are connected and it's hard to know when you're in one and go to another. At certain times of the year the fishing is good in the caves."

While he talked, Carlos handed me a crudely sketched map of the area. Marie had done most of the drawing with Carlos sitting at her side, he said. I studied the chart and made note of the fact that some of the caves were no more than fifteen feet at the mouth while others might run a half kilometer or so.

"Lots of fish down there," Carlos reflected. "A man could make a decent livin' if that was all he had to fish."

While Carlos occupied himself in keeping us headed toward some as yet unidentified point, I noticed that the Admiral and Rainbow were distracted by something else. The Admiral was standing up, pointing down at the water. Some twenty yards behind us I could see two vortices trailing out from a good-sized dorsal fin. When the creature got a little closer I could identify the wide mouth, broad nose, and dark stripes on its gray back. It was a tiger

111

shark, which in all probability had come inside the reef to feed the previous evening. Carlos watched it catch up to us and eventually veer off to port.

"Sharks. I don't like them," he said. He was scowling. "I know this one. He stays inside the channel and sometimes he follows me."

"Nasty-looking fellow," I observed. I could have shown off a bit and identified the tiger as a Galeocerdo Cuvier, but so far Carlos seemed to be the kind who put more stock in people prone to plain talk. "But then, I guess they aren't much of a threat in shallows like these. Right?"

Carlos shook his head. "Inside the reef waters one day I saw a tiger shark attack a cow that was cooling itself in two feet of beach water. It dragged the cow under, and the water turned red." He took a long drag on his cigar and exhaled a pungent gray-purple cloud. "The whole episode," he said, "didn't take more then three or four minutes."

I was still watching the beast cruise back and forth no more then thirty or forty meters from the *Mezcal* when I heard a commotion in the back of the boat. Rainbow was on his feet again and pointing. The Admiral was interpreting.

"He—he says it happen about—about here," the Admiral informed us.

Carlos looked up and down the length of the waterway. He was frowning. "We're still in the shallows of the channel—not in the channel itself," he said. "The water in most of this area inside the reef is no more than thirty to forty feet deep. In the channel it's maybe seventy feet deep. I've fished here, close to the barrier before the fish go down to cooler water."

I was looking over the side, staring down into the water. It was clear, but it was doing a good job of hiding its treasure because of the reflection of the sun. "Are you certain this is the place?" I asked.

Rainbow was nodding. He continued to gesture. It was a stabbing motion and he was excited. "Rainbow see boat. Right here."

Rainbow's sudden exhilaration caused Carlos to turn on the *Mezcal*'s fish finder. It was a Korean War vintage L-4 sonar/probe unit. He continued to steer the small craft in a slow counterclockwise circle around the place where Rainbow was pointing. At the same time, he was trying to find something on the L-4 scope to justify Rainbow's excitement.

"I don't see anything," I complained.

"There's something on the scope," Carlos confirmed, "thirty-three to thirty-five feet down.

"You don't suppose it's the *Baja Lady*," I said. "What luck," I chirped. "First day out, first image on the old fish finder and we've found it." I was winking at Carlos and envisioning a rewarding return flight to SFO not later than two days hence.

"How long is this *Baja Lady* yacht of yours?" Carlos asked.

"Forty-eight feet."

He shook his head. His expression was solemn. "Then this isn't the one you're looking for," he said. "What you are looking at on the scope can be no

113

more than thirty feet in length, maybe even less."

"This isn't it? This isn't the *Baja Lady*?"

Carlos was still shaking his head, scouring the nearest point of the reef looking for reference points. "This may be the same wreckage I discovered three or four years ago. It's hard to tell. In shallows like these inside the channel, there's often a three- or four-knot current. In such a strong current, wrecks will shift from time to time."

I was listening and trying to overcome my disappointment. At the same time, I was straining, looking down into the water, trying to make something out of the shapeless image on the L-4 scope. Admittedly, it looked like anything but a yacht, but I was still hoping Carlos was wrong. Finally I asked, "Could it be the *Baja Lady* with the bow nosed into one of the caves?"

Carlos nodded. "Anything's possible."

"Okay, then," I pressed, "could the yacht have broken up? Maybe part of it is back in the cave. Maybe that's where the rest of it is."

A sardonic smile was beginning to play with the corners of Carlos' mouth behind the moustache. "What you see down there could have happened five weeks ago, five years ago . . . perhaps forty years ago, perhaps more. Who knows? If no one knew where this particular yacht was going and no one ever came looking for it, why should anyone know what happened? I'll show you many wrecks like this, if you wish. The Magdalena channel is littered with the wreckage of many like this."

I looked back at the Admiral and then Rainbow. Even though they could hear what Carlos was saying, they still sported expectant expressions. No doubt they were anticipating that I would dash to the back of the runabout, shake their hands, and hand them another twenty-five green ones. Maybe they were expecting even more than that. When I instead informed them that Carlos was convinced they had led us to the wrong wreck, Rainbow began eyeing me. Then he muttered something to the Admiral that sounded suspiciously like, "I don't trust this gringo."

Behind me I could hear Carlos questioning whether I was a good enough swimmer to want to dive down and take a look at the wreck appearing on the scope. "According to the finder, it's no more than five fathoms," he said. Then I heard him mutter, "If the damn thing is working."

I did some quick reconnoitering to determine if diving was even halfway feasible. If the tiger shark was gone, maybe. If he was still hanging around, definitely not. Unfortunately, the brute was less than thirty meters from the *Mezcal*, cruising about, biding his time, waiting for someone to do something dumb—like getting in the water to poke around a five-year-old wreckage.

Then I was distracted by something in the stern. Rainbow had suddenly unleashed an outburst that consisted of few words and a copious amount of gestures. He had the anorexic Admiral locked and loaded in the listening position.

115

"What's wrong with the big guy?" I asked. "He sounds upset."

The Admiral was glaring at me. "He—he is upset. He says he—he doesn't know why—why he came out—out here. Rainbow thinks—thinks you and—and—the captain are not—not listening to him."

I glanced back at Carlos and headed for the stern. "All right," I said, "we're both listening. Now just exactly what is it you wanted to tell me?"

Rainbow was a couple of inches taller than yours truly but probably enjoyed a two-hundred-pound weight advantage. He waited until I backed off before leaning close to his spindly confidant and whispering in his ear. When he finished, the Admiral drew himself up to his full five feet two inches, squared his shoulders, and relayed what his man mountain friend had told him. "He—he says he knows—knows he saw the boat—boat—boat you are looking—looking for—break up. One minute it—it was there, the—the—the next minute it was gone."

"Ask him why it sank. Did it explode? Was there a fire? Ask him if he remembers how it happened."

The Admiral turned back to his friend, repeated my questions, and listened as Rainbow again bent down to whisper in his ear. When the big man was finished, the Admiral turned to face me again. This time he was scowling. "Rainbow—likes to—fish—fish at night," he stuttered. "He says he was—out—out here fishing between the reef—and—and the shore and there was a full moon. He says he was just sitting there—minding—minding his boat when he saw—saw—this thing come—come down—down from out of the sky and hang like a bright—bright light right over the—the—yacht. Then, all of a—a—sudden, while he was watching, it—it—began shooting—shooting green and yellow rays down—down at the boat. He—says—says the water was—swirling—swirling around and then—then—there was a loud sucking sound and the yacht just disappeared. No—no explosion. No—no noise. No anything except—except quiet. Then the—the flying thing—thing went away."

"Wait a minute," I said. "Are you telling me Rainbow told you a saucer with a ray gun sank that yacht?"

I could tell by their expressions that both men were impressed with my ability to condense what the Admiral had told me into so few words. They looked at each other and then at me. The thing that bothered me was that I actually was able to understand what the Admiral had told me.

Most everyone knows I consider myself to be both a patient and a tolerant man. More often than not, the frailties and foibles of the human condition amuse me. But this was not one of those times. The mid-afternoon Baja sun was hammering down on me, I was where I did not want to be, doing something I did not want to do. I was feeling extremely perturbed and decidedly unsettled.

Instead of overreacting, I counted to ten and slowly repeated, for Carlos's benefit, exactly what the Admiral had told me. Then, having regained a modicum of control, I walked back to the helm and sagged down in the pilot's seat. "Sorry," I sighed. "It would appear I brought you out here on a wild goose chase. Apparently our friend Rainbow is the kind who sees saucers and hears the water making sucking sounds."

The *Mezcal*'s skipper glanced back over his shoulder before he looked at me. He was smiling. "I'll tell you what bothers me even more than that," he said. "His buddy, the Admiral, believed every word Rainbow was telling him."

Journal: No. 5

Saturday, June 7

There is an old Furnace family saying that a great deal can be accomplished when efforts are focused. So when I, along with Carlos and the rest of the intrepid *Baja Lady* search team, finally returned to the docks at Las Cuevas, I was inspired to report to my colleagues back in California. No small chore. It was already early evening.

I knew it would be chancy trying to find the unholy trio on the weekend, but I had the advantage of knowing that both Bro and Dara in all probability would be at home after spending a good portion of the day at the office. Bro was a sure bet, because that's what CEO's think they are supposed to do on weekends—play golf in the morning and stay home

119

and play family in the afternoon. Dara was a longer shot, because I always slip her a little extra money when she goes in on Saturday to tidy up my paperwork. Whether or not she would still be at the office depended on whether or not she needed money.

Amy would be the real long shot in the trio. A person can't expect to find someone of her bore and stroke sitting home on a Saturday night waiting for the phone to ring.

To contact all three, I had to race from Las Cuevas, where I had established my temporary headquarters, to the only working telephone in the area. This, as I have previously pointed out, is inconveniently located at the exit of the Transpeninsular Highway.

True, we're talking here of a distance of no more than eighteen miles (one way), but eighteen miles on the road from Highway 1 to Las Cuevas may well be the equivalent of forty or fifty miles driving time, given the assortment of potholes, detours, and other impediments.

Once I got to the phone, I managed to get through to all three of my neglected confederates. The first call was to Amy Reed, the second to Roger, and the last to my perpetual connection to reality, dauntless Dara. It should come as no surprise that each responded to my call with essentially the same opening volley, "Where the hell have you been" or words to that effect.

I opened my conversation with each by explaining that my journey thus far had taken me to the tiny village of Las Cuevas on the shores of Bahia Magdalena. I further revealed that even though my original source had indicated this was the site of the *Baja Lady*'s reported demise, thus far I had been unable to verify that as fact.

That tiny bit of news seemed to assuage them. None of them bothered to inquire if I was eating my vegetables or getting the proper amount of sleep. Only one, Amy, even bothered to ask me about the weather. It was also she who had the most intriguing news. She had learned that a great deal of import had been attached to certain security provisions in Unitrieve's handling of the CARTO Project—understandable and not at all uncommon when dealing with the minions of Uncle Sam.

Before she could elaborate, however, I interrupted. "When we had our first conversation about Unitrieve, your primary concern was their financial stability. Now you're talking security problems as well. Why?"

"One leads to the other," Amy responded. "While you've been vacationing in sunny Bahia Magdalena, I've been doing some very serious digging. The situation at Unitrieve is even worse then we first thought."

"What do you mean, worse?"

"I mean their financial problems are a lot worse than we imagined, and the firm's security practices, especially as they relate to the CARTO Project, have a number of people at the DOD very concerned."

"Real people or government types?"

"Both."

"Elaborate," I said.

"Okay," she said, "let's start with the fact that I recently learned that just eight weeks prior to his disappearance, the same consortium of bankers Tyler Rowland and Jacob Hake have been working with for the last eight years refused to either lend Unitrieve any more money or give Unitrieve an extension on their current loan."

"Wait," I said, "let me guess. You're going to tell me why."

"According to my sources, gross mismanagement of funds in the CARTO Project start-up phase, and evidence of continued questionable financial practices during the design and development phase."

"Are your sources reliable?" Not a frivolous question.

"The best, A. J. Insiders at Unitrieve and one of Unitrieve's bankers. All right, now couple that little bit of background info with what else I've learned . . ."

Even though the sun had worked its way to the west and the world to the east was darkening, it was still uncomfortably warm. The phone booth I was standing in had spent the day soaking up heat, I was sweating, and there were three very impatient-looking people waiting to use the phone. Despite all that, I urged Amy onward and upward.

"One week after Rowland and Hake were told 'no' by the bankers, Rowland disappeared for ten days—"

"Then this isn't the first time he has slipped off the face of the earth?"

"True, but it is the first time he has disappeared with a forty-eight-foot yacht for more than three weeks. You don't hide something like that under the bed."

Amy had a point, but I did too. "My point is," I said, "it's entirely possible our boy Rowland could just up and reappear like he has in the past."

"You disappoint me. You haven't asked me where Rowland went those ten days," Amy scolded.

"Okay, I'll play your game. Where did he go?"

"China. More specifically, Beijing."

"How do you know that?"

"I'm sitting here at my desk looking at a copy of his most recent American Express credit card invoice. Everything is here, including the name of the hotel he stayed at in Beijing. Would you like to know how much money he spent entertaining Chinese dignitaries?"

"Not important," I said, "and it may not be relevant. Lots of people go to China these days. You may be attaching significance to something that has no significance. Maybe he and his wife wanted to get away for a few days, eat a lot of rice, that sort of thing."

"Mrs. Rowland did not go with him," Amy said, "but someone did."

"Who? Man or woman?"

"I'm still trying to find out."

"Hmmmm," I said, trying to make it sound like I

thought Amy had uncovered information of some import. To be quite honest, though, I wasn't certain if I thought it was important—or why I thought it essential to bolster her ego.

Then I suggested she contact some of the bigger yacht brokers up and down the West Coast to see if anyone had requested service for or tried to palm off a forty-eight-footer on them in the last few days.

"Already done," Amy informed me. "That was one of the first things I checked on."

After that it was all downhill. Amy and I exchanged a few pleasantries, and I again promised to call her, this time no later then Monday night. Then, without letting the three people waiting to use the telephone get excited about their prospects, I dialed Bro Roger. His opening sounded similar to Ms. Reed's. "Where the hell have you been?"

I reminded him he was the one who had insisted I cooperate with Ms. Reed and her cohorts at Cal Maritime. "I'm using a small village by the name of Las Cuevas as my base of operations," I informed him. As usual, whenever I'm having a conversation with Bro, I resort to a matter-of-fact business tone. That seems to work best with Roger.

Instead of trying to console me, he informed me that the project director on the Pony program had called him earlier in the day to inquire when I would be conducting the shakedown runs. When Bro told him I was out of town, the man replied that was unfortunate. He along with his team of stout-hearted technicians had completed the laboratory evaluations of the Pony, and now it was ready to be trundled off for a test or two in open water.

"You're the one that sent me on this," I reminded Roger and hoped I sounded like I was working. "In the meantime, tell Hennings and his people to get their lab reports together and give you a copy. I'll be there in plenty of time to do the testing."

"I'm quite sure you will," Bro sneered.

After that, I quickly ended the call to get on to the next, Dara. She was still at the office. Good girl. Her greeting was no more original than the other two, and, if possible, she was even less enthusiastic about hearing from me. I assume this was not because of any personal dislike but rather because she was ready to shut down her work station, pick up her purse, head for the door, and call it a day. Bonus earned.

"Do you know the code to my private closet in that little conference room next to my office?" I asked.

I could hear Dara huff. "I have the code or key to everything in this division," she assured me. "If you didn't give me the code or key, I managed to get them elsewhere."

"How?"

"Don't ask. Now, what is it you want from your little hiding place?"

"My diving gear."

"Oh, going to do a little recreational diving after the hard day's work?"

"Never mind the venom," I hissed, "just make certain everything I'll need is in that sea bag and ship it down here the fastest way possible."

"Aye, aye, sir," she snapped.

The Taurus limped back into Las Cuevas somewhere around ten o'clock. One tire was low, no spare, no jack, no tire pump, and one wheel was wobbling. The latter was the victim of the largest pothole in the history of potholes. Making it back to Las Cuevas was one thing; the question now was whether or not the car would have enough grit to make it back to the rental agency at La Paz.

I parked at the side of the hotel, walked up on the veranda, stepped over the dog, and found Carlos right where I had left him three hours earlier—sitting in a rocking chair, cigar in one hand, a bottle of Budweiser in the other. This time, however, there were two men with him. "Join us, amigo," he said.

There is a theory that if you are married to the same person long enough, you will eventually begin to look and act like that person. It's a good theory, and I buy it in part. But I have observed another, somewhat similar phenomenon. If an individual hangs around with other folks of the same persuasion or occupation long enough, sooner or later they too will begin to take on many of the same characteristics.

Captain Carlos's companions were at least a partial validation of that theory. Like Carlos, they were raw-boned, dark, and weathered men who looked like they had labored long and hard for the privilege of being called "Captain." Because of that, they had also earned the right to sit next to Carlos on the biggest veranda in all of Las Cuevas. So when Carlos invited me to join the three of them, it was like being invited into the big boys' club.

"A. J.," Carlos rumbled, "want you to meet a couple of friends of mine." His voice was thick, and his smile listed slightly to port. There was every indication that Captain Carlos had indulged in too many Dos Gusanos with Bud chasers. He managed to point to the man on his left, who, like Carlos, was a big, bulky, substantial-looking man with thick gray hair and a full gray beard. "Meet Viktor Yulanov. He's a former Russian Navy man. Came here twenty years ago, and he's been fishin' these waters ever since."

Yulanov looked me up and down and grunted his appraisal. "Do much fishin'?" he asked.

I shook my head.

Carlos wasn't done. "And this is my oldest friend, Bo Bo Acosta. When he was a boy he fished these waters with my grandfather."

Of the two, Acosta appeared to be the one who might be the most receptive to the idea of an occasional tourist in Las Cuevas. He smiled, and we shook hands. Yulanov appeared to have more of a KGB or GRU mentality. He did not offer to shake hands.

I was still in the process of sitting down when Carlos invited the Russian to repeat what he had been telling him earlier. "Tell Abraham what you told me about that Chinese fishing trawler."

Yulanov had a thick, decidedly Russian accent. Even though he had taken up residence in the Baja several years earlier, his English, while not good, was much better than his Spanish. "I tell Carlos," he began, "Chinese fishing vessel is still working waters inside reef."

I looked at Carlos and repeated the words, "Chinese fishing vessel?" Then I remembered our conversation from the previous evening. "A bit unusual, isn't it? Technically, when they're fishing inside the reef they're fishing in Mexican waters—aren't they?"

Carlos agreed with me. "In the past we've reported such violations to the Mexican Coast Guard, but they're too busy with drug patrols. Before, it was the Japanese. Now it's the Chinese. When the Coast Guard does come, it slaps their hands and tells them to move on. But in a day or two they're back."

Yulanov took a long, healthy swig of whatever it was he was drinking, wiped his hand across his mouth, and stared down at the dust. He was shaking his head; clearly an indication of his dismay at whatever it was he was about to tell me. When he spoke, his voice had somehow managed to become thicker. "I tell my friend Carlos, five weeks ago I locate place where fishing is good. I mark spot. I go back and fish same waters every day for whole week. Twice I come back to Las Cuevas at night with so many fish Acobar make one trip for everyone else in village and one just for Yulanov."

"Tell Abraham about the boat that does not fish," Carlos urged.

Yulanov seemed only too happy to have the opportunity to continue to vent. "One morning I go back same place where I have been fishing many days, but Chinese are anchored right over place Yulanov marked with flag. When Yulanov tell them they are poaching, they tell him to go away."

Acosta confirmed Yulanov's story. "Big boat," he repeated, "like Viktor says, like a trawler." Then he looked at Carlos. "Viktor is right when he says it looks like a fishing boat, but it does not act like one."

"Tell him about the net they put out," Carlos pushed.

The light was such that it was hard to tell exactly what Viktor Yulanov looked like. The veranda's half-moon shadows conspired to conceal his features, but the smoldering resentment was evident in his voice. "When Yulanov get close to Chinese boat, they use loudspeaker. They tell Yulanov to go away. They tell Yulanov they have nets and longlines out, but Yulanov not see a longline reel on deck."

"They don't even have their scuppers blocked off," Acosta chimed in. "When they dump their nets, what is to keep the fish from washing back into the water?"

"That net, it's not like any net Yulanov see before," the Russian continued. "Net it is made of some kind of metal wire material. Radio beacons attached to it."

Acosta was easier to read. He was equally perturbed, but the light was such that you could see the indignation in his eyes. He had the habit of gesturing with his hands when he talked, and he spoke so fast it was sometimes difficult to catch up with him. "Viktor said he saw what happened when one of the *Americano* pleasure boats was passing through on its way south. Viktor said the *Americano* happened to get too close to the net, and one of the men from the Chinese vessel came out in a little inflatable dinghy and told the *Americano* to go away because they were conducting experiments."

"Experiments?" I repeated.

Bo Bo nodded. "They say experiments."

Listening to the three old salts from Bahia Magdalena was fascinating fare, but it wasn't doing much to help me find answers to the Rowland riddle. They were talking about a Chinese fishing trawler, not the *Baja Lady*. What I was looking for was someone who might have seen or heard a forty-eight-foot yacht taking it on the chin in waters that were partially visible from the very porch we were sitting on.

What I had told Amy, Bro, and Dara was true; so far, I had very little to show for my efforts. Doubts? Indeed, I was beginning to have them. Maybe I was in the right place and maybe I wasn't. Maybe Love Handles had his information about the *Baja Lady* all wrong. Uncertainties, vacillation, and skepticism had me thinking that just about anything was a possibility.

I listened to their conversation awhile longer before deciding it was time to turn in. As I started to get up, Carlos stopped me. Yulanov had been whispering to him. "Viktor would like to know if you would be willing to ride out to the reef and take a look at the Chinese trawler."

"Won't he be fishing tomorrow?" I asked.

Carlos explained that tomorrow was Sunday. "We do not work on *domingo*. Everyone in Las Cuevas goes to church."

"Everyone but Yulanov," Viktor laughed. "Yulanov *un agnostico*."

"Perhaps that is why you have so much trouble with the Chinese," Carlos laughed.

"Why not?" I said. "Let's go have a look at this Chinese annoyance of yours. Where and when?"

Viktor and I agreed on a meeting place and time and I bade the three men good night. Given my sleeping accommodations, I did not know how easy it would be to go to sleep, but on this particular evening it didn't matter. I had plenty to think about while I was trying.

Sunday

For the first time in the three nights since I had arrived in Las Cuevas, my sleep was not interrupted by strange noises, barking dogs, roosters, or the Baja sweats. Even the rather distressing contraption that Carlos had had the audacity to call a bed when

he rented me the room proved incapable of deny-
ing me a somewhat satisfying night's sleep.

Since the Chinese trawler had been the subject
of our conversation prior to retiring for the night, I
spent a good part of the bedtime hours with visions
of Chinese fishing trawlers dancing in my head. The
fact that I was getting a double dose of Chinese was
proving to be rather interesting. Somewhere in that
fog-induced zone known as presleep I found myself
wondering if I was having some kind of grade B
epiphany.

In college I spent a couple of summers working
on a boat that took wannabe ocean anglers out for
a day on the briny. I baited hooks, chummed,
cleaned fish, and swabbed the deck each afternoon or evening when the boat returned to port.
When I finished my second season on the *Day Joy*,
the skipper saw to it that I was summarily fired. Reason for dismissal, unknown. I suspect, however,
that it had something to do with the man's daughter. But that's another story.

What did the job do for me? I had saved enough
legal tender to buy a few beers while clawing my
way through my junior and senior years of college.
In addition, I could boast that I had been to sea and
learned how to survive in calm waters. At no time
did I subject myself to the decidedly more rigorous
and adventurous life aboard a commercial fishing
craft in hostile weather.

I crawled out of bed, subjected myself to yet another cold-water shower, and dressed. In the dis-

tance I could hear the solitary sound of church bells. That caused me to wonder just how many of the locals, including Jean Jean, the Admiral, and Rainbow, would be bowing their heads in prayer. While I was still musing about that, I saw Viktor Yulanov trudge by the hotel headed for the pier. He was dressed for the occasion: black blousy pants, white dress shirt, and sandals. Around his neck he wore a battered set of binoculars, and he was carrying a gunnysack, contents unknown. I had no idea what Viktor Yulanov believed important enough to carry with him when he took someone out in his boat.

I went downstairs. The hotel's barren dining room was deserted. Marie had doubtless joined the others in the pilgrimage to the village chapel—but she had left breakfast on the table for me. Reminiscent of a blintz, it was a pancake of sorts with what appeared to be a jellied substance wrapped up in it. Delicacy or not, I wolfed it down, braved her scalded coffee for the second day in a row, and set out in search of Yulanov. I found him at the pier, grumbling about the heat and untying his boat.

Unlike his friend Carlos, Viktor Yulanov held title to only one craft. He had named it *el billete* because, as he explained, it represented a whole new way of life for him after leaving Russia. Yulanov, I learned, hailed from Kiev and had spent twenty years in the Russian Navy back in the days when his country referred to itself as the USSR. By the time we had left the bay and pulled out into the channel, he had revealed even more about himself. Somewhere along the line I got the impression that he was in his late fifties and he had never taken the time to get married.

Curiously enough, I had the impression that Viktor had decided I was okay. Why? Probably because I agreed to take time to ride out to the spot where the Chinese were playing havoc with his livelihood, and because Carlos had already put his stamp of approval on me.

As for *el billete*, it appeared to be thirty-eight, perhaps forty feet in length. It was powered by a noisy, oil-soaked diesel that seemed to miss every fifth beat. The fish hold was in the middle of the boat, separated from the motor by a thin piece of oil-stained plywood. The wheelhouse was nothing more than a sheet of tattered, sun-rotted canvas held in place by four steel rods. While Viktor had obviously practiced old-world frugality with the amenities on *el billete*, he had been a virtual spendthrift when it came to electronics; he had both a radio and loran. The problem was I did not see an antenna.

We were still plowing our way at a brisk four or five knots across the channel when Viktor began gesturing, pointing at an object in the distance. Slowly that object began materializing into a craft unlike anything I had ever seen before. Like Acosta had said the night before, the Chinese fishing trawler was no fishing trawler. It was at least 120 feet long, and it looked very, very military. The only thing missing was a forward deck gun. If Viktor had pressed me to classify it, I would have termed it a hybrid between a launch and a cutter.

We were still several hundred yards from the craft when I realized that an aluminum-hulled Boston whaler with a two-man crew was skipping across the water racing toward us. One man was manning the outboard, the other was standing in the bow. He had binoculars trained on us. He was still a good thirty to forty yards from us when he dropped the binoculars, and began waving his arms and shouting, *"Prohibido el paso!"*

Viktor was slowing, explaining that we were being told to keep out.

By then the craft was close enough that I could get a good look at the occupants. I've been around all kinds of water, seen hundreds of seamen, and even more men who make their living on fishing boats. Just like the Chinese trawler wasn't a trawler, the two men telling us to stay away weren't fisherman. Fishermen don't wear uniforms.

I looked at Viktor, then back at the two men in the outboard. They appeared to be neither imposing nor menacing, but they did possess the demeanor of men who were used to having their orders obeyed. As near as I could tell, they did not appear to be armed, but it was easy to picture them brandishing semiautomatic rifles.

Through it all, Viktor was scowling. At the same time, he did not seem inclined to speak up. That's when I decided to take a crack at it. I was at least six to eight inches taller then either of them and probably outweighed each of them by a good seventy or eighty pounds. "By whose authority?" I demanded.

The minute I rattled off the English, the two men in the outboard appeared to change their attitude. The one who had been tending the motor stood up. Now he was the one doing the talking. Actually, he was shouting, a necessity since he was trying to be heard over Yulanov's diesel. "You speak English, that is good." When I didn't react, he continued. "I will explain. We are a research vessel from the university in Zhengzhou. We have requested that you come no closer because we have deployed a network of very sensitive electronic instruments."

"How long do you intend to be here?" I shouted.

"We will be finished shortly."

While all of this was going on, I was able to get a relatively good look at what both Acosta and Yulanov had described the night before as "a wire net all the way around the Chinese vessel." It was wire all right, and it was also at least technically a net. But it was a net with a difference. I had encountered a similar net the previous year while good old FSORC was testing a new submersible in the Bahamas. What Yulanov and Acosta were calling radio beacons were actually feedback sonar units. Expensive toys for Chinese boys.

Where what I said next came from, I will never know. All I knew was that I was shouting to make myself heard above the din of Yulanov's engine. "I am a representative of the Mexican government, and I am here at the request of the Mexican Fishing Council," I said. "They have registered a complaint. You are interfering with their fishing, and you are inside the international boundary of Mexican waters."

There was a reason for my not so thinly veiled insanity. If it wasn't a fishing trawler, it sure wasn't a research vessel either. I had grown up crawling in, around, and over Furnace maritime facilities, and that included boats of nearly every description. Not only that, my current position as D.O. at FSORC enables me to do a certain amount of skulking around at such places as Woods Hole and Pacific Research. I feel reasonably confident that I know a research vessel, regardless of what flag it is flying, when I see one.

What I was looking at was not a research vessel, it was a salvage vessel—a thinly disguised salvage vessel trying to pass itself off as a research vessel trying to pass itself off as a trawler.

So—why were they doing it? Maybe that wasn't the right question. Maybe the right question was, what was it trying to salvage?

"I demand to see your captain," I said.

The expression on the faces of the two Chinese sailors could best be summed up as "Who does this clown think he is?" I had the feeling this was the first time, on this sojourn at least, that anyone had challenged their right to be there or demanded to see their captain. It was easy to believe that up until now the sheer size of their mother ship had allowed them to muscle their way through and bully the Mexican fishermen.

The one standing in the bow of the boat was straining to be heard over Yulanov's diesel. "We will inform our captain that you wish to speak to him," he shouted. As he did, his partner was already turning their skiff around and heading back to the mother ship.

Thirty minutes later there was still no sign of the aforementioned captain or any indication that his arrival was imminent. There was, however, a noticeable increase in activity on deck and the number of men I could see walking around, making themselves visible. I had the feeling this was their idea of a way to do a little posturing. Since the ship's manpower compliment was probably forty men or so, I figured the odds against us were about twenty to one.

I watched what was going on for several minutes and cautioned Viktor not to expect much. On balance, our unexpected appearance on the scene hadn't resulted in much more then a minor inconvenience for the Chinese.

Nevertheless, we waited, and while we waited, we were being subjected to more than our share of a blistering dose of Baja sun. Viktor had sweated through his white Sunday shirt and was forced to tie a bandana around his head to keep the sweat out of his eyes. Yours truly wasn't faring a whole lot better. I found myself seeking refuge under the tiny canvas canopy that constituted the roof over *el billete*'s wheelhouse. As shelters go, it left a lot to be desired.

When it became apparent that the captain wasn't coming, I decided it was time to try something new. I looked at Viktor and told him I was ready to concede that the Chinese had won round one. "They can wait us out and they know it. While they wait, we boil in the sun."

Viktor gave me one of those pained looks that people give people who have just summed up the obvious. "You are saying there is nothing Yulanov can do about this?"

"No way. First of all, we don't give up just because our uninvited Chinese visitors put on a show of muscle, primarily because I think I just figured out a way to discover what our uninvited visitors are up to."

I didn't know what Viktor was expecting, but he was looking at me like he was anticipating the unfolding of a plan as convoluted as the Normandy invasion. It wasn't. But when he wanted to know what I had in mind, I had to tell him to wait. Why? Because I didn't know if there was a way to do it, or even if it would work if we tried it.

"How long," I finally asked, "would it take us to swing down, then out beyond the barrier reef?"

Yulanov did a little mental arithmetic before he answered. "Forty, maybe forty-five minutes."

"Good. Next question. Once we're out there, do you think you can get us close enough to see what's going on onboard that ship? But still be far enough away that they are not likely to see us?"

Once again the Russian had to think about it. Then his face lit up. "I know a place. There is out-cropping on barrier reef, just inside buoy, it stand several feet out of water. Chinese not likely to see us there." When he finished he looked up at the position of the sun and intensified his smile. "When we get to outcropping, sun will be at our back. That also in our favor. It will be more difficult for Chinese to see us because they will be looking into glare of sun off water."

With Viktor taxing the trawler's ancient diesel, *el billete* coughed and wheezed her way around the southern end of the reef and came up on the wind-ward side. Along the way, Yulanov indicated that he had fished the ocean side of the reef many times and he knew it well. I believed him when he nestled his old barge into some shallows less then forty yards from the outcropping he had described ear-lier. After he dropped anchor, it took Viktor and me less than five minutes to untie and launch the pram lashed to the stern and row into the reef. Whoever it was that said "Plan your work and work your plan" knew what they were talking about.

I peeled off my shirt and folded it into a small cushion where I could brace my hands. Then I dialed in Viktor's binoculars. They were salty, old, and had seen better days, but at slightly less than one hundred yards, I was getting a better than anticipated view of what was going on aboard the ship that everyone in Las Cuevas was calling a fishing trawler. I studied the scene for several minutes and handed the binoculars to Viktor. "Tell me what you see," I said.

Viktor Yulanov steadied his arms against a flat spot on the outcropping, adjusted the binocs, and zeroed in. His commentary was clipped and concise. "Divers. I count two—no, three. They have hoist over side. They are bringing up something."

"Can you see what it is?"

Viktor was shaking his head. "It looks like . . ." He put the binoculars down and looked at me. He was frowning. "What kind of research would they be doing on cushions?"

"What are you talking about?"

"Salvage net is full of cushions," Viktor said.

"Flotation devices?"

Yulanov was nodding.

"Pillows?"

"No, bigger, like kind used on furniture."

He handed me the binoculars, moved aside, and I wiggled back into position. Viktor was right, they looked a whole lot like furniture cushions.

"Can you see what they do with them?" Viktor asked.

I couldn't tell him for the simple reason that what our Chinese visitors were doing wasn't making a whole lot of sense. The contents of the net were being spilled out on the deck and immediately attacked with knives by two sailors. They were cutting the cushions into sections. Two other men were assigned the task of sifting through every scrap, fragment, and remnant. I had no idea what they were looking for, but they were sure being thorough.

If Viktor Yulanov was looking to me for an explanation of the activity onboard the ship he kept referring to as a trawler, he was going to have to look elsewhere for his answers.

"What we do now?" the Russian asked.

"I don't know," I admitted, "but I think it's time we hightailed it out of here. For the time being at least, we don't want them to know we're aware they're conducting a salvage operation."

By the time *el billete* hacked and wheezed its way back to Las Cuevas around the north end of the reef, Viktor managed to get it secured at the dock, and we walked back up to the hotel, it was midafternoon. The sun was no longer just a source of annoyance, it was a first-class blister maker and I had the mother of all sunburns.

I was looking for shade and a cool place on the hotel veranda to drop my tortured body when I saw Carlos and Bo Bo walk out of the dining room. They were still wearing their church clothes. Standing in the doorway behind them was Marie, the cook. When she saw me she headed for her bottle of cactus salve.

I dropped down on the porch next to Carlos and

listened while Viktor gave his fellow fishermen a summary of the day's activities. He concluded with what we had been able to see from our vantage point on the reef. When he was finished, Carlos turned to me and asked what I made of it.

"Well, to start with, the Chinese fishing trawler isn't a Chinese fishing trawler. Nor does it appear to be a research vessel, like the two men who approached us would have us believe. Unless, that is, they are researching the effect of salt water on furniture cushions."

"So what's our next move?" Carlos pushed.

"Well, if I had the right equipment, I would suggest we do a little exploring of our own. When I called my secretary last night, I asked her to ship my diving gear down here. With any luck at all, it should be here in the next couple of days."

"Then what happens?" Carlos asked. Acosta and Yulanov had been reduced to the role of attentive bystanders.

"I go down and take a look around," I said.

"But you forget they've constructed a wire net made of metal around the area where they're conducting their research."

"Not research," I said. "Salvage is more like it."

Carlos looked at me and laughed. He repeated the word "salvage" and looked at his two friends. "This time I think you are wrong, amigo. We've been fishing these waters for many years, we know what's down there. Except for a few old wrecks like the one I've already shown you, there is nothing in the channel out there worth salvaging. If there was, the *americano* insurance companies would have been down here long before now."

I hated to admit it, but Carlos was probably right. At the same time, my personal epiphany had just elevated itself to stage three. My reasoning goes something like this. If someone had lost a vessel of value out there and filed an insurance claim of any size, someone like Sebastian Frank and his Depth Finder crew would have been down here poking around by now. But suppose the Chinese were the only ones who knew about this particular ship-wreck. If that was the case, it was entirely possible they were camped over the very thing I had come to Baja Sur to find.

None of this, of course, was a theory I was ready to postulate. At least not yet. At the moment it was too much of a shot in the dark. I decided to try another approach. "What about the caves? Do you really know what's in those caves?"

Carlos was shaking his head. "Fish perhaps, and sharks. We have all tried to fish the caves. If we troll, the sharks will usually get it before we can get it in the boat. If we're netting, the sharks will shred our nets. It's easy for the sharks; our nets are old."

I was still kicking around how much I wanted to tell Carlos when I heard something that I realized I hadn't heard much of lately—the sound of a car or truck. Moments later, a seventies-vintage Dodge pickup rumbled up to the front of the hotel. A man of considerable girth was driving. His companion was a lad of no more than ten or twelve. The boy jumped down out of the truck, took off his hat, and inquired where he might find a Senor Furnace. He tried to give it an exotic twist; he pronounced it "Fur-Nace."

I stood up. "I'm Furnace," I said. "What seems to be the problem?"

The lad took out a piece of paper, unfolded it, and turned it right side up. He was pointing to himself as he began, "Me, Chico. I work at *lonchería* on highway. I answer phone. Call is from a Senorita Reed. She tell Chico she is looking for Senor Furnace. She tell Chico Senor Furnace is staying at hotel in Las Cuevas. She tell Chico if he get Senor Furnace to come to telephone, Senor Furnace will give him handsome reward."

By the time the lad had finished, I was down off the porch and heading for the Taurus with Chico right in step. I knew what I intended to do, but I was already preoccupied with the idea that my only means of getting back to the Transpeninsular Highway where there was a working telephone was a carriage endowed with an all-but-flat tire, no spare, and a wobbly wheel.

As I made ready to shut the car door and turn the key in the ignition, I realized that Chico was standing next to the car, holding out his hand. "*Veinte americano dólars, por favor.*" he said.

To my way of thinking, twenty dollars was a bargain. I peeled off a portrait of Jackson, thanked the lad, handed him the twenty, and started to shut the car door. Bro Roger would have agreed. I was looking at a future entrepreneur. With a few more like him, the Baja's future economy was assured.

"And twenty dollars for my father too," he said. His second demand was in English. I winced, slipped the money-grubbing little urchin another twenty, muttered an obscenity or two, and tried to close the door, but his hand was in the way.

"Don't you want the telephone number where you can get in touch with Senorita Reed?" Chico asked.

"How much is it going to cost me this time?" I sighed.

If Carlos, Bo Bo, and Viktor hadn't been watching, I might have slugged the kid.

First Chico looked at me and then his father. The lad was giving me a lesson in international trade. "It should at least be worth twenty dollars," he said. I couldn't believe how much the kid's English had improved between his first and third demand.

I paid the little thief another twenty to ransom a number where I could get in touch with Amy, stuffed it in my pocket, and finally managed to get the door closed. While I was doing it, I was wondering where I was going to bury the sixty dollars on my expense account. My other concern was what it would cost me if the Taurus failed and I needed a lift.

Attractive Amy picked up her receiver on the second ring. "I thought we agreed to get in touch Monday night," I complained. "It's only Sunday."

"I know what day it is," she snapped. "I waited two hours for you to return my call. I finally gave up and decided to take my shower. The moment I got in the shower, you called. Now I'm standing here soaking wet."

It occurred to me that I would have rather been wherever it was Amy was instead of standing in an oven called a Baja phone booth.

Before I could ask why it was so important that I call her, Amy launched into that very subject. "Are you familiar with a woman by the name of Elizabeth Carter?"

I had to think a moment. Between the diet of mescal and the Baja sun, my brains were a bit toasted. "Elizabeth Carter," I repeated. Finally the bell rang. "Tyler Rowland's administrative assistant?" I guessed.

"Good boy," Amy applauded.

"What about her?"

"She called me. She said she wanted to talk to me, but only if I would be willing to guarantee her that everything she told me was off the record. She said if I repeated anything she said to anyone at Unitrieve, she would deny it and file defamation of character charges against me."

"But I take it you went anyway?"

"Wouldn't you? I spent my lunch hour with her yesterday. Let me tell you, that girl can put away the bloody Marys. What I learned is, this whole thing with Tyler Rowland, Unitrieve, and the *Baja*

Lady is a great deal more complicated and convoluted then we first thought."

"How so?"

"Can't explain it over the telephone. This is face-to-face stuff. I've already called your brother; he's sending one of the company planes down to get you. The plane is scheduled to pick you up at the airport in La Paz at eight o'clock tomorrow morning."

"Tomorrow?" I winced. "Eight o'clock. I'll have to drive a good part of the night."

"Poor baby," she said.

Journal No. 6

Monday, June 8

Alluring Amy met me at a small private airport in Oakland where Bro Roger keeps the Furnace flying fleet and promptly whisked me off to the trendy Bay City Club for some noontime sustenance. Timing and thoughtfulness, dutifully appreciated.

Amy's choice of eateries was one of SFO's "in" places for the lunch bunch. Predictably crowded. The noon-hour crunch had started to subside, but even so there were still a goodly number of the financial district hoi polloi waiting for tables or a place at the BCC bar. Nevertheless, Amy prevailed. She somehow ushered us past the club's host and a throng of less fortunate patrons, through a tangle of tables, to a semi-remote booth in the back of the room. While Amy indulged herself with what the club called a "lite portion" of coriander-crusted tuna, I opted for the man-sized special, the BCC's version of Asian-marinated lamb. And for the first time in all too many days I had a cold Corona. Our Mexican neighbors may know how to make good beer, they just don't know how to drink it.

In less time than it takes to tell you about it, Amy had her glasses on, her computer fired up, and had assumed her "all business" posture. Then, with everything in place, she tilted her pretty head to one side, either waiting for my report from the Baja or ready and eager to get the old conversational ball rolling.

"So, where do we start?" I finally asked.

"Let's start with what you found out," she said.

"In a nutshell, zero, zip, nada," I said. "No hits, no runs, no errors." Then I added, "But I do have a hunch."

"Ready to tell me about it?"

"Can't. Still germinating."

Amy chewed on her pencil while I was talking. It was the first time I could recall seeing her manifest anything close to an anxious gesture. I had the distinct feeling she was impatiently waiting for me to finish my part of the report so she could tell me what she had turned up.

"I talked to several people in the village near where my sources told me the *Baja Lady* sang her swan song," I said. "I even had one of them take me out to the spot where one of the locals said they saw a yacht go down. It was a yacht all right, but it wasn't the *Baja Lady*." I did not mention the Chinese salvage vessel, nor what I was beginning to suspect might be under it, because as yet I could figure no logical reason for the *Baja Lady* being there.

Amy leaned back in her chair. "Do you think you were on the right track?"

I shrugged. I was getting good at it. I was doing a lot of it lately. "When we talked on the telephone last night, you said you'd had an interesting conversation with Rowland's administrative assistant, Elizabeth Carter. Right?"

Amy was drinking vodka collins. She was on her third one by the time she had finished her lunch and the waiter began clearing away the dishes. "Well, I knew it was a long shot, but sometimes long shots pay off," she started. "I decided to call her and I decided to be up front with her. I told her who I was, where I worked, and that my boss at California Maritime had been hearing some rather disturbing rumors about Unitrieve at his club. Rumors he said he would be more comfortable with if someone he trusted could check them out."

"That's all it took to get her to talk?"

Amy was smiling. "I'll let you in on a little secret. A secretary either worships her boss or hates him with a passion. If she's behind him one hundred percent, she'll do everything she can to protect him. If she wants to torpedo the taskmaster, she'll do anything she can to shoot him down. Guess which kind Carter is."

While Amy was cluing me in on the secret lives of secretaries, I wondered which category Dara Crawford fit into. "So which species is Ms. Carter?"

"Clearly the latter. Once she got started, Elizabeth Carter has a hard time talking about her boss without using language that would get her kicked out of a pool hall."

I hated to admit it, but Amy's report was getting interesting. I pushed myself away from the table, ignored my coffee, leaned back, and waited for her to continue. Apparently, Carter had done some real dirt-dishing.

"So what did she have to say?"

Amy was chomping at the gossip bit. "Are you ready for this?"

I nodded.

"Let's start with the fact that Elizabeth Carter and Tyler Rowland had an affair that lasted almost two years. According to Carter, Rowland made all the usual promises, including the one about leaving his wife and marrying her."

I shook my head. "All of which tells me that Ms. Carter is somewhat gullible if she thinks Rowland would actually divorce the sister of Unitrieve's CEO so he could legally bed down with her. In my book, that would be tantamount to both career suicide and paramount corporate stupidity."

Amy was in agreement. "The way Carter tells it, when Rowland told her their toe-tangling days were

over, she threatened to blow the whistle on him if
he didn't do the honorable thing."

"Let me guess. The honorable thing in this case
was a position as his administrative assistant at a
very attractive salary. Correct?"

Amy had more. "Carter pretty much confirmed
what we had already learned about the Unitrieve
financial situation. The coffers are all but empty,
and their financial sources aren't coughing up the
funds to help them get over the hump. I asked Carter if she thought the situation was desperate, and
she said she thought the word 'desperate' was un-
derstating the situation."

"I assume she knows all of this because she has
access to Rowland's files, and she could prove what
she's telling you."

It was Amy's turn to nod.

"Hell hath no fury . . ." I muttered.

"Indeed."

For some reason it seemed appropriate that I try
to form some conclusions. "Okay, given all of this,
what else does your boss want or need?" I asked.
"You now know Rowland is missing and so is the
Baja Lady. We know that they now have a working
model of an entirely new computer language using
random numerical syllabification. We also know
they have done some top secret archival work to
validate the program's efficacy. In other words,
everything they've done, works."

Amy finished her third vodka collins and ordered

a fourth. I was hurrying my report. I felt compelled to finish before she collapsed.

"And we also know that the DOD is taking them to task for poor security practices. What else do you need? It sounds to me like the powers that be at California Maritime have enough information to start making some decisions. And it appears to me that unless they like the idea of getting caught up in what could eventually become a very nasty legal situation, now is the time to make their move."

Amy pursed her lips and frowned. Her eyes were just a tad glassy. "Are you saying you think California Maritime would be wise to divest themselves of their Unitrieve stock?"

I held up my hand. "Wait, and listen carefully. That's not what I'm saying. My sources tell me California Maritime is holding nearly ten percent of Unitrieve's common stock. If that's the case, we're talking dollars and cents far beyond old A. J.'s fiscal comprehension."

Amy was listening. "Aren't you eager to see where all of this leads?" she asked. "Aren't you just the least bit curious?"

"You know what they say about curiosity."

"Don't quit on me now, A. J.," she said. She suddenly sounded sober. "First of all, I don't think of you as a cat, and as far as our investigation goes, we're just now getting to the juicy part. I now know why Tyler Rowland went to Beijing, and I know what happened while he was there."

The end was in sight, or so I thought. "Okay, put a wrap on it," I said.

"According to Elizabeth Carter, when Unitrieve's bankers turned Hake and Rowland down, Rowland told his brother-in-law that he needed to get away for a few days. Hake told him to go . . . and while he was at it, figure out a way to get the long-term money they needed. So, unbeknownst to Jacob Hake, Rowland bought a couple of airline tickets to China and struck a deal with the powers that be in Beijing."

"Deal? What kind of deal?"

"To start with, he torpedoed Hake and the company. For some unspecified financial consideration, Rowland agreed to sell the Chinese the code keys to the recently developed random numerical syllabification language."

"He agreed to do what?"

"You heard me right. According to Liz Carter, someone was able to breach security at Unitrieve three days after Rowland returned. Two days later, Rowland told Carter he had the syllabification code keys and asked her if she was going with him. She says he told her he had made provisions to meet a Chinese agent and exchange the CARTO contract code keys for a very handsome sum of money. When she asked him how much, he wouldn't tell her."

I was stunned. Rowland had done what? I asked Amy to repeat it. She did. It didn't sound any better (or smarter) the second time. If Tyler Rowland had offered to sell the Chinese the key to the random numerical syllabification code, he was asking for big-time trouble from people with recognizable acronyms on their jackets like CIA and FBI. Playing fast and loose with corporate funds can get a man a prison term. Playing fast and loose with Uncle Sam's secrets can get him shot or hung. Maybe both.

"Your friend Carter didn't agree to meet him, did she?"

"She not only agreed to go with him, she helped him hide the CARTO code keys on board the *Baja Lady*."

Suddenly I was very nervous about asking what seemed to be the next logical question. I was wondering if I should be talking to one of Bro's battery of lawyers instead of Amy Reed. If I knew where the CARTO random numerical syllabification code keys were and failed to get that information to Uncle Sam, would I be considered an accessory? Throwing caution to the wind, I said, "Where?"

Suddenly Amy was acting coy. "Wait a minute. Just exactly what do you plan to do with this information?"

"I think someone better be notifying the appropriate contract compliance officer in the DOD."

Maybe Amy's response shouldn't have surprised me, but it did. "If that's what you intend to do with it, then I'm not going to tell you. If you blow the whistle on Elizabeth Carter and the DOD ends up pulling the plug on Unitrieve, thousands of people will end up losing their job, Unitrieve will go down the tube, and to make matters worse, California Maritime loses a ton of money on their investment. If the latter happens, and my boss finds out I had been in a position to see that it didn't happen, my career as a project specialist with California Maritime is o-v-e-r."

"Then from here on out, you're on your own," I announced. "Old A. J. is walking away, and my story is going to be, I saw nothing and I knew nothing."

"You can't."

"Why not?"

"Because I need your help. I know this sounds corny, A. J., but you are the one person who can keep this whole thing from turning into a disaster."

I knew better than to ask but I did anyway. "Just how do you figure that?"

"Because you know how to find things underwater."

"What does that have to do with it?"

"If the *Baja Lady* is on the bottom of some big body of water, who better to find it?"

"What do you mean by 'it'?"

"The CARTO Project code key."

I started to laugh. "Amy, my dear, before yours truly or anyone else can find the code keys to the CARTO Project, they would have to find the *Baja Lady*. At the moment, that presents us with a not so small and very real problem. No one seems to know for certain just exactly where the *Baja Lady* went down . . . if indeed she really did go down."

"But you think you know, don't you?"

"It's a long shot."

Amy was still smiling. "There's more to the Carter story," she persisted.

"If you've got something else to add to what you've already told me," I said, "now's the time. Otherwise, as far as I'm concerned, the ill-conceived search for Tyler Rowland and his float-ing pleasure palace is over, done with, and terminated."

Amy glared back across the table at me. "Is there anything I can say that will change your mind?"

"Nothing I can think of," I said.

Tuesday

The lunch between the charming Ms. Reed and yours truly went on for another twenty minutes or so without the fair colleen adding anything signifi-cant to what had already been said or revealing anything that made me change my mind. On the other hand, all was not tranquil in the A. J. main-frame. More than a few pieces of china were still rattling around in my mental galley. Some, obvi-ously, could be disposed of by my simply walking away from our little tête-à-tête. Others, like the Chi-nese salvage boat posing as a fishing trawler/ research vessel, would likewise eventually fade un-til it became just so much mental clutter. But until it did, there was one item I still had to deal with. If I quit now, I would never know if the *Baja Lady* was down there under that Chinese salvage vessel.

On the other hand, I was upset with myself for having been so blatantly cavalier in my handling of the entire Rowland and *Baja Lady* affair. I'd asked questions all right, but not necessarily enough, or not necessarily the right ones. Plus, looking back, I could see where there were a number of other factors and elements I should have confirmed, validated, or made certain of before becoming involved. I hated to admit it, but the winsomeness of the fair Ms. Reed had a lot to do with that.

The more I thought about it, the less I liked what my behavior audit was revealing. I had actually put the test schedule and delivery of the Pony Project in jeopardy. Not good, and definitely not smart.

In my parting with Ms. Reed there were the usual expressions of regret, apology, and sorrow. She held out hope until the last minute, and when I didn't relent, she turned off her computer, took off her glasses, and finished her fourth and final drink. Brave soul, that girl. "I hope there are no hard feelings," I said as she stood up.

She said nothing, gave me a resolute smile, held out her hand, and we shook hands. It was all pretty sober, one of those stiff upper lip occasions during which I had the decency to avoid saying something silly like, "I'll give you a call sometime."

As I watched her walk out the door several other like-minded male heads also turned to admire the scenery.

* * *

R. Karl Largent

Since Amy had picked me up at the airport, I ended up taking a taxi from the BCC to the Furnace corporate offices on Sutter Street in the financial district. My plan called for me to inform Bro that I was safely back in the ZI and let him know that the handshake agreement to help California Maritime untangle the web of mystery at Unitrieve had been terminated. Bro was in a meeting, unavailable. Predictable and not that unusual.

So instead of laying reality on Bro, I ended up using his office to make a number of telephone calls. The first was to Dara to tell her to see what she could do about having my diving gear shipped back to SFO from Las Cuevas.

The second call was to Laurie Phillips, a onetime romance with whom I now maintained an infrequent passionate, occasionally professional liaison.

When we met, Laurie worked for a yacht broker. Now she was doing the brokering. Laurie was busy, couldn't take my call, but managed to get back to me within ten minutes. As usual we exchanged pleasantries for several moments before Laurie got around to asking me what was on my mind.

"Long shot," I said, "but by any chance are you familiar with a Gardini-designed, San Diego-based forty-eight-footer named the *Baja Lady*?" I paused long enough to give my former lady love a chance to think before I went on. "A fellow by the name of Tyler Rowland purchased her a little over a year and a half ago. Maybe even before that."

Why, if I had already informed the fair Ms. Reed

160

I was through chasing my tail on the *Baja Lady*/
Tyler Rowland affair, was I still poking around in
the Unitrieve ashes? Well, probably because I
would hate to go down in anyone's book as a quit-
ter. And I had the feeling that was exactly the way
Amy Reed was branding me when she walked out
of the BCC earlier that afternoon. At any rate, the
reason behind the call to Laurie was that if I learned
anything of value, I could pass it on to Amy and
her friends at California Maritime.

Laurie giggled. It wasn't the kind of hollow, frivolous titter usually associated with youth. This was
the decidedly full-throated feminine sound that
women are prone to make when someone buys
them a diamond or makes a veiled indecent over-
ture. "Do I know the *Baja Lady*?" she said. "Believe
it or not, A. J., I brokered that deal—my first one of
any size. Made a bundle and bought myself a Jag-
uar to celebrate."

Bingo. "What can you tell me about it?" I pressed.

"Come on, A. J., you know that kind of information is confidential."

"I said, what can you tell me? I'm not asking for
specifics, Laurie. I'm looking for the kind of information that will eventually lead me to the conclusion that earlier today I made the right decision."

"You're not making any sense," she said.

"Probably not," I admitted. "I think I was out in
the Baja sun too long. I'm not even sure I know
what I do know. For example, did Rowland pur-
chase or lease the *Baja Lady*?"

161

Laurie giggled again. This time it sounded portentous. "Neither," she said. "Look, A. J., suppose I tell you this much. Rowland's wife bought it for him for an anniversary present two years ago. She called it a coming-home gift. Not sure what that means, but I have a hunch, knowing his reputation."

"Reputation?" I repeated.

"Local joke. Keep your legs crossed when you're around Tyler Rowland."

That stopped me for a moment. Finally I managed to ask, "Where did Mrs. Rowland get that kind of money?"

"If you read the *Wall Street Journal* instead of using it to clean up the oil leaks under that Cobra of yours, you would know that Rita Rowland, the former Rita Hake, and her brother Jacob at one time controlled forty-nine percent of Unitrieve common stock. The way I heard it, little Rita not only could afford it but was prepared to buy Tyler a whole lot of toys if he stayed home nights and took care of his homework."

"All of this is on the level?" I asked. "You're not just regaling me with another girl-getting-even-with-a-guy fable, are you?"

"Out there in the trenches it's general knowledge," Laurie assured me.

I waited several moments before I asked my former romp the sixty-four-dollar question. "I know California Maritime is the insurer on the *Baja Lady*. Who is the insurant?"

"Tyler, the Straying," she said.

"Rowland?"

Laurie thought my incredulous reaction funny enough to laugh this time. "I assume the super-wealthy live by a different social code than people like you and me, A. J. Apparently, when you give someone a multimillion-dollar yacht as a gift, you don't attach strings. Trust me, Rita Rowland bought and paid for the *Baja Lady*, and she is paying the insurance premiums as well. If something nasty should happen to Rowland's floating Eden, Tyler Rowland is the one who collects."

I knew I couldn't ask how much, so I said, "Lots?"

"Lots," Laurie confirmed.

Ever the skeptic, I said, "Straight skinny?"

"Straight skinny," Laurie verified. "Like I said, I brokered the whole deal, including the insurance. In this case I know what I'm talking about."

I had intended to call several other people, including Poker Palmer, my old service amigo, following my conversation with Laurie Phillips. Instead I found myself thinking about her revelations. I was still doing so when Bro Roger got out of his meeting and returned to his office. He called me. We exchanged small talk, chatted about business for a few moments, and moved on to other things. I neglected to tell him I had informed Amy Reed that Furnace Standard in the person of myself would no longer be assisting her in her efforts to solve the mystery of the disappearance of Tyler Rowland and the *Baja Lady*.

Still without wheels (mine were still bedded down in the company hangar at the airport from the time I caught the flight to La Paz), I convinced Roger to drive me out to pick up my car. Once again, despite a protracted conversation covering numerous topics, I failed to mention the termination of the search for Rowland and his toy.

The drive back to Sausalito gave me an opportunity to play mental tag with some of the possibilities beginning to emerge in the saga of Rowland and company. One of my nephews had presented me with one of those small, hand-held voice recorders the previous Christmas. I decided to rescue it from the glove compartment, checked the batteries, and began to talk, picking through my thoughts.

Possibility number one: Without the necessary funding, Unitrieve was in danger of going under. Jacob Hake, with a family fortune behind him, could live with disappointment. Tyler Rowland, unable to accept that fate, ran. Something goes wrong. Boat goes down. Bottom line: the world is minus one very nice Gardini-designed yacht and one boy computer genius who his friends claim has trouble keeping his pants zipped. If this were the case, we're talking no cabal, no skulduggery, no intrigue. I come to the conclusion that there are too many elements of intrigue for possibility number one to have any validity.

On to possibility number two: Same scenario, different twist. This one is replete with devious machinations, some of which were hinted at by Laurie

Phillips. Suppose our boy Rowland really did go to China with a deeper, more sinister purpose than to see the Great Wall and entertain his current consort. Perhaps Amy was right as well. Maybe there was something to it besides vindictive lies being passed on by a former torch. Perhaps he really did go there to sell them the code key to the hottest DOD contract to come down the pike in many, many moons.

After all, Laurie Phillips was right on another score, and she hadn't been an overnight guest at my Sausalito pad in over a year. In all likelihood, I would not have been caught so far off base if I had not been using the *WSJ* for purposes other than what it was intended.

Since it was soon apparent that I was chasing my tail trying to develop theories about Rowland and his Unitrieve connections, I decided to change my attack. The first question being, why was Jacob Hake reluctant to let his sister report the fact that her husband had been missing for almost a month? A point both curious and deserving of further speculation. Was it enough to accept Hake's reasoning? Maybe. Maybe not.

The way I saw it, there was a darn good chance that if Rita Rowland had been allowed to get the right people involved early on, Tyler Rowland's whereabouts would not have had the opportunity to become the foggy tangle it had become.

And of course, why was I doing what I was doing? Wasn't all of this rather pointless? Had I not just informed Amy that she could no longer count on my involvement in the Unitrieve problem? I put the voice recorder down and for the fourth, maybe fifth time that day, resolved to forget about every aspect of the Unitrieve situation (except, of course, Amy Reed) and get on with my life.

So much for reaffirmation. By the time I was again rejoicing in the clarity of my thinking, I was pulling into my driveway. Home again.

I entered through the garage area just so I could steal a covetous glance at the Cobra before going on to the more mundane activity of checking my phone messages.

The first message was from Leland Powers of San Fran homicide. He wanted to know what I knew about a woman by the name of Elizabeth Carter. Then he casually mentioned, I suppose because he knew I was interested, that they were close to making an arrest in the Templeton murder. Obviously, he did not say who the suspect was.

There were several other calls, but none quite as intriguing as the last one, the one from Elizabeth Carter. She left a number where she could be reached. Once again, resolution forgotten.

Before I returned her call, however, I had to put myself to a test. What did I actually know about Elizabeth Carter? I sifted through the prior knowledge to see what I could remember about the woman who, according to Amy, was a quick draw on bloody Marys and carried the title of Tyler Rowland's former lover and current administrative assistant.

One: I had talked to her once on the telephone; sexy voice, calculating, noncommittal, professional sounding. Two: According to Amy Reed, Ms. Carter at some point in the past had an affair with Tyler Rowland. When Rowland broke the affair off, Carter retaliated by insisting on a position and pay package that would assuage her wounds and ensured a certain amount of discretion. Impressions gained from these two bits of knowledge about Elizabeth Carter? Intense. Strong. Clever. Devious. And maybe more woman than Tyler Rowland could handle.

Also according to Amy, Carter at various points had revealed interesting bits of information neither Amy nor I were aware of when we started. Plus she had confirmed others that up until Rowland's sudden disappearance were little more than guarded suspicions. The most important of the latter being that the bankers had said nay nay to the Rowland/Hake request for additional funds.

I picked up the phone and promptly dialed the number E. Carter had left on my answering machine. She was where she said she would be, and before I realized it I heard myself asking what I could do for her.

"Thank you for returning my call," she said. I was getting an array of mental images of Elizabeth Carter, and words like seductress, siren, and temptress were having their way with me. After hearing her opening volley, there was no doubt in my mind about who had seduced whom back in the early days of the Rowland/Carter affair.

Elizabeth Carter didn't believe in small talk. She was off and running. "Amy Reed called me. She tells me you've decided not to continue . . ."

Before we go on, two reactions here. One, I was surprised that Amy Reed and Elizabeth Carter had established the kind of relationship that, after only one or two meetings and one or two phone calls, the two women were hot-wired. Two, it sounded as if Amy Reed had taken what I said about being through with the whole Unitrieve situation as my final word on the matter. That surprised me. From the night of our first meeting, Amy Reed had impressed me as being decidedly more persistent when it came to getting what she wanted.

"Is there anything I can say or do to make you change your mind?" Carter pushed. When someone says something like that, particularly when they sound like Elizabeth Carter, there is the ever-present and often regrettable male tendency to say something tasteless. Instead I heard myself saying something reasonably free of innuendo.

"I'm afraid not, Ms. Carter. If you've talked to Amy Reed, I feel certain she explained why I've decided to back out of the search for your employer."

"And that's exactly why I want to talk to you, Mr. Furnace," she replied. "Amy did talk to me." She paused. "We all know that what Tyler Rowland has done is inexcusable. Like you, I am aware he has put his company in serious jeopardy." She paused again. This lady was long on stage management.

"But I think I know a way to undo much of what has been done."

"How?"

"Return the code keys before their theft has been discovered."

"I'm glad someone at Unitrieve realizes how serious this situation has become," I said. "If what Amy Reed tells me is accurate, your boss, when he is caught, could well be charged with treason. Defaulting on a government contract is serious enough. But it is an entirely different game when the charges are treason."

"That's why it is imperative that I talk to you," she insisted.

I had to admit it, Elizabeth Carter was cool, sedate, and composed. She had no intention of letting me off the Cal Maritime hook. I was getting the feeling that Amy Reed had handed me off to Elizabeth Carter to see what she could do about keeping me involved.

"I'll be happy to talk to you about all of this sometime," I said.

"How about now?"

"Sorry," I said. "I've got a house full of people and—"

"You do not," she replied. "I'm sitting in my car, using my car phone, two houses down the street from yours. You came home less than ten minutes ago, and up until then your house was dark. Now don't disappointment me with some absurd story about a bevy of friends hiding in the dark to spring a surprise party on you." Then she added, "You may as well relent and talk to me."

When I opened the door, I knew why Tyler Rowland had succumbed to Elizabeth Carter's charms. They were fatal. She was the antithesis of Amy Reed: dark skin, dark eyes, ultrasultry, and very, very enticing. Tall, not overly voluptuous. The signal was loud and clear. She was telling me in no uncertain terms, *You may have been around the block, sonny boy, but you haven't tangled with anything quite like E. C. . . . at least not yet.*

"Won't you come in?" I said.

Elizabeth Carter stepped into the room, peeled out of her khaki-colored raincoat, and handed me a six-pack of Amstel. "They're cold," she said. "Amy said you liked your beer cold." She was wearing a beige sweatsuit with flowers embroidered across her chest and lace around the collar and cuffs. Attractive but hardly serviceable as workout clothes.

"How about a beer?" I said.

E. C. was shaking her head. "No, thank you, but I would enjoy anything with a little vodka in it."

I didn't have to invite the woman into what I sometimes refer to as my den, as Ms. Carter seemed intent on conducting her own tour of the premises. I worked up a vodka martini for her and decided to wait until she was through prowling. Eventually she drifted back into the den and seated herself close to the fireplace. No fire. The gas was turned off. This is California. What you see in California isn't always what you get.

"Are you eager for me to get started?" she asked. She was sipping her drink and smiling. A nice beginning.

"It all depends on what you intend to do."

"Actually, it depends not on what I am about to do but on what you are about to see." She looked around the room. "Where is your video tape player?"

I used a small hand-held remote to open what appeared to be the doors to a walnut gun closet. It revealed all the accouterments of TV watching, including the tape player. The sultry Ms. Carter nodded approval, stood up, walked across the room, and inserted a video cassette. It took several seconds to materialize, but there it was, a screenful of a room with lavish appointments. There were two people in the room. One was a woman. The other, Carter informed me, was none other than Tyler Rowland.

I was a bit surprised. Instead of looking like a bedroom athlete from one of the soap operas, Rowland had some substance to him. I thought he looked a little bit like Clark Gable. He was holding a small metal canister.

"What you are looking at," Carter informed me, "is the salon on the *Baja Lady*." As I watched, Rowland, using a screwdriver, removed a wood panel covering the bulkhead and inserted the canister. "That," she said, "is a hermetically sealed canister

171

containing the code keys to the random numerical syllabification."

"And that, if I heard you right, amounts to a first-class security violation," I observed.

"So much for understatement. Amy described you as a rather exciting man, Mr. Furnace. Under the circumstances, I did not expect you to be quite so puritanical. But let's call a spade a spade. Once the Chinese are in possession of the code, what we have done will be viewed, not as you call it a mere breach of security, but as an act of treason."

"If they don't shoot you," I said, "turning the code keys over to the Chinese is likely to get you locked up for the rest of your life. You realize that, don't you?"

Elizabeth Carter had a different vision. She was smiling and shaking her head at the same time. "I don't think so," she said. "You see, I've decided not to go through with it. I want to turn—what is the term?—state's evidence. When I do that, I throw myself on the mercy of the court. But in order to do that, I need to be able to hand over that canister, unopened, to the proper authorities with the code keys still in it—as proof of my total contrition."

Elizabeth Carter had caught me off guard. "Even if someone can find the *Baja Lady*, it won't work," I said.

She was still smiling. "Oh, I think it will. All I need is the canister to present a very convincing story. As for the canister, I know you'll be eager to help me locate it. Why? Because it will save jobs. It will save a company. And it will save lives."

"Sorry," I said. "Not interested." Determined to be a gentleman despite the drift in the conversation, I started to ask Ms. Carter if she would like a refill on her drink. I stopped when she held up her hand.

"On the contrary," she said, "you are more interested than you realize. The only problem is, you don't know it because you haven't heard my little caveat to this whole proposal."

"Which is?"

Instead of answering me, she reached for the rewind button, hit it, waited, and played the tape a second time. "Watch the tape carefully," she advised. "As you watch, you will note that it is quite impossible to identify the woman in the video. All the viewer knows is that it is a woman with dark hair. In fact, the only reason you know who it is is because I told you."

She was right. As I watched it, I realized it could have been anyone. She waited for what she was telling me to sink in before she continued. "In other words, Mr. Furnace, even if this video tape was in the hands of the authorities, this is hardly condemning evidence that little Elizabeth was in any way involved in this sordid affair."

"I'm waiting," I reminded her. "You used the word '*caveat*.'"

"It's very simple. I will hand this tape over to the authorities and I will tell them that you and Tyler were working together; that you are as deeply involved as anyone."

My initial reaction was that Elizabeth Carter was mired somewhere in a sophomoric fantasy that she could worm her way out of a very nasty situation by trying to implicate others. True, a convoluted plot leaves a convoluted trail, but no matter how complex and twisted it may be, ninety-nine percent of the time it is a trail that can be followed. I didn't say so, of course, but what was worrying me more than I cared to admit was that other one percent. I decided to test her.

"Suppose I agreed to continue," I said. "Just exactly what is it you want me to do?"

"I want you to find the *Baja Lady* and recover the canister. You've seen the tape. You know where it is. I've practically led you to it."

"As I explained to Amy earlier today, finding something on board the *Baja Lady* isn't the problem, depending, of course, on what caused her to sink. Finding the *Baja Lady* is the tough part. Locating and then getting to your boyfriend's floating pleasure palace is going to be a great deal more difficult than you think it is."

Liz Carter was carrying a very small purse with quite a bit in it. Other women, a little less secure in the role they were playing, might have resorted to a briefcase. That wasn't E. C.'s style. She rummaged around in her purse, took out a piece of paper, unfolded it, and began to read.

"Abraham Joseph Furnace. DOB: 4/6/60. Single. POB: San Francisco, CA. Adopted. Educa-

*tion: Prep School: Forest Academy, Biloxi, MS,
Stanford University, Palo Alto, CA, US Navy Special Forces (file sealed). Profession: Director of
Operations at Furnace Station Oceanic Research Center, Seal Island, CA. . . ."*

"There's more," she said. "Want me to go on?"

I shook my head. "How much did you have to pay for that?"

"Not a thing. I got it off the internet. It also told me that you are generally considered to be an authority when it comes to underwater investigation and submersibles. I think Amy is right, you are the logical person to recover that canister from the *Baja Lady*."

I wasn't about to interrupt the lady. She was working up to her big finish and had reached the point where her voice needed to soften to sound convincing. She did it. "I need your help, Mr. Furnace. I've made a terrible mistake and I want to rectify it."

Surprisingly enough, there were real tears etching their way down her cheeks. "I know what you may think of me, but I don't want my name on some police blotter, and I don't want my family to be ashamed of me."

I was looking (maybe even hoping) for some kind of sign that this wasn't just another beguiling belle playing mind games with a bone-headed bachelor. But that sign never came. As my old college roommate used to say, "Never try to BS a BSer."

R. Karl Largent

"I think you better find someone else," I said. As I did, I stood up, offered to give her back what was left of the six-pack, and escorted her toward the door. "And the sooner you start looking for that someone, the better. In this case I'm just not your man."

She stopped at the door just long enough to inform me that when the FBI or CIA uncovered the theft of the random numerical syllabification code keys, one of the first people she intended to implicate was A. J. Furnace.

"Sticks and stones may break my bones"—I smiled—"but accusations will never . . ."

For a moment there I thought she was going to try to slap me. But the gesture wilted in the inception stage and she turned instead and headed down the street toward her car. Then, as I closed my door I had a sickening thought. Elizabeth Carter just might be crazy enough to do what she threatened to do. Charges that I was involved in a plot to steal top secret government software might not get me sent to prison, but it sure could hurt FSORC's relationship with all those government contractors.

Journal No. 7

Robert Benchley, I'm told, once said, "I do most of my work sitting down; that's where I shine." It's a shame the great man and I weren't confederates, because in many ways we are similar. To para-phrase my soulmate, "I do most of my thinking when I am lying down, that's where *I* shine."

Despite being grateful to be back home in a com-fortable bed, I did not sleep well. I spent much of the night tossing, turning, and thinking.

What did I think about? Tyler Rowland and his blasted boat, of course. Where was he? What had happened to him? And what had happened to the *Baja Lady*?

It is also possible that some of my insomnia was

triggered by a wee bit of not liking myself for not seeing this episodic adventure through to its conclusion.

The fact that I had walked away from the mission Ms. Amy and I had agreed on was all the more difficult to understand because, in my mind at least, I felt I finally had a handle on what had happened or was happening. My session with Elizabeth Carter had filled in many of the remaining gaps. And to top it off, now that I was no longer obligated to find the *Baja Lady* and her missing master, I was convinced I had a pretty good idea where she was. As for Rowland himself, who knows?

So for the umpteenth time, when I should have been sleeping, I found myself sorting through what just a couple of days earlier looked like a hopeless mélange.

The whole sordid scenario started with the bankers telling Hake and Rowland the cupboard was bare. No more cash, hard or cold.

Let's start with Jacob Hake. One, Hake is a very wealthy man. According to my sources, he has more money than Budweiser has bottle caps. Two, if he has been properly trained in money management (a reasonable assumption), he knows better than to prop up a financially challenged Unitrieve with his own personal fortune, even if it is his company.

After Hake comes Tyler Rowland. From what I've been able to learn so far, the guy gives evidence of being more than slightly wonky. Up until a few weeks ago he was living the good life, making mucho money, and according to people in the know, was a computer language wonder boy. As an illustration of how bright he is, he even married the founder's sister. On the negative side, the lad appears to be seriously ethically and morally challenged. Rounder Rowland, has all the symptoms of being in deep squat.

So what am I left with? Inference, guesswork, and assumptions. First assumption, based mostly on hearsay: Hake has informed Tyler Rowland that if the Unitrieve ship goes down, Tyler baby goes with it and in all likelihood, the marriage. For Rowland, the end of his marriage has to equal the end of the free ride on Rita Rowland's money. It is not a case of her dumping him. It is a case of him dumping her.

Satisfied that I have correctly worked through the first part of the equation, I turn my attention to Rowland's reaction to this messy megillah. What would he do? Confronted with no job, no money, no future in his marriage, Rowland might (perhaps already has) decide to sell the most valuable thing he could get his hands on. What would that be? The code keys to the random numerical syllabification project.

Next question. Who would be interested?

Answer: Russia would be a possibility. But the old Bolsheviks still thumping around the Kremlin are broke. Castro. Same scenario. Who does that leave? A whole bunch of Middle Eastern troublemakers and the boys in Beijing. And where did our boy Tyler go? He went to China.

Next assumption: Rowland, while in Beijing, cut a deal with the Chinese to sell them the code keys to the CARTO Project. He comes home from Beijing, pilfers the code key, enlists the aid of Elizabeth Carter to help him put the code key somewhere on board the *Baja Lady*, and takes off for his rendezvous with the gang of however many.

I sat up, turned on the light on my nightstand, and began scribbling the essence of my hypothesizing on a scrap of paper. That, incidentally, is usually the test of whether or not I'm on the right track. Does it still make sense when I see it in black and white?

Back to the postulating. Here we have to make several more assumptions. The first assumption being that Elizabeth Carter's self-incriminating revelation about helping hide the code keys to the CARTO project is true. If she knew about the theft and had not reported it to the proper authorities, she is, like Rowland, in a heap of squat. Added to that is the admission that she was actually Rowland's accomplice. She said she had helped him hide the object behind a panel near the mirror in the *Baja Lady*'s salon. What she failed to reveal, if in fact she knows, is what Tyler Rowland intends to do after the code keys and the money change hands. Even supposing she does know, the likelihood of getting her to reveal what her former paramour had in mind when the deal is done is highly unlikely. Unless it didn't include her. Conclusion? Tyler's disappearance was something Carter hadn't counted on.

Next assumption: Tyler Rowland, with the CARTO Project code keys safely tucked away behind a *Baja Lady* bulkhead panel, departed his San Diego marina with every intention of rendezvousing with the Chinese. But something went wrong. The question was, *what*?

Which brings us to still another question: Was the Chinese salvage vessel that was masquerading as a fishing trawler, sitting inside the barrier reef near Las Cuevas, the vessel Tyler Rowland was supposed to rendezvous with?

If the rest of my assumptions are anywhere near on target, that's exactly why the Chinese and their counterfeit trawler were there. And the fact that they are still there speaks volumes. It is telling us that Tyler Rowland and his friends from Beijing never completed their deal. If they had, the Chinese would have set sail for home long before yours truly arrived in Las Cuevas several weeks later.

So why wasn't the deal completed?

The more I thought about it, the more I realized there were a number of possibilities. One, Rowland's yacht blew up before the deal could be consummated. Two, the Chinese did their own double cross: Rather than pay Rowland for the code keys, they took the code keys by force. If possibility number two had any merit, that would again indicate that something had gone seriously wrong.

So what conclusions can be reached based on all of the above? One, as yet the Chinese still do not have and are still trying to find the CARTO Project code keys. Two, since they had sent a salvage vessel to the rendezvous point and gone to all the trouble of making it appear to be a less-than-conspicuous-looking fishing trawler, they had intended some kind of chicanery from the outset.

Three, the Chinese salvage vessel was anchored directly over what was left of the *Baja Lady* and they were still looking for the code keys as recently as last Sunday morning when Viktor Yulanov and I showed up.

Four, our Chinese visitors have no intention of letting Carlos, Viktor, Bo Bo, or anyone else fish the waters close to the area they have staked off . . . because the wreck of the *Baja Lady* is somewhere down there and they aren't through sorting through the wreckage.

By the time I had figured out enough to make me change my mind about going back to Las Cuevas, it was almost four o'clock in the morning. Even so, I continued to replay the scenario over and over in my mind. Finally, I reread my scribbled notes and roughed out a plan of action.

That plan still needed some of the rough edges smoothed out, but the essential ingredient was a phone call to Ms. Reed to tell her I had changed my mind. Again.

*   *   *

My morning routine, after a nearly sleepless night, was fashioned around a hot shower, a shave, and buttered oatmeal laced with real cream. Guilt more than anything else made me also consume eight ounces of iced vegetable juice. All in all, a worthy eye-opener. After that, I was on the phone to Poker Palmer. If you don't catch Poker early in the morning, you are not likely to catch him at all. If and when he doesn't go fishing, he heads for the bar. In his case, downstairs. Poker once confided that his room over a Gloucester bar was perfect for a man of his bore and stroke.

A word or two about Poker is in order here. He was baptized Elmer George Palmer, but dropped that appellation when he went into the Navy. The Navy—in fact, Norfolk—is where Poker and I were first thrown together. He hails from a five-generation Gloucester, Massachusetts, fishing clan. He fished before he went into the Navy and he fished there for a while after his medical discharge. That medical discharge was the result of an underwater explosive he was testing going off prematurely and blowing his left hand off. As Poker tells it, being a one-handed fisherman just didn't work out.

Bottom line, he borrowed some money, bought himself a day charter, and for the past several years has made his living taking would-be anglers out for half- or whole-day charters.

Back to the Navy. We're still not allowed to talk about what we did in those days. Suffice to say,

Poker and I were part of a very secret, highly trained group of twenty or so men who were trained to pilot L-7a underwater sleds while performing eradicative duties to things in places no one ever heard of.

Lady luck was with me. Poker had run into heavy rains before his charter had even cleared the harbor. "Them candy-asses wanted no part of a four-foot chop so I turned her around and brung 'em in. Got my money though, even if they didn't get any fish. Candy-asses—they shoulda been wearin' dresses."

I waited until Poker was through with his assessment of his clientele. And I knew he was finished when I heard him stop long enough to light the inevitable cigar and ask what prompted my call.

"What are you doing for the next week or so?" I asked.

"Probably sittin' on my ass wishin' I had opened my charter business down in Florida someplace," he growled. Then he explained. "There's a string of low-pressure areas movin' up the coast; cloudy skies, winds out of the north. Pissy-ass weather. When the weather gets like that I don't see many payin' customers." Finally he asked the question he knew I wanted him to ask. "Why?"

"I'd like to put you on the FSORC payroll for a couple of weeks."

I knew Poker was grinning. He always claimed the one thing he liked about the Navy was that he could count on a payday. Paydays refueled his poker habits. "What's the project?"

"FSORC has just finished building a couple of second-generation, high-tech sleds for one of the maritime research centers. They are part of something called the Pony Project. They come in two exciting flavors, open and closed cockpit. Thought you might like to help me do a little testing."

"Where and when?"

"Down off the west coast of the Baja Sur close to Bahia Magdalena."

Suddenly, clear across the continent I was getting negative vibrations. "What's wrong with your regular crew?" Poker asked. "And why aren't you testing down in the Caribbean like you usually do?"

"It's a long story."

"Good. I like long stories. Gives me something to look forward to. How soon do you want me there?"

"The sooner, the better. I'll wire you a ticket and your first week's pay within the hour. Pick it up at the airport. You know the airline."

There was a flurry of phone calls after that. The first was directed to Ms. Amy. It's frightening how charming I can be when I put my mind to it. I apologized profusely, informed her that a good night's sleep had changed my mind, and told her that if she still wanted my help, I was ready to return to Las Cuevas and renew the search.

That was the easy part. I wasn't quite certain how I was going to put the pieces together just yet, so I neglected to mention the fact that I was taking some serious hardware and an old Navy sidekick back to Las Cuevas with me.

"When are you leaving?" she asked.

"Possibly tomorrow. Why?"

"Because I'm going with you," she said, "and I need to know how much time I have to get ready."

The Pony I and Pony II were designed and built to fill one East Coast research center's need for a hybrid, state-of-the-art, multitask-capable, independent underwater sled. A tall order. They were not designed to be operated on a tether, umbilical cable, or otherwise surface-supported. FSORC's charter was to build something multifaceted and agile, something akin to a surface sled with deep-water capabilities. Both units were designed to be operated like a torp device, but their maneuverability was expected to exceed the jockey's manipulation of fore, aft, and vertical thrusters. FSORC engineers had enhanced the sled's performance by coming up with a new use for an old idea, a stabilizing gyro. Used in helicopters, it was the first time it had been designed into a one-operator underwater craft. In theory, at least, there would be no performance degradation and no disorientation despite the depth and loss of visual cues.

Both versions were equipped with radar, sonar, and GPS accessibility, port and starboard manipulator devices, video cameras, and a battery of lights that would enable the sled jock to record almost any kind of phenomena encountered.

On the Pony I version, the pilot straddled the submersible like a horse. A saddle of sorts had been molded into the upper shell. The Pony I's controls were on a telemetry display immediately in front of the cockpit. In addition to a beacon tracker and buoyancy controls, there was also a makeup air monitor. On both units, we had installed an arsenal of practical weapons and tools unique to conducting underwater research. My favorite, though, was a prod gun with six chambers housing six-inch-long stainless steel darts dipped in TRH.5R and encapsulated in acrylic bubbles until they were ready to be fired. The lads in the chem lab claimed a single dart could stop a ten-foot, one-ton shark. Anything bigger than that might require more than one.

In the final analysis, the only significant differences between the I and II versions of the Pony were an encapsulated cockpit and a few personnel amenities. In the Pony II, the sled jock got in and pulled a watertight canopy over himself. The Pony II could therefore be operated with or without the sled jock wearing diving gear, because, unlike the Pony I, it was equipped with a self-contained life support system.

Finally, the Pony I was twelve feet long. The Pony II was a full twelve inches longer. Both, because of size and weight, were designed to be easily transported to their deployment site.

That same evening, at roughly fifteen minutes after seven California time, I was straddling a bar stool at Polo Bob's. P.B.'s place, as most of us refer to it, is a small, congenial watering hole near the airport where Bro Roger constructed a hangar to house the three shiny planes that constitute the Furnace Standard air fleet.

Beside me, looking more like a weather-beaten reprobate than a man with numerous Navy-honed skills, sat Poker Palmer, fresh off his flight from Boston and ready to depart for points south.

I have already said that Poker is minus his left hand. He now comes equipped with a state-of-the-art stainless steel prosthesis that enables him to do everything he could do before he lost the hand. To hear him tell it, he can actually do more. "I used to be so damn clumsy I'd stab myself with a fork. Now I can twirl a plateful of spaghetti with the best of 'em."

Poker's transition from East to West, rainy weather to something more agreeable, had him dressed in a grungy short-sleeved cotton turtleneck and sporting a gray-flecked beard that was almost as shaggy as his eyebrows. He wore granny glasses, had gray eyes, gray hair, and a gray complexion. The majority of the time he had an inexpensive cigar clenched between his teeth. I should probably add that he is strong, very strong. Years earlier, in a bar in Manila, before he lost his hand, I saw him break a beer bottle in half with his bare hands. He was planning to use the top half in what he referred to as "a minor disagreement." After that, I informed him it would have been less wasteful but just as impressive if he had used an empty bottle.

Our first half hour was spent getting caught up. He told me in rather explicit fashion how his relationships with Coreen, Laverne, and Margot had ended (this was the first time I had even heard about Margot), and moved on to the series of repairs that had been necessary to keep *Gladys Ann* seaworthy. He concluded with, "Glad you called, A. J., the old bank account was gettin' hammerhead low. Lots of foul weather. Charters are damn few and far between this season."

At some point during all our catching up, Poker finally got around to inquiring why I had put him on the Furnace payroll. I glanced at my watch, wondering if I had enough time before Amy joined us to fill him in on everything I knew and suspected. When I realized it would be another thirty minutes before she was scheduled to arrive, and another thirty before the Bandeirante was fueled and ready to depart for La Paz, I decided to get started.

I began by telling him everything I knew about the convoluted situation at Unitrieve, and added sketchy profiles of who I considered to be the three or four main characters. That took all of fifteen minutes. After that I gave him a blow-by-blow description of what had happened while I was in Las Cuevas. Then, just to be certain, I again paraded him through the cast of characters, even including some I was reasonably certain had nothing to do with the eventual outcome of the story. I still hadn't delved into my hoard of assumptions when Amy arrived.

Let's be honest. Polo Bob's type of clientele don't often see a happening like Amy Reed. There were eight men in the place including Polo Bob himself. By the time I helped her up to the bar, six of the eight were in love and the other two were wondering how to get rid of their current wives. Even Poker was impressed.

Introductions took thirty seconds. Amy ordered a beer and said, "I might as well be one of the boys."

Despite her willingness to drink straight from the bottle, I knew that Poker and I were in complete agreement on this one. There was nothing Amy Reed could do that would make her "one of the boys."

I glanced at my watch again and reminded the lady that the flight would be leaving shortly. "Last chance. Are you certain you want to go through with this? I feel I should warn you, I have yet to find a place in all of Las Cuevas that makes a decent martini."

Amy laughed. All the same, I had to admit I was beginning to wonder about the lady's employer. Why was a man (or company) so concerned, perhaps even paranoid about California Maritime's relationship with Unitrieve that he (they) were willing to send an employee all over the West Coast to check out rumors? True, Bro Roger usually takes care of these situations at Furnace Standard, but even I was certain there were more efficient and economical ways of validating scuttlebutt.

Still, if the charming Ms. Reed's employer was willing to spend the bread for her adventures, I was determined to enjoy her company. And from the look on Poker's face, he shared my enthusiasm.

The EMBRAER EMB-110 Bandeirante made it to La Paz on schedule with fuel to spare. Since the 110 was Bro Roger's aircraft of choice and the one he used most frequently, it was equipped with amenities that made the six-and-one-half-hour flight a hedonistic adventure.

Amy boarded, promptly retired to the spacious restroom, and emerged several minutes later in what looked like an ensemble every woman headed for the wilds of Baja Sur would select: field jacket, island shorts, field cap, and desert boots. Only the heart-shaped earrings seemed a bit much.

Thirty minutes later she had curled up on a small couch in Roger's airborne office, leaving Poker and me to do the scheming and masterminding. No problem. We work well together.

I had arranged for one of FSORC's trucks, complete with a fifty-three-foot enclosed trailer and loaded with two state-of-the-art but untested submersibles, to head south from FSORC earlier in the day. With two drivers, and orders to "keep the pedal to the metal" throughout the night, I figured they could be somewhere close to Las Cuevas by noon the following day. A good distance can be accommodated in thirty hours of hard driving.

Also earlier in the day I had procured a useful Dell notebook (pilfered from the FSORC QA lab would be closer to the truth), and had Dara load Pony I and II test data, relevant blueprints, and operating procedures. These I turned over to Poker and told him to start earning his pay. I figured that by the time we landed in La Paz, he would know more about how to push buttons and get results on the two Pony submersibles than I did.

We landed around midnight, plodded our way through customs, caught a taxi into town, and bedded down for the night at the Hotel los Arcos. Poker and I shared a room. Amy slept alone.

Poker and I managed to stay awake, trying to figure out how we would go about getting a good look at what the Chinese salvage vessel was guarding so closely. By the time we finally dozed off, it was almost morning, but we had a plan.

Wednesday

Sunrise in the Baja can be a delightful experience or a disappointment. I got lucky. The tenth day of June dawned the way every Baja-bound tourist hoped it would when they booked their vacation. Spectacular colors, gentle breeze off the sea of Cortez, delightful quiet.

But since neither Amy nor Poker was up to enjoy it with me, I took an early morning stroll down Malacone, located a small cafe that indicated by a sign in the window that they served *el café solo* and *el desayuno* and spoke *inglés*. All true.

I finished, had a second cup of *café*, called the car rental agency, made certain I didn't get the same tired Taurus, and made provisions to pick up the car at the hotel. This time they handed me the keys to a road-weary two-year-old Cavalier. Like the Taurus, it had more dust and road grime on it than paint.

I hustled Poker and Amy out of their rooms and had the hotel dining room rustle up something hot, black, thick, and loaded with caffeine. I also ordered a sack of *bocadillos de quesos* to help them stave off hunger pangs. If they didn't care for cheese, that was their misfortune.

I was eager to get to Las Cuevas. If I had calculated correctly, the Furnace family's corporate truck with two multimillion-dollar submersibles would be arriving in Las Cuevas somewhere around the noon hour and I wanted to be there when they were unloaded. With luggage for three jammed into the Cavalier's trunk and the spillover piled in the backseat, Poker, cigar clenched firmly between teeth, rolled his window down and rode shotgun. Amy was relegated to the backseat with the extra suitcases.

We stopped at the Pemex station, fueled up, and headed up Highway One. By the time we had cleared La Paz and were headed north, Amy was already sporting a thin sheen of perspiration on her forehead. It was eighty-six degrees and the Cavalier's air-conditioning wasn't working.

*   *   *

R. Karl Largent

With a display of deft driving skills, I managed to avoid most of the potholes on the road to Las Cuevas, buzzed past the church, pulled up in front of the hotel without a name, and hit the horn. It took a while, but eventually Marie appeared on the porch, wiping her hands on her apron. At first she was frowning, but when she recognized me, she managed a welcoming smile. "Senor Furnace," she cooed, "welcome back."

Poker was impressed. Amy wasn't. She was out of the backseat, stretching, mopping her forehead, and casing her surroundings. "I count eleven what I assume to be houses, four establishments of some calling, one rather dubious hotel, and a church," she said. Then she looked at me. "This is Las Cuevas?"

"Kind of overwhelming, isn't it?" I grinned.

"And what is the population?"

"It depends on whether or not you count dogs, pigs, and chickens," I informed her.

Amy managed a restrained laugh. I knew then that she hadn't completely lost her sense of humor. Nevertheless, the body language was easy to read. In no uncertain terms, without uttering a word, her posture was telling me that if she had it all to do over again, she would have opted for a tour of duty at some other site. Acapulco maybe.

I helped Poker unload the luggage, lugged it up on the porch, and informed Marie that my associates had been shortshifted on their first Baja Sur breakfast and that they were looking forward to her

194

culinary artistry. She gave me her standard girlish giggle and promised to take care of the situation. After that, I inquired as to the whereabouts of Carlos. She informed me that the village's number one fisherman and only innkeeper had headed up the beach toward Jean Jean's after she had sent someone to inform him that a "great truck" had arrived with *la máquina* for Senor Furnace.

Moments later I was headed up the beach with Poker and Amy in tow.

To unload the two submersibles, all an individual has to do is press a couple of buttons, the hydraulics take over, and the subs are unloaded on rubber-tired dollies that transport them easily from trailer to water. The unloading was witnessed by Poker, Amy, Carlos, Viktor, Jean Jean, Bo Bo, the Admiral, and yours truly. The only local who wasn't there was Rainbow. Rainbow, according to the Admiral, hadn't been seen since the previous morning.

Luck was with me. I had arrived just in time to make certain the submersibles were tucked away, out of sight of passing boats, and sheltered by two large canvas canopies. The trailer with necessary spares and several hundred thousand dollars' worth of on-site testing gear was backed into position beside the two subs, and an electronic security system, complete with video monitors, was activated. The two men who had escorted the submersibles from FSORC were also technicians who would be able to set up the test parameters before they returned to SFO.

It was then that I pulled a slightly perplexed-looking Carlos aside and told him what I had in mind. I started by explaining I was reasonably certain the yacht I had been looking for on my first trip was probably somewhere under the Chinese vessel masquerading as a fishing trawler. I did not go into all the reasons why and how I had come to that conclusion. Nor did I tell him about Elizabeth Carter's claim that she had helped Tyler Rowland hide the code keys behind a bulkhead panel. What I did tell him was that I intended to use the Pony sleds to help me learn what had happened to the *Baja Lady*. "And that's where you come in," I finally added. "I'm going to need your help."

Carlos is the kind of man you want for a friend. His only question was, "When do we get started?"

By mid-afternoon Phase One of the plan was ready to swing into action. Poker, yours truly, and slightly more than 350 pounds of electronics and diving gear were loaded aboard Carlos Martinenez's twenty-one-foot yard boat.

Getting to that point, however, had taken considerably more dialogue, planning, and patience than I anticipated. First there was the matter of verifying that the Chinese and their counterfeit trawler were still anchored over Viktor Yulanov's favorite fishing spot inside the reef. Viktor was no help. He indicated he had spent the better part of the last three days repairing his nets and hadn't been back to the place where the Chinese vessel was anchored. Only Bo Bo was around to vouch for their presence, and that had been late Monday afternoon.

Then there was the matter of convincing Amy that this was neither the time nor place to flaunt her pretty blond presence in front of our Chinese visitors, for the simple reason that when we checked out the site where we believed the *Baja Lady* had gone down, we wanted our Chinese friends to think we were nothing more than three hardworking locals out for an afternoon of catching fish. That was hardly a salable premise if they spied Amy.

In the end, the fair Ms. Reed bought my story, but she groused and made it patently clear she didn't like it. As she stepped away from Carlos's yard boat, I heard her mutter something about chauvinism and witnessed a pout developing.

After that had been taken care of, there was the matter of rigging a tattered old oil-stained tarpaulin between the tow bar and the stern under which we hid the diving equipment as well as several pieces of electronic gear. As a final precaution, I made certain I was packing my Type 59, 9mm Makarov.

In addition, I knew that Poker was packing something for the occasion, I just didn't know what. Over the years I have learned that his tastes in personal weapons are subject to frequent change.

As we motored away from what served Las Cuevas as a port and began sputtering our way out toward the reef, I again found myself trying to sort

197

through a webby tangle of variables, facts, and assumptions.

In bringing the submersibles down to see what our Chinese friends were trying to keep everyone away from, I was testing the submersibles and I was keeping my word to Bro Roger. In addition, I was hoping what Elizabeth Carter had told me was true.

For the most part, I believed her. What I did not understand was why she had revealed her involvement to a perfect stranger. By doing so, she had implicated herself in a situation that, if the FBI or CIA found out, could get her in all kinds of major-league trouble.

Plus I was now convinced the *Baja Lady* had gone down. More to the point, I was convinced that she, or what remained of her, was nestled up at the base of a barrier reef in roughly thirty-five to forty feet of water, and that the Chinese figured they had squatter's as well as salvage rights.

Third question. Was the *Baja Lady*'s demise totally unexpected? Answer. You bet. That was the only logical answer. Otherwise Rowland would have made arrangements to get the code keys to his Chinese confederates and they would have been on their way back to Beijing long before this. The fact that they were still hanging around led to my next point. There wasn't much doubt in my mind that whatever was supposed to have come off between Rowland and whoever he was rendezvousing with just plain hadn't happened.

Why? Unknown. But, for whatever reason, the

transaction hadn't taken place and the Chinese did not have what they wanted, i.e., the code keys. And they were convinced it could be found somewhere in what remained of the *Baja Lady*.

All reasonable assumptions, I thought. But that's all they were—assumptions.

By mid-afternoon the glint of Baja sun on Baja water made visibility somewhat hazy. Hazy enough that we were less than a half mile from the bogus trawler when it began to emerge from the heat haze. I instructed Carlos to kill his motor, he did, and for the next several minutes we maintained silence and drifted closer. I was reasonably certain the Chinese knew we were there even if they hadn't actually seen us. It was safe to assume that their sonar had already picked us up. That was a given. On the other hand, if we could pull off our little fishermen ploy and stay far enough away from their vessel to keep from annoying them, I figured there was a good chance they would leave us alone.

Unlike my Sunday adventure with Viktor Yulanov, this time we appeared to have caught the Chinese with their defenses down. The only sounds we could hear were the wave action against the ocean side of the reef. I took out the binoculars and handed them to Poker. "Tell me what you see," I said.

Poker Palmer is the kind of man who has an edgy, sometimes quirky smile. You are much more likely to see him smile when he is disquieted than when he is amused. At the moment, his expression was stolid. He studied the strange craft for several minutes before I was able to read his expression. "It might fool Hollywood," he finally muttered, "but not someone who's been hanging around the docks at Gloucester half their life."

When Poker handed back the binoculars, I was able to get my own look at what was going on. I could see two men in the wheelhouse and two more lounging near the ship's working boat at the stern. What had been rigged to look like a mizzen mast and boom was actually a cluster of antennas including a receiver for synoptic data.

Finally I pointed at the net. As a submersible jock, Poker has his equals. But he has no peer when it comes to figuring out a way to get past the type of warning device the Chinese had deployed. Uncle Sam had spent a great deal of money teaching him how to get through, around, over, and past riggings of the very type he was looking at. Unless our Chinese friends had invented a whole new kind of underwater barricade technology, it wouldn't take long for Poker to figure out a way to get us past it.

"How far from the net to the vessel?" I asked.

Poker squinted into the haze. "Four, five hundred yards," he guessed. "Less on the vessel's port side because it is anchored closer to the reef."

"How far from where we are now to the net?"

"Another two hundred yards, give or take a few."

"When we were out here last Sunday we could see some kind of security sensor attached to the cable on top of the net. I figure we must have got

200

a little too close for their comfort, because they hustled a couple of goons out to tell us to go away."

Poker had already figured out what I needed to know. How close could I get to the security net without triggering some sort of alarm? And how could I get through the security net with more than just diving gear?

"You keep 'em occupied," he said; "and I'll do a little survey work. You and Carlos make like you're out here to catch some fish . . . just in case one of them happens to be watching us."

Carlos caught on. He made certain that anyone watching us would see our apparent preoccupation with the deployment of a fishing net. At the same time, Poker slipped behind the stretch of tarpaulin, peeled out of his clothes, and slipped over the side wearing nothing more than his skivvies and scuba gear.

Years ago, Bro Roger and I agreed that I would be the one who determined whether a unit was ready to ship or had to go back to the shop for more work. Over the years I've taken some eighty-odd different submersibles and sleds down for their first test, only to surface and give FSORC's waiting engineers the old thumbs-up or thumbs-down signal. So what have I learned from those test runs? One, patience. Two, waiting is tough. Test runs seldom go as planned, adjustments have to be made, sometimes the best efforts result in failure, and on at least two occasions I was lucky to get out with my life.

In any case, whenever I surface after a test, one

of the first things I hear is how those who were waiting on the surface became concerned when one or more aspects of a test run appeared to put both the craft and the pilot in jeopardy.

This time it was me doing the waiting. Poker was the expert, the master, the old hand, the specialist. But that didn't stop me from holding my breath and muttering an appeal to higher powers.

When his head finally popped through to the surface again, he was on the starboard side of Carlos's boat. Pro that he is, he had made certain he surfaced out of the salvage boat's line of sight . . . just in case the Chinese were watching. He grabbed hold of the gunnel with one hand and peeled off his mask with the other. At the same time, Carlos was helping by hefting his air tanks back into the boat.

"Well, at least we know what we're up against," Poker sputtered. "One thing for sure, your Chinese friends sure as hell ain't fishin' inside that perimeter net of theirs. They aren't foolin' anyone. Someone ought to tell them that net of theirs gives them away. Anyone who knows anything about fishin' knows those one-way intrusion alarms will do a helluva lot more to scare the fish away than anything else. They've got that net rigged with sensors arranged in a five-by pattern, similar to the ones in Nam."

"What about the net? Can we get through it?"

"Not through it. But I think we can get under it. On the far side, the net appears to be hung up on the reef. There appear to be several places where we could get one of the sleds under the skirt bottom. It would be a tight fit, but I think it can be done."

I reached down to give Poker an assist back into the yard boat, but he waved me off.

"I saw something," he said, "and I want to take a closer look." He signaled for Carlos to lower his tanks back into the water, squirmed back into his harness, checked his regulator, and secured his buckles.

By the time I had glanced back at Carlos, Poker had again disappeared beneath the surface. The second time he was down less than ten minutes. He popped through to the surface, grabbed hold of the gunnel with his steel hand, and hefted a large piece of charred wood into the boat with the other.

"Take a look at that, old buddy," he said. "I think I found what we're lookin' for."

Carlos scooped it up, studied it for several minutes, and handed it to me. He was shaking his head. "No way of tellin' whether it's the one you're lookin' for or not. Not much to go on, but my guess is it's part of some pleasure boat's deck trim. They don't use burled teak and number one brass on workin' boats."

I studied Poker's prize piece of water-soaked debris while he shimmied into the boat, shed what was left of his diving gear, and pulled on his trousers. While he fumbled for a cigar, he explained what he had found. "Main channel's clean as a

203

whistle. Damn near looks like it's been vacuumed. Someone, probably your pals on that phony trawler, has been draggin it. Even so, there's wreckage scattered all along the base of the barrier reef. It starts maybe two, three hundred feet south of that big outcropping on the coral ridge and disappears under that net your Chinese friends have deployed."

"Can you see what they're anchored over?"

Poker shook his head. "There's something there, but it's too far away for me to tell what it is."

There's a feeling a person gets when something they've been piecing together suddenly starts to jell and shows promise. In the last forty-eight hours I had done a whole lot of conjecturing. The chunk of water-soaked, charred teak with its strip of broken brass trim suddenly made it look like I might actually be on target.

Behind me I could smell one of Carlos's rope-thick cigars being lit. He and Poker were high-fiving. "All we need now is a little tequila," Carlos grinned.

"Then head for shore," I said. "I'm buying."

Journal No. 8

By seven o'clock the next morning, the entire "Let's find Tyler Rowland and his yacht" team had assembled in the combination dining room/bar/lobby of the Las Cuevas hotel and Marie was lighting their fires with her *café solo*. Poker, who I am convinced could handle Sterno if that was all there was to drink, was already on his second cup. Amy, on the other hand, was demonstrating a little less enthusiasm. I had watched her take one tentative sip, but that was the extent of it.

We had returned to the Las Cuevas docks after Poker had recovered the debris from the Bahia Magdalena channel. To a man we were in agreement that the fragment came from a pleasure craft, probably expensive, and probably fairly good-sized. Teak and brass aren't used on cheap boats. The question was, was it the *Baja Lady*?

More important to Carlos and his friends was the fact that on the way back to the docks he and I had worked out a deal. In return for the Las Cuevas fishing fleet helping the SFO contingent search for the remains of the *Baja Lady*, we would help them get rid of the sham Chinese fishing boat.

Carlos loaned me his charts of the channel and pointed out the holes, caves, and anomalies in the reef. The most intriguing aspect of which was a pair of almost parallel tunnels through the reef that just might be big enough to give us some latitude in how we approached the coral ridge.

Amy, still somewhat disgruntled that she had been unable to accompany us to the site where Poker had found the piece of debris, pointed out something neither Poker or I had picked up on. The charred, roughly thirty-six-by-eighteen-inch scrap of teak was somewhat convex, not standard in a deck application, and there was evidence of fracturing in both the surface grain and varnish.

"Which would indicate?" I asked.

Amy was pleased with herself. "It would take a great deal of energy, maybe even a violent impact of some kind, like an explosion, to distort the decking in that fashion."

"Meaning?" Poker asked.

"I think there is a strong possibility that whatever you find down there may have exploded."

I looked at Poker. What the lady was saying made sense.

"Just a passing thought," Amy shrugged, "but if we are lucky enough to find what is left of the *Baja Lady* under that make-believe Chinese trawler you keep talking about, and if it did explode, that means that what's left of the *Baja Lady* is likely to be scattered all over the place. If that's the case, it's going to be even more difficult to find those government code keys. Even if we do know where Rowland and Carter hid them."

It was almost as if someone had shouted "fire." The minute Amy uttered the words "government code keys," Poker Palmer's veil of cool was suddenly a lot less serene. "Code keys?" he repeated, "What's the lady talking about? Government code keys?"

The proverbial cat was out of the bag, and I knew Poker wasn't going to like it. "A project Unitrieve was working on," I finally said. I was hoping it would be enough to satisfy him.

It wasn't. Poker's feathers were ruffled. "You didn't tell me this cockamamie enterprise of yours had anything to do with government stuff. Next you'll be telling me it's top secret material."

Amy glanced at Poker and then back at me. "You didn't tell Mr. Palmer what we're looking for?"

Carlos, Viktor, and Bo Bo were also staring at me.

Thanks to Amy Reed, my integrity was suddenly in question, as well as my ability to lead the project. I could feel my face getting red. "Would it make

you feel any better," I said, "if I told you the code
Amy is talking about isn't actually government
property . . . yet? To the best of my knowledge, Unitrieve hasn't signed off on it."

Poker was scowling. "I'm sure that little formality
will be a great consolation when the feds haul my
ass off to Leavenworth for getting involved and vi-
olating the terms of my probation. Have you forgotten, I'm still treading water from that last stunt
you pulled down in Florida?"

I glanced in fair Amy's direction, looking for an
ally. She was ignoring me.

"Okay," I said, "the reason I failed to mention it
was I was convinced that Poker would have balked
at coming if I had told him I needed help recovering stolen government documents."

"You got that right," Poker grunted. He was no
longer smiling.

I set my cup down and tried to explain. "Less
than forty-eight hours ago I talked to the person
who claims she helped Tyler Rowland hide the
code keys to the random numerical syllabification
project behind a bulkhead panel in the salon of the
Baja Lady. Now, when I didn't go straight to federal
authorities with that information, I was consciously
acquiescing to Ms. Reed's appeal for help. I was
also aware that I was putting myself in jeopardy."

"And the rest of us as well," Poker fumed.

"Look. It's a simple equation. If we get caught,
we're in trouble. If we recover it, turn it over to the
proper authorities, we're home free."

"And what happens if we don't find it?" Poker pushed. "What happens if they find out we knew that this whatever the hell you are calling this thing had been stolen and we didn't report it?"

Poker was backing me into a corner.

"I don't know," I finally admitted. "But if any of you feel like it's too risky, now is the time to bail out."

No one walked out of the room.

With Poker still glowering and muttering about being incarcerated, I gathered the five of them around me and began detailing my plan. "Let's start with you, Carlos. We're going to need your fishing boat. You're going to be our cover on the ocean side of the reef."

The captain of the two largest fishing trawlers in Las Cuevas was frowning. "What do you mean, 'cover'?"

I unrolled one of his charts and began pointing. "All you need to do when you leave here is proceed out into the channel, making sure the Chinese know you're there. Head north, sail out around the north end of the reef, and come back to where you'll take up position due west of the Chinese but with the reef between you and them."

"Then what?" he asked. Amy's unexpected revelation had made everyone edgy.

"Throw out your nets. You may as well see if you can catch some fish during all of this. You're my main decoy. Instead of you watching them, I want them preoccupied with watching you."

I could tell that Carlos was skeptical. Poker and Amy's talk about government involvement was bothering him. Still, he hadn't indicated an unwillingness to go along with the plan. He took out a cigar, used an oversized knife to cut off the end, lit it, exhaled, and looked at Viktor and Bo Bo. "What about them?"

"They do the same thing," I said, "except they both anchor inside the channel and start fishing. The only requirement is that they make sure they anchor where the Chinese can keep an eye on them."

Carlos began to laugh. "Now I see," he said. He leaned forward and slapped Bo Bo and Viktor on the back. "We are the decoy for our gringo friend here. If they start shooting, better him than us, huh?"

"Exactly," I said. "We have to assume the Chinese are using some sort of optical scanner to observe everything on the surface. Likewise, it's an equally safe assumption they're using some sort of sonar device to monitor what's going on below the surface. So here's the plan."

For the moment at least, the collective nervousness about being involved with stolen government documents appeared to have dissipated.

"Viktor, if you station yourself near the south end of the reef you'll be the closest to the Chinese. That means they will be watching you the closest. Keep your distance. Don't get too close to their net. Make it look like you have some kind of problem with your equipment. I don't care what it is, as long as you make a lot of noise repairing it. How are you at acting?"

Viktor grinned. "My wife and I went to the Moscow Circus once."

"Good enough. When they see you pounding on your equipment, try to look annoyed and harassed. Chances are they will probably be watching you with binoculars. Put on a good show."

Bo Bo was waiting and smiling. The talk of government documents appeared to have bothered him the least. "I think I know. You want me to head for the north end of the waterway. When I do we will have them surrounded."

"You got it," I said. "If you make enough noise, it will mask the sound of the submersible props. We'll be working both the channel side and open-water side of the reef. Poker will sled sidesaddle with Viktor's boat and use him for cover. While Viktor puts out his nets, Poker will slip away and work the eastern side of the net. In the meantime I'll catch up with Carlos, use his boat for cover, and try to find out if one of those caves tunnels through to the channel side of the reef."

Finally it was Amy's turn. "Where do I come in?"

"You're going to be the class monitor. You'll be working out of Viktor's boat, but you'll have to keep out of sight. Have Viktor rig up a place where you can observe the topside activity on the trawler. Poker and I will be working in the dark, and both Viktor and Bo Bo won't be able to get to the COM D to warn us if anything happens. You'll be our

R. Karl Largent

surface eyes and our warning system. If our Chinese friends see or hear something that makes them suspicious, they'll launch a couple of their deck boats, and unless you warn us, we'll be sitting ducks."

Amy was pleased. "I can be a hell of a lot more than a distraction," she reminded me. I was beginning to think the girl had a death wish.

"According to Carlos's charts, we'll be working in approximately thirty-five to forty-five feet of water. That means we get the bad with the good. We can't use the sonar on the submersibles, because the Chinese would be able to nail our location. Without the sled sonar, we need good visibility to find the wreckage. At that depth we should have it. By the same token, if the water is clear enough, we'll be visible from the surface."

"Not good," Carlos assessed.

"All this means, Amy, is that you'll be manning the radios and we'll be depending on you. We'll have it set up so that you'll be able to communicate with each of the submersibles and the technicians back in the trailer. Whatever you do, though, keep chatter to a minimum. The more you transmit, the easier it will be for them to lock on to your signal. If they do that, they won't have trouble locating the sleds."

I had said everything I intended to say and they were still with me. That was the important part. I looked around the table. "Any questions?"

There were no questions.

*　　*　　*

212

It was one-thirty in the afternoon when we finally got started. Much later than I had planned. I did not know how long the operation would take, but I wanted to avoid working in the dark for the simple reason that our underwater probe lights would be visible to the Chinese on the surface.

Following our morning briefing, a second but equally disconcerting situation developed. Carlos had learned from the Mexican Maritime Meteorological broadcasts that an early-season low-pressure area was rapidly developing two hundred miles south of Bahia Magdalena. It was forecast to move north and intensify.

By the time we had informed everyone what was happening, I had taken the opportunity to review with each member of the team what was expected of them, the captains had rounded up their crews, and everyone appeared ready. As far as the crews were concerned, their captains, despite the late hour getting under way, were simply trying to put some fish in the hold before the bad weather set in. The deckhands knew nothing about the sleds.

The initial stages of our plan came off without a hitch. Viktor was the first to leave. Amy tested the COM D with her initial transmission. As base, she was using the code numeral one five aught aught. Viktor had been instructed to respond with the preceding number, one four niner niner, when he was in position at the mouth of the harbor. I was banking on the Chinese thinking there was something more to the code than a simple vocal distraction for the radar operators. When a person is trying to divert someone's attention, every little bit of confusion helps.

Viktor had been instructed to wait at the entrance to the harbor until Poker was able to sidesaddle the Pony II into position beside the Russian's boat. He had a distance of less than a quarter mile to negotiate.

Exactly twenty-five minutes after Viktor confirmed his position, it was Carlos's turn to move out. Amy documented his departure with her signature code. I made note of the time and slipped into the water aboard the Pony I. It would be a good half mile before I could cozy up to Carlos's boat and create one image on the Chinese radar just as Poker had. Until I was able to rendezvous, like Poker, I was vulnerable and probably real visible on the Chinese radar. If they weren't at their stations, crossing the channel and snuggling up to Carlos's trawler would have been a whole lot easier.

Radar was one thing. Radio transmissions were another.

The second dangerous question was whether or not the Chinese were actually monitoring our radio transmission. If they were, Amy's occasional four-digit code combinations and the responses probably sounded like gibberish. That's what we wanted them to think. Even so, Amy further complicated their monitoring by introducing her own wrinkle. She was communicating in a monotone that sounded a whole lot like it was computer-generated. It may have been effective, but as Poker later pointed out, not nearly as sexy.

I started breathing a little easier when I realized it was all coming together. At 1447 local time, Poker was in position beside Viktor's boat. At 1531LT, Amy informed the team I was in position next to Carlos's vessel. At 1601LT, Amy relayed the word that Bo Bo Acosta had dropped anchor north of Viktor's position and was holding fast. At 1630LT, on Amy's inviolable count, Poker and I were cut loose from our respective tows and began operating under our own power.

For the benefit of the technicians back at the trailer, I activated the GN-t unit, which monitors and records the sled's performance. GN-t is a maritime version of the black box. For the record, the Pony I was operating just like it was designed to operate. Important because even though the sled design for the Pony I was a proven one, in any new model there are always questions and maybe even an element of doubt—especially when the FSORC engineers add new performance features and make extensive design changes. In the case of both the Pony I and II, the sleds were loaded with features that weren't—up until this very moment—field tested.

In one sense, the Pony models were hybrids. They were, to quote Bro Roger, "a fusion of the latest underwater sled and submersible technology."

Unlike Poker, who was encased in a claustrophobic acrylic bubble on his sled, I was literally riding an underwater crotch rocket with more sophisticated electronic gear than we had previously built into any combination of our units.

In the final analysis, the Pony I was faster and more maneuverable then the Pony II, but the II could go farther, deeper, and sustain the mission for a longer period of time. There were other trade-offs, but for personal reasons I preferred the mobility and freedom afforded by being able to park and leave the sled if and when the occasion demanded.

Tight places and heights are not my cup of tea.

For the first several minutes of the dive I maneuvered the Pony through an underwater jungle that masked the real nature of the reef. In the process, I was testing the Pony I controls and comparing Carlos's chart to the sunken network of nooks, crannies, and places for entities to hide. What I was looking for was the two parallel caves the chart indicated existed near the base of the reef—supposedly at a depth of between six and seven fathoms.

On the plus side, visibility was good. The water was even clearer than I had anticipated. On the negative, it had taken longer for me to locate the cave area than I had hoped. I was approaching an elapsed dive time of twenty-nine minutes when I heard the first of two transmissions; one from Poker, the other from Amy. They were coded, and it took me a moment or two to decipher. In Poker's case, he was informing Amy he had discovered addi-

tional wreckage and debris similar to what he had
discovered on his first dive.

When Amy took over, she gave the coded message once, then repeated it. This time it wasn't what
Poker and I wanted to hear. Apparently, the Chinese did not like the fact that they were surrounded
by our makeshift fishing fleet. In response they had
launched two skiffs, each one containing two men
wearing diving gear. Since I was on the ocean side
of the reef, I felt reasonably certain I was safe from
whatever mayhem our Asian friends had in mind.
Poker was the one with a problem.

As for our code, aside from the fact that it was
taking me longer than I had foreseen to figure out
what the number clusters stood for, it was working.
We had designed the combination of digits and an
occasional word or two to sound like gibberish,
and that's exactly what it sounded like. In addition,
Amy was proving to be one clever improvisor; in
addition to throwing in an occasional line of pig
Latin, she was repeating each transmission to make
certain that both Poker and I were aware of what
was happening on opposing sides of the reef. Each
time she paused, I hit my transmit button twice in
rapid succession to verify I was receiving and com-
prehending the message.

At the same time, I was starting to get lucky in
my own quest. I had finally located what appeared
to be the two parallel caves Carlos had marked on
his chart. On the first count, he was right, the caves
were parallel, almost as if someone had drilled

through the reef in that fashion. On the second count, he was wrong. Neither cave was large enough in circumference to accommodate the sled. As Bro Roger would say, if I got through that cave, it would be a matter of sheer commitment. If I wanted to see what was on the lee side of the reef bad enough, I was going to have to swim through. But I wasn't certain the larger of the two tunnels could accommodate a diver wearing tanks.

For an admitted claustrophobe like myself, this was no small issue. Just getting through the reef cave to the tunnel was going to be a big test of my resolve.

It took a while, but the temptation to inform Amy and Poker that I was aborting the mission and returning the Pony I to the surface finally passed. When it did, I managed to maneuver the sled into position so I could use the console-mounted G-10 laser to determine the cave's length. The measurements I was getting varied from fifty-five to sixty-one feet in length. Just long enough for me to get a bit hyper. In addition, the cave was only just large enough for a diver to get through. And then only if the diver pushed the air cylinders through the tunnel ahead of him.

The entire exercise was rapidly becoming a less than compelling assignment.

After I saw how narrow the tunnels were, it also took a while to convince myself that I was actually going through with the insanity. When and if I did, I knew I would have to inform Amy that I would be out of contact for the next thirty to forty-five minutes. Even though I was wearing an open-circuit helmet and inside a tunnel, I was convinced I would be too close to the bogus trawler to acknowledge or get my free hand to the response button. In the tunnel there would be as much danger of the Chinese hearing me as there was of them spotting me on their radar screens.

I was closely monitoring my mission time. I was already at MT: 35, and my rendezvous with Carlos was scheduled for MT: 105 with a ten-minute cushion. All of which meant my thirty to forty-five minutes inside the net wasn't giving me much time to get everything accomplished.

I kept telling myself the plan was simple. Park the sled outside the reef. Fill the sled's ballast tanks and worm my way out of my tanks and dive gear. At one point I started to remove the emergency oxygen supply from the sled. I was planning to tuck it in the vest strap of my diver's harness as a kind of insurance policy. At the last minute I decided against it.

Step one in the sequence was to pray that there was enough room in the tunnel for man and equipment to make it through to the other side. Step two called for me to push the air cylinder pack into the tunnel ahead of me. Step three was to crawl in, and step four was to start monkey paddling and clawing my way through the tunnel. Step five was to say a littler prayer if and when I reached the other side.

If I accomplished all that, I was banking on coming out on the lee side of the reef and somewhere inside the Chinese security net. If I emerged somewhere other than where I needed to be, the whole drill would have been in vain.

I anchored my safety line to the D-ring on the cowling of the sled, made my final contact with Amy-base on Viktor's boat, and crawled into the tunnel.

Irrational or not, those who experience a phobia of some kind know it can be a very real and frequently debilitating sensation. Over the years I've learned that when I'm encased in a submersible but able to see out, things are okay. It's the not being able to get a good look at what is going on around me that makes matters mentally dicey.

Less than ten feet into the tunnel I felt the first traces of sweat begin to trickle down behind my dive collar, and I checked my air usage. I knew from experience that it was too soon to be out of control, but I was aware that my pulse had quickened and breathing was accelerated. I checked my watch to determine the elapsed MT, double checked my regulator, and in an effort to lessen the tension, released my grip on the tanks long enough to flex my fingers.

All the while I could hear Amy's transmissions. She was still broadcasting in a monotone and informing Poker that the two rubber skiffs continued to confine their surveillance to an area inside the perimeter of the security net. Good news for Poker. Not so good for me. He was outside the net, and if

I made it through the tunnel I would be inside—I hoped. It also meant that sooner or later our meddling Chinese playmates would be searching along the reef where the water was less agitated. When you are diving in reefs, less agitation equals better visibility. At the moment, though, I was focused on getting through the tunnel and wondering—if and when I cleared the tunnel—if I would be inside the security net.

At the same time, I was listening to Poker inform the surface that he had discovered what he was estimating to be at least a ten-foot-by-ten-foot hole in the security net. Amy repeated the dimensions for verification. As she did, I felt the tanks grind to a halt. I pulled the cylinders back and shoved them forward a second time, hoping the obstruction was minor. It wasn't. That old feeling of being closed in was becoming even worse. I couldn't go forward, and there wasn't enough room in the tunnel for me to turn around and head back toward the entrance. My only option appeared to be to try to chisel away at the ridge of fossilized coral.

I checked my elapsed MT. It was reading 41.22, and I was clearly beginning to experience the initial stages of elevated agitation. Every phobia sufferer recognizes it. At that point, I knew I had reached a level of excitation such that if I wasn't able to get through the tunnel, I would begin to feel something akin to what they call "the sweats." Everyone who has ever experienced a severe reaction to some phobia is familiar with "the sweats." They are the second stage in the escalation of anxiety.

Over the years I've learned that only so much rationale seems to work when one is trying to avert the onset of a panic attack.

Underneath it all, I knew there wasn't any real reason to panic. But I knew that if I didn't get my emotions under control, my head would take me out. According to my gauges I had plenty of air and as far as I knew, I was not being presented with threats to life or limb. Nevertheless, there I was and the gods were orchestrating a game consisting of cold sweats and alarm

I reached back as far as possible, lunged, and jammed my eight-inch dive blade into the reef scab three or four times.

Nothing.

It was like chipping away at a piece of concrete. I tried again and again until I had established a kind of frenzy. Each time I did, I realized my use of air had accelerated and I was losing strength. I could feel a salty, irritating, vision-impairing sweat begin to trickle down, under my face mask, and into my eyes.

I had reached the point where my vision was blurred and my throat was getting raw. I realized my mixture was probably too rich, but at the moment there wasn't a great deal I could do about it. The reef had become my enemy, and worse yet, the reef was winning. At the same time, the still rational part of my brain was beginning to wonder what kind of progress I could make if I began trying to inch my way backward.

I began thinking about something I had read. I think it was George S. Patton who wrote about his battles with Field Marshal Rommel, "Retreat was never an option." Maybe not, but I wonder what he would have said, if he had been wedged in an underwater tunnel off the coast of Baja Sur.

That was still in my head when the reef gods suddenly decided to get involved. The fossilized ridge of centuries-old, perhaps eons-old, coral suddenly began crumbling under the assault of my dive knife. I wasn't through yet, but as I began to inch my way forward again I could feel and hear my air tanks scraping and grinding against the roof of the tunnel. I was moving, and as near as I could tell, everything was still intact.

I could also hear Amy. She was warning both Poker and me to be careful. Both skiffs had deployed a diver. The divers, she warned us, were armed with spear guns.

Suddenly luck was on my side. I was on the verge of emerging from the tunnel on the lee side of the reef when the Baja sun suddenly became my compatriot. With the glare, I couldn't see the diver, but I could see his shadow on the rocks just above me. This time he was the seal and I was the shark. I backed into the tunnel as far as I could and kept out of sight until my Chinese friend was convinced there was nothing amiss. Twice he swam within thirty feet of me, each time looking in every direction but mine. I didn't know whether or not I would have used it, but I found myself with a death grip on the TRH.5R dart gun and a finger planted near the trigger housing.

He disappeared for a moment, and I ran a quick check on my equipment. According to my gauges, I was some forty-three feet below the surface and I had used close to sixty percent of my total of 105 minutes of mission time. I was till trying to feed the data into my dive computer when he circled back again. I continued hiding until he was again satisfied there was no threat and began working his way north along the reef.

Relief was temporary—either way he went he would still be inside the security net—and as long as he was inside the net he would be in a position to return.

I had to give Carlos Martinenez credit. He had been wrong about the tunnel's size, but he had been right about everything else: their location and the fact that they went all the way through to the lee side of the reef. Plus he had been right about the deployment of the security net. In places where the net had been deployed too close to the reef, it had managed to get hung up on reef outcroppings. That made him two for three. Two for three is good.

The bottom of the security net was tangled on the outcroppings at several points along the reef. Had I known as much and if there had been a way to get the Pony I into position without being picked up by their radar, the whole tunnel ordeal could have been avoided. As it was now, I was going to have to retrace my way back through the tunnel to retrieve the Pony I. Not a task I was eager to tackle.

The thought had occurred to me that I could tell Bro the Pony I was lost in testing. It wouldn't be the first time we had lost a test model. A twenty-one-footer destined for delivery to Woods Hole two years earlier was still lying somewhere on the bottom of the Pingre Trench off the southern coast of Jamaica. A very big, very aggressive shark had a lot to do with that one. In the end, though, the thought of undergoing the inevitable Bro Roger inquisition held even less appeal than threading my way back through the tunnel.

I waited another couple of minutes until I was reasonably certain my adversary was gone, buckled back into my dive harness, adjusted my gear, and moved into the search area. It didn't take long to figure out why the Chinese had deployed their net where they had. It had nothing to do with research and even less to do with fish. The fragmented remains of what I now was convinced was the *Baja Lady* were randomly scattered over the bottom of the Bahia Magdalena waterway like pieces of a derelict puzzle. Not only that, there was plenty of evidence the Chinese had been systematically combing through the wreckage section by section.

I headed straight to the remains of what had to be the ship's salon. If Amy's hunch was right and the *Baja Lady*'s demise was the result of some kind of explosion, the salvage effort had one thing going for it: While most of the bow and much of the stern were scattered around the floor of the channel in little pieces, the cabin, the foredeck, and much of the vessel's interior in the center section appeared to be pretty much intact.

As I surveyed the wreckage, I was mentally going back through the photographs Dara had obtained from the *Baja Lady*'s builders when she first started making inquiries about the vessel. The photograph of the ship's deckhouse showed what Elizabeth Carter was calling the salon. I think the reason I remembered that particular photo was because at the time I noticed that there was a mirror and a small safe under a built-in desk on the starboard side. The explosion had taken care of the mirror, but I doubted if it would have destroyed the safe. Why did I remember the safe? Probably because a safe is not one of the appointments I would have thought of requesting if I was having a ship's interior designed to my tastes and specifications.

According to Elizabeth Carter, though, that was not where she and her former playmate had stashed the code keys. She indicated that Tyler had decided to remove one of the salon's bulkhead panels, conceal the item in question, replace the panel, and ignore the more obvious safe. Again the question, why? Why have a safe installed if you aren't going to use it? Second question: If I was a Chinese diver and I was looking for something important, why wouldn't I think the safe was a likely candidate to contain what I was looking for? Curiously enough, there was no evidence the Chinese had even paid attention to the safe.

If you don't want someone to find something, don't hide it in the obvious place. If Rowland had made a deal to deliver the code keys to the Chinese and he was planning to meet the Chinese to hand it over, he would have had the code keys with him, or at least where he could conveniently lay his hands on it.

So if Rowland himself was on board and planning to rendezvous with the Chinese, why would he feel it necessary to hide the code keys? Answer: A person doesn't hide things in a safe, a person puts something in a safe to keep it safe. Obviously, Rowland had something else in mind. The question then becomes, safe from whom or what? Was there someone else on board besides Rowland? Was it someone Tyler Rowland didn't trust? Is it possible there is another player in this convoluted little drama? Someone that as yet I didn't know about?

At a depth of approximately forty feet, inside the Chinese security net on the bottom of the Bahia Magdalena channel, I was swimming toward all that remained of the *Baja Lady* and questions were again racing through my head. Without spending much time poking around in the wreckage, I could tell that the Chinese had been busy people. The furniture was gone, the place had been gutted. No doubt the divers figured that was where Rowland had stashed the goodies, in the furniture. In the process, they had discovered what Amy and I had already been told: The code keys weren't there.

Swimming around and through what was left of the *Lady*'s once ultraluxurious deckhouse and studying its layout, I was convinced I was in the right place. It had to be the place where Carter and Rowland had stashed their prize. At the same time, it occurred to me that Rowland would have had to feel something akin to sick to his stomach if he could see his floating pleasure palace now. The deckroom's lavish appointments had been slashed, gutted, torn apart, and otherwise wasted. Desecrated. Opulence reduced to rubble.

When the *Baja Lady* sailed from SFO, the deckroom was festooned with large windows on both sides of the vessel. Now the glass was intact in only two of the six windows. Were the other four blown out when the *Lady* exploded? Or did the Chinese break them out in the process of looking for the code keys? It probably didn't matter.

Amidst a whole lot of rubble, litter, and confusion, I was trying to determine which bulkhead panel would be the most likely place and which the least likely place to hide the code keys. Of the several, four appeared to be possibilities. When I pounded on the four, two sounded hollow, two sounded as though there might be something a bit more substantial than empty space behind them. Using my dive knife, I pried at the edge of the panel that seemed the most unlikely place to hide something.

I had managed to loosen the corner of the bulkhead panel that butted up against the bar when I felt it. If you dive often enough and deep enough, something happens to your sensory bank. You develop a kind of personal sonar, a danger-sensing device somewhere near the brainstem. It's a survival thing, primal and aboriginal. It operates like an alert system, making you acutely aware of your vulnerability. Seconds, maybe even microseconds before you are attacked, broadsided, or incapacitated, an alarm goes off. If you're agile enough and lucky enough, you may have just enough time to assume some sort of a preventive posture. If you're not, that particular micro-miniature interval in time may do nothing more than warn you that suddenly your sorry life is going to be just a tad more miserable.

At any rate, I knew something was coming at me from behind and I spun around. When I did, all I could see was mask, fins, what appeared to be some kind of menacing-looking cartridge-powered spear gun, and some guy with an attitude. Before I could decide which way I needed to go to get out of his way, he managed to make solid contact just below my helmet with the handle of his spear gun.

It hurt. I winced, stumbled backward, and lost my equilibrium. I was still reeling around when I realized he was coming at me again. I tried to duck, but he brought his knee up and connected with that vulnerable area just under my chin. That second blow, in addition to making me feel like my brains had been run through a blender, momentarily dislodged the cover and diaphragm on my breathing apparatus.

I twisted my helmet back into position and backed away. All I needed was a little room, my dart gun, and the opportunity to aim it. Fortunately, I was able to attain all three. And just like it says in the sales literature, "The TRH.5R has the power to help you turn the tide of battle with any aquatic adversary."

With one six-inch stainless steel dart liberally coated with piralexon, the tide was turned. The dart buried itself in the meaty part of his thigh with only an inch or so still protruding. Predictably, he dropped his spear gun, grabbed his leg, and spun away streaming blood.

There was only one thing wrong. If my bleeding adversary was able to communicate when he arrived topside, he would doubtless scream for hordes of reinforcements. I still hadn't peeled away any panels and explored deckhouse bulkheads, but I was fairly certain this was not the time. While my flailing assailant was trying to cope with his increasing discomfort, I slipped up behind him, grabbed a fistful of face mask, gave it a violent twist, and peeled it away from his face. With that, he had only two options; he could either head for the surface or become the main course for some creature at the bottom of the Bahia Magdalena channel. He chose the former, and I headed back for the tunnel.

With all the unscheduled activity, it occurred to me it had been a while since I had checked my elapsed mission time. Not good dive management. Especially when one is confronted with an uncompromising tunnel to work through. Then, when I did try to get current readings, I realized my militant pal had at some time during our brief squabble managed to render useless more than half the gauges on my LS system. To top it off, I could tell that either I had picked up a pinhole leak in the high-pressure hose to my air supply or one of the helmet valves had been knocked out of adjustment. At the depth I was, it wasn't a panic situation, but it could get a little sticky if I got stuck in that tunnel again.

Once again I peeled out of my dive harness, shoved the air cylinders into the tunnel ahead of me, crawled in behind them, and began clawing and paddling my way toward the ocean side of the reef. If Rowland's U.S.-based investigation team ever held an advantage in this search scenario, we had just lost it. The Chinese now knew we were there, and they had made it abundantly clear they wanted us out of there.

By now, my bleeding adversary was probably floundering around on the surface waiting for someone to pull him on board. And depending on how quickly they could get ready, he probably had several buddies preparing to head down to the wreckage of the *Baja Lady* to administer what they considered to be a sound dose of comeuppance.

This time I was in luck. I cleared the tunnel with a minimum of hassle, informed Amy I was out of the battle zone, climbed aboard the sled, and

R. Karl Largent

plowed my way back to the surface. If Bro Roger
had been waiting on board Carlos's boat for me to
give him a test report, I would have reported that
the Pony I had performed quite admirably—but
only if we were evaluating the relatively minor tasks
of taking me down and bringing me back up again.
Beyond that, it hadn't been much of a test.

By the time we were able to get everyone back to
port and assess the damage, it was almost eighteen
hundred hours. There was still plenty of sunlight,
the temperature continued to hover around the
eighty-five-degree mark, and Marie was giving us
our ration of good news for the day. The *teléfono*
repair crew had been there. Las Cuevas once again
had phone service, and Amy promptly took advantage of it. She said she needed to call her boss and
report the day's progress.

In the conversation that followed, Poker confirmed Amy's earlier report that he had discovered
a sizable hole in the *Shanchu Fhin*'s security net.
"Big enough," he said, "that I think I could have
slipped the Pony II through without setting off any
of their detectors."

Amy began nodding. "I could see everything the
Chinese were doing. I don't think they ever de-
tected that there were two of you down there. I
think they locked on to A. J. and that was as far as
they got."

Amy's observation about the Chinese not being
aware of Poker, valid or not, triggered a whole new

line of thinking. The three of us hadn't as yet discussed it, but we now had a problem that we didn't have earlier in the day. The likelihood that we would catch the crew of the *Shanchu Fhin* off guard a second time seemed unlikely. The Chinese knew we were in the area now, and in all probability all we had really done was wake them up. In addition, one of their own had actually encountered the enemy, taken a six-inch stainless steel dart coated with piralexon in his leg, and managed to claw his way back to the surface.

Now they had more than suspicions, they had a description of the intruder and had doubtless reached the conclusion that they were no longer dealing with just a bunch of disgruntled local fishermen. They were dealing with someone who was just as interested in the wreckage of the *Baja Lady* as they were. But—and I had to believe this was our ace in the hole—it was unlikely that they knew about the submersibles.

If I continued to accept the premise that the *Shanchu Fhin* was still deployed over the wreckage of the *Baja Lady* because they still didn't have the code keys in their hot little hands, it seemed equally reasonable to assume they would remain there until they found them. So it seemed unlikely we could wait them out. It also seemed likely they would redouble their security and do everything in their power to make certain we didn't find the code keys before they did.

Finally, when I was through speculating, Poker

finished his cigarette, ground it out in the hardpan, and shrugged. "Okay, so they know we're there. What's our next move?"

Amy was frowning and shaking her head at the same time. "I don't know what our next move is, but the important thing is, we're making progress. We now know the *Baja Lady* did go down. We know where it is located. And we know what's left of it. Earlier in the day we were only guessing on all three counts. Plus we now have every reason to believe that if Rowland and his Chinese friends had consummated their deal, it isn't likely they would still be hanging around and taking such drastic measures to keep us away from the wreckage."

". . . And the code keys are still stashed behind one of those panels in the deckroom," Poker added. "But which bulkhead panel is it, and how do we get to it now that the Chinese know that someone else is interested in the wreckage?"

We had been mulling the situation over for hours and still hadn't come up with anything that all of us agreed would work. The best we had been able to come up with was the old diversion ploy—hope that while the crew of the *Shanchu Fhin* was preoccupied with a distraction we could send our man in. We did agree that in order to make it work, it would have to be hit and run. Get in and get out.

We were still looking for our distraction when Marie announced *la cena* was ready. I figured that with any luck at all, a healthy dose of spicy Mexican chow might wake us up and spark an idea or two.

After dinner we again sat on the porch of the Las Cuevas Hilton swapping stories and drinking beer. Poker, like me, initially had a degree of difficulty learning to drink warm Budweiser, but when Carlos offered him one of his rope cigars to go with it, all was right in the Palmer world.

Later, when Carlos and Poker drifted down to the pier to check out the next day's weather forecasts, Amy and I lapsed into a prolonged conversation about her background. The session carried us all the way from her early days in public school in Atlanta to graduate school at Auburn in Alabama. Her first kiss happened in the second grade, and her first real boyfriend was a young man who washed taxicabs. She went on to say that when she got out of college she thought about applying for a position with the FBI.

"But I wasn't qualified, and when that didn't happen I just sorta drifted from one thing to another, I learned to do and did just about anything that paid decent money. After all, a girl has to eat. All of which, I suppose, explains how I ended up with Cal Maritime. They were recruiting in New York at the time, offered me a package I could live with, and I thought the idea of living in San Francisco sounded appealing. You know the rest. My first assignment was to chase down the rumors my boss was hearing about the deteriorating situation at Unitrieve.

"Now all of sudden I'm in a godforsaken place

called Las Cuevas, trying to fend off hordes of sand fleas and drinking warm beer."

Admittedly it was brief, but I consoled myself with the fact that I now knew more about Amy Reed than I did before. But it still wasn't as much as I wanted to know. Then she began again. "So, A. J., aren't you the least bit curious about what I've learned about you?"

"Why should I be? There isn't that much to know, and what little there is is public knowledge. All a person needs these days is a Furnace Standard annual report."

"Trust me, any girl who flies off to the Baja with some guy and his buddy, especially when his buddy is named Poker, better do a little checking on the man before she departs. That is, unless she doesn't care whether or not she returns with her reputation intact."

"Sounds like you did a little digging."

"Some. You're forty-one years old, the operations director of the FSORC division of Furnace Standard, you're not married, never have been, you're not gay, and you don't have a police record."

"Except for the not being gay part, you could have learned all that from that annual report I was telling you about."

"But I didn't." She smiled. "I made a lot of calls. I talked to some of your friends. That forty-one-year-old wealthy bachelor part of your résumé makes you intriguing. Whether you know it or not, the girls are conducting an A. J. watch. I guess you'll just have to hope that what they told me is on the up and up, huh?"

I shrugged. The truth is, for the most part I was hoping she would find something else to talk about.

Hope is one thing, reality another. Amy was on a roll. "I guess the only question I have now is, just exactly what does someone do when they are involved in so-called Navy Special Projects?"

"You spend your time getting prepared for any eventuality," I said.

"Like?"

"Jump school, scuba school, how to survive in hostile weather, that kind of stuff. If you had made it into the FBI, you would probably have been exposed to some of the same training."

Amy leaned back against the porch railing. She gave me her most coquettish smile and shook her head. "No, thanks," she said. "If that's the case, I'm glad I didn't make it. I very much prefer fragrant candles, expensive perfume, fresh flowers, and French cuisine. The old *Nyoka, Queen of the Jungle* routine isn't my thing."

It is difficult to say how and where the conversation would have progressed after that, because at that point Marie joined us on the porch and I saw Poker and Carlos lumbering back up the street from the docks. The conversation had been intriguing. Time had passed, and it was later than I realized. Las Cuevas was bedding down for the night. Daylight had been reduced to a few pencil-thin pastel slashes on the western horizon, and the only sounds being generated featured malcontent gulls, an occasional barking dog, and someone somewhere playing a radio. When I cocked my head to one side in an effort to determine where the music was coming from, Marie informed me it was probably the Admiral. She explained that for years the Admiral and Rainbow preferred to fish at night, and with Rainbow being gone now for two days, the Admiral seemed lost. "He is probably somewhere out there fishing," she concluded.

Like the conversation with Amy, the one with Marie piqued my interest enough to pursue it further, but Poker cut it short. He climbed up on the porch and plunked down on the steps beside me. "I think you better read this," he said. "Me and Carlos hung around long enough to hear the latest NOAA weather forecast for this region. Good thing we did—looks like we've got a problem brewing."

Carlos elaborated. "They've upgraded that tropical storm a couple of hundred miles south of Cabo San Lucas to hurricane status. They say it's moving north-northeast at roughly eight to ten miles an hour."

"This time of year?" I said.

"Been a mild winter," Carlos conceded, "and an even warmer spring. Fishing has been poor." He lit one of his cigars and slumped down on the steps beside Poker. I had a hunch Carlos and the rest of the Las Cuevas contingent had been through it all before. The word "hurricane" didn't seem to be throwing him off stride.

"Is it likely to hit us?" I pushed.

Carlos thought for a minute, then shook his head. "Not likely. Usually they drift to the north-northwest away from Bahia Magdalena. But I haven't heard of one this close to land before." He handed me a piece of paper. On it he had scribbled the NOAA 2100 GMT forecast.

Warning. Hurricane Celia moving NNE 8 to 10 KTS—forecast increasing storm winds 55 to 80 KTS . . . maximum winds 72 KTS gusting to 82 KTS near center—seas 12 to 15 FT.

I folded the piece of paper and stuffed it in my shirt pocket. As if our friends aboard the Chinese salvage ship weren't enough, now we had a hurricane to deal with. The National Oceanic and Atmospheric Administration is generally right on target, and, like it or not, they were saying a hurricane was headed for Las Cuevas.

Journal No. 9

Friday, June 12

Conversation on the front porch of Carlos's place lasted until shortly before twenty-three hundred hours so that we could check NOAA's 2300 weather forecast. According to NOAA, there was no significant change in the Baja weather forecast—except that the center of the developing hurricane was continuing to move north-northeast instead of the usual north-northwest. And, NOAA noted, the storm was developing at a slightly accelerated pace.

At the broadcast's conclusion, Poker made a few inquiries about the type and extent of precautions the Las Cuevas fishing fleet had taken the last time a hurricane brushed the coast of Bahia Magdalena.

"That was ten years ago," Carlos reflected. "We

dogged down the hatches, tied down everything that looked like it could blow away, covered the windows, made certain we had plenty of drinking water, a case of batteries, and plenty of fuel for the generator."

Marie was listening and she authored another of her musical little laughs. "The captain was just as careful about making certain there was plenty of beer, cigars, and tequila," she added.

"You must have made it through it okay," I said.

Carlos was nodding and smiling. "The real damage was up at Jean Jean's place. Blew it clean away. We found parts of it up and down the beach for weeks. The only thing the storm left behind was a bushel of tomatoes, a handful of peppers, and a bucket of lard. On the whole, though, the village didn't experience much damage."

On our way back up from the beach I began thinking about our Chinese friends anchored out in the channel. True, they were much safer there than they would have been on the ocean side of the reef. Still, I had to wonder if they were aware that mother nature had conjured up a rather nasty tropical storm for them and as of 2300 hours it was headed straight for them.

Despite the fact that the *Shanchu Fhin* had sent hostiles with gas-charged spearguns after me, I was in no hurry to see the entire crew of any ship deep-sixed by a hurricane. But if seventy- and eighty-mile-an-hour winds slapped them up against the reef, that was a distinct possibility.

241

R. Karl Largent

"Think we should warn them?" Amy asked when we returned to the hotel.

I told her it was safe to assume the Chinese had all the maritime electronics in the form of GPS, loran, and radio gear they needed to know that a good-sized storm was approaching and take the necessary precautions. In truth, I figured they had a whole lot more going for them, but I didn't see any reason to go into that with Amy.

By the time we were safely back in the hotel, the first tentacles of the storm had already begun to infiltrate the peace and calm. Some high cirrus clouds had begun to claw their way across the sky from the southwest, the moon was all but obliterated, and it was much darker to the south. All in all, it was looking like a prelude to bad weather. Cirrus, followed by low clouds of high density, accompanied by falling pressure is a pretty good indication of rough weather.

The arrival of the first clouds is usually accompanied by a freshening wind and falling pressure. When I checked the old Freeman barometer on the hotel porch, that was happening. Where we had been enduring an oven-dry heat earlier in the evening with little more than an occasional breeze, I saw Amy don a sweater as she walked around the porch bidding the rest of us good night.

She had been gone for several minutes when Poker began speculating when and how we could get back inside the *Shanchu Fhin*'s security net.

He lit a cigarette and leaned back against the

242

porch railing. "Know somethin'? This storm may just turn out to be a blessing in disguise for us. While the storm keeps the crew of the *Shanchu Fhin* busy battling Celia topside, we could launch the submersibles, hug the bottom, avoid most of what's brewin' up on top, go with the current in the channel, and maybe get another chance to do some pokin' around in Rowland's boat." When he finished, he took another drag on his cigarette and exhaled. He studied the pall hanging over his head. "Think it'll work?" he asked.

I didn't know. More important, I didn't have a feel for working a sled in a shallow, narrow body of water like the channel. Six to seven fathoms of water isn't all that deep. My only experience operating an underwater vehicle like the Pony I during a tropical storm had come during a late-season storm in the Caribbean two years earlier. But there I had the advantage of being able to operate at a depth of eighty feet, a lot deeper than we would be at any time in the Bahia Magdalena channel. I relived that experience, trying to recall the nuances and subtleties of operating a craft under the surface of a raging storm. Finally, when I felt confident I had thought it through, I looked at Poker.

"I suppose it could work," I agreed, "but I guarantee you, getting those submersibles launched in that kind of weather will test the old intestinal fortitude."

Poker leaned close. "You know what they say." He grinned. "No balls, no bullion."

*   *   *

I don't know how long I had been wrestling with my pillow when it began to rain, but rain it did. At first it was just a sprinkle, not enough to settle the dust. But rain in the Baja Sur is a lot like rain in California—it seldom rains, but when it does, it gets serious about it. Most of the time, Bahia Magdalena survives on three or four inches of rain a year. And most of the time, as Carlos had already pointed out, tropical storms and hurricanes tend to drift out from their point of origin to the north-northwest. All of which tends to leave places like Las Cuevas with scant rainfall.

Nevertheless, as Carlos also pointed out, in the Baja Sur it is the wise man who prepares himself at any time of year for any kind of weather.

The first spotty, sporadic rains associated with Celia began about two-thirty in the morning. I was awake when the rain started. The approaching storm was accompanied by a definitive increase in surface winds and occasional but distant cloud-to-cloud lightning. Once again I was reminded that lightning can have its origin a long way away and still appear to illuminate the sky overhead.

The thunder at that point was even more remote. I lay there listening to the approaching storm for several minutes before I got out of bed, pulled on a pair of trousers, groped my way down the stairs through the dark, and ended up on the porch. Amy was already there. She was wearing a dressing gown made of some kind of diaphanous material that billowed in the wind, and her short blond hair was likewise being ruffled. I wasn't surprised when she said, "I love thunderstorms. I used to sit on the roof of our sorority house down at Auburn when we would have a spring thunderstorm. My roommate thought I was half nuts, and when our house mother learned I was doing it, she forbade me to go up there."

"Dangerous," I assessed.

"Life is dangerous," she replied.

After that, we stood there for quite a while, watching the storm and knowing that nothing either of us said would be recorded for posterity or held against us.

The next morning, the rain had stopped and there was nothing to prove that it had ever happened. Dust had been dampened, but hardpan was still hardpan. The Baja sun was nowhere to be found.

The color of the day was chimney-sweep gray. Amy was touching me on the arm. I liked that, but I was also aware she was trembling. In addition to coping with the sensations of Amy, I was desperately trying to order my thoughts. When I did, I realized I was looking up at someone who looked as if she were living in a nightmare.

"A. J.," she finally managed, "Carlos sent me. They want you down at the pier."

I swung my legs over the side of the bed. Everything seemed to be working. There was still a degree of wobble in the main frame, but I managed to work my way around that, pulled on trousers, a T-shirt with the words *Coast Guard* emblazoned across the chest, and donned a pair of sandals. All in all, I considered it to be a successful reentry into the land of the awake.

Amy followed me down the stairs, across the dining room, out on the porch, and began gesturing. The activity she was pointing out was taking place down at the dock. I could see three men, two of whom were Carlos and Viktor standing on the pier looking down at a forlorn-looking dory in need of a paint job. There was a man standing in the boat, and they all had flashlights.

"Mind telling me what this is all about?" I said.

Amy didn't answer but continued pointing.

"Are you coming with me?" I asked.

She was near tears. She shook her head.

I started down the street toward the dock only to become aware that Amy had changed her mind. She was following me. The closer I got to the three men, the more it was obvious that they were waiting for me. By the time I walked out on the pier, I also realized that whatever it was that had captured their attention, it was lying in the dory.

I looked down, felt my stomach do a slow roll followed by a fast dive straight down to where Marie's fare from the previous evening still resided. At that point, Carlos and Viktor were standing next to me. The third man, the one I had been unable to recognize from the hotel porch, was the Admiral. He was crying.

Sloshing around in the bottom of the dory was a dirty brown canvas tarp covered with oil stains. In the center of the tarp was what was left of the Admiral's friend, Rainbow.

I did a double take, hoping I could do what I knew I had to do without throwing up. The head, the neck, and the shoulders were still pretty much intact. The rest of what had once been a very large, very muscular man was either mangled or missing.

I looked at Carlos. "What the hell happened to him?"

"Shark," he said. "Maybe one, maybe more than one."

I stepped down in the boat, held my breath, and peeled the folds of the tarp away from the body. A tangle of white and pink sun-bleached organ and muscle remnants dangled down from what was left of the area where the abdomen used to be. The right arm was missing, chewed off at the shoulder, and smaller fish had made short work of Rainbow's facial features.

"That tiger shark we saw in the channel a week ago?" I asked.

Carlos and Viktor both nodded. I looked back up the pier at Amy. The look of shock on her face revealed just how unnerved she was. I started to get out of the boat, and the Admiral reached out to stop me.

"You see this?" he asked. He leaned down and rolled Rainbow's massive head to one side. There was a large hole in the back of the neck several inches below the base of the skull. The flesh around the wound had been ravaged still further by sea creatures. "That—that not—not caused by shark," he said.

The Admiral could probably count the number of times someone had said he was right about something on the fingers of one hand. This was one of those times. The gaping hole in the back of his friend's neck had not been caused by a shark. Sharks don't carry weapons.

I swallowed hard, chewed on my lip, and tried to wait until I had my stomach under control. When I did, I crouched down to get a better look. The best way to describe what I was looking at would be a puncture wound—a very large puncture wound with a circumference about the size of a golf ball. When the blow was delivered, the instrument that dispatched it, in all probability a speargun propelled by a gas-charged cylinder, did its job with considerable force and efficiency. When whoever did it pulled the trigger, there was never any doubt about the outcome.

It didn't take much imagination for me to paint a mental picture of what had happened. Rainbow had been attacked, perhaps by the same diver that had attacked me. In all probability, the blow didn't kill him. It may have broken his neck or it may have rendered him unconscious. Perhaps it only stunned him. At this point it was impossible to tell. Either way, the trauma was just below the base of his skull and was obviously the beginning of the end. Either momentarily or permanently paralyzed, there wasn't much Rainbow could do about his situation and he started to drown. With any luck at all, he died before the shark or sharks got to him.

As I stood there looking at the mortal remains of Rainbow, a multitude of new questions started popping up. It was further proof that the Chinese were convinced the code keys were still stashed somewhere in the wreckage of the *Baja Lady* and that anyone outside of the crew of the *Shanchu Fhin* was there for no other purpose than to stop them from finding those keys.

Still, killing Rainbow didn't make a whole lot of sense. Rainbow was fishing. No diving gear. Nothing to indicate he was looking for the code keys. The *Lady*'s wreckage was underwater. Rainbow couldn't have been poking around in the wreckage, and he couldn't have been a threat, because he wasn't a diver. So what was Rainbow doing that got him killed? I looked at Carlos. "How long do you figure he's been dead?"

The captain shrugged and hesitated, reluctant to say. "Judging from what's left of him, three, maybe four days. Hard to say, with what that shark did." He had turned to the Admiral. "How long since you seen him?"

The pencil-thin little man with the well-worn, cut-off khaki-colored shorts and a length of cotton rope serving as a belt tried to remember. It was hard for him. "Three—three—three days," he guessed.

I stepped out of the Admiral's boat and looked

at the faces around me. All of a sudden, the search for Tyler Rowland and the *Baja Lady* had taken on an entirely different character. In a very short period of time it had become a great deal more serious. It was no longer a detached, semiabstract search for a man and a boat none of us were really familiar with. Now Rainbow was dead. Not just dead—killed. It was no accident. Judging from the wound's location and severity, it had been intentional.

Amy said it best when we were walking back up to the hotel, "I thought coming down here would be sort of a lark, you know, an adventure, kinda like one of those survival games. I never figured on people dying in a game."

It took the better part of the day to put the pieces back together. We carried Rainbow's body back up to the hotel, Carlos cranked up the ancient ice maker out in back of the hotel and covered the body with ice. "Haven't used it in months," he said. "Back when fishing was good, we used to catch enough fish that we had to ice down what Acobar couldn't take in one trip."

Carlos finally managed to get a call through to the *comisario de policía* at Mulege to inform them of Rainbow's death. He was careful. He told them he believed the cause of death was a fishing accident. Later he explained. "I was buying time. If I tell them we think he was killed by someone aboard that Chinese fishing boat, they will be here in force.

If that happens, it'll be impossible for you and your friends to find what you're looking for in the wreckage."

What Carlos was saying made sense. In recovering the code keys, if all we had to do was contend with the crew of the *Shanchu Fhin*, that would be tough enough. Throwing the Mexican *policía* and possibly even the Mexican Coast Guard into the equation would make it twice as difficult. I agreed with Poker; if that happened, there was a good chance we would be restrained from diving the wreck site altogether.

With that in mind, we decided to delay making a decision on whether to call the *policía* back and inform them we had found a hole in the back of Rainbow's head until after we had made a second dive.

As for the Admiral, he was proving to be inconsolable. Finally, Carlos sent Marie to get Jean Jean to stay with him. She was able to pump enough of her tequila into him during the course of the afternoon that he finally fell asleep. After that, Amy and I called Carlos, Viktor, Bo Bo, and Poker together to figure out how we could best utilize the approaching storm for dive cover. By late afternoon two things had become abundantly clear.

One, NOAA forecasts and reports from several ships south and west of Baja Sur were reporting rapidly falling pressure, waves in excess of six feet, and winds out of the south-southwest blowing consistently in the 22-to-29-knot range. To keep tabs on

251

the storm's progress, Carlos sent Viktor down to the docks where the *Desastrada Mujer* was tied up.

Viktor's sole purpose for being there was to monitor the emergency VHF channel and the *Mujer's* single sideband radio. The sum total of all this was that the eye of the storm was starting to shear out toward open water. It was beginning to look like we were going to miss the eye of the storm, but we were still in for some nasty weather.

Two, despite several hours of trying, we had failed to come up with any kind of dive plan that seemed even halfway clever. But we did have a plan. The plan depended on two elements: storm and luck. Simply stated, we intended to use what we could of the storm for cover. Using Carlos and Bo Bo's experience in the channel during a blow as a guide, we decided to wait until the wave height in the channel reached the forecasted eight to eleven feet and the winds maxed out around thirty-one to thirty-five knots with occasional higher gusts.

According to Viktor, the weather people were forecasting conditions in the channel to continue to deteriorate until somewhere around midnight and to stay that way until between four o'clock and dawn. If that was the case, that meant we would have roughly four hours to get another look at what was left of the *Baja Lady*.

By the time we were through hashing and re-hashing our plan we had convinced ourselves we had considered, if not all, then most of the critical variables in the equation. Getting to the *Baja Lady* for look number two was beginning to sound easy.

By eight o'clock that evening we had both Viktor and Bo Bo conducting what we were calling a "mission watch" aboard the *Desastrada Mujer*. The two men were recording and relaying every piece of weather information they could get their hands on. Fortunately, NOAA's forecast wasn't changing much. They were recording winds in the eye of the storm at seventy knots. At the same time, they were confirming that the center of the storm continued to plow its way to the north-northwest. Ships near the vicinity of the eye of the storm were confirming that the worst of Celia was nearly 125 miles west of Bahia Magdalena. Even so, Carlos's assessment of the forecast conditions in the channel was simply, "It'll be choppier than hell."

I figured we could live with that.

In order for our plan to work, though, the officers and crew aboard the *Shanchu Fhin* had to be convinced they were safe in thinking the storm was the least likely time for us to make a second attempt at combing through the wreckage of the *Baja Lady*. How would we do that? We had a plan, not brilliant, but workable. First, we would make certain our Chinese friends could see the lights of the Las Cuevas fishing fleet anchored in the harbor. Second, we would make certain they could monitor a steady line of chatter between Bo Bo, Viktor, and Carlos

R. Karl Largent

all talking about the storm. Ergo, no fishing boats, no threat.

Both Poker and I were counting on the combination of foul weather and darkness to provide the cover we needed. Hopefully, a little harbor savvy and conventional logic on the part of the Chinese would convince them it was highly unlikely we would pick the middle of the night in the middle of a storm to make another dive attempt. That same stream of logic was telling us the weather in the channel would be rough enough to keep our Chinese friends aboard the *Shanchu Fhin* occupied. Those that weren't required topside would probably be relegated to duties below. Those on deck would have their hands full with the weather. Hopefully, they would not be busy worrying about what the Las Cuevas fishing fleet was doing.

It was a little after ten o'clock when Poker and I finally managed to muscle our way up the beach in the rain, wind, and darkness to the trailer where the submersible sleds were housed. We had slightly less than two hours to make the necessary changes in equipment for a night launch and to dolly the Pony I down to the water. We had agreed I would handle sled duties and Poker would monitor the telemetry equipment in the trailer.

By the time we got to the trailer we were soaked. Poker unlocked the door, crawled in, lit a cigarette, and complained he wasn't being paid enough for all the grief he was being put through. I said nothing to Poker, but it was the second time in less than

254

twenty-four hours that I wished I had insisted the FSORC engineers stay with the test facilities instead of putting them on a plane and sending them back to SFO.

Some two years earlier, FSORC engineers had developed a number of working prototypes of two multicolored situation display units to replace conventional instrumentation in the console of a underwater sled. Unfortunately, I had left the original SD units along with a working prototype of the pilot model (known as the Courier I) scattered over several square miles of the Caribbean when the sled's FA-2a engine exploded. It was a harrowing experience that resulted in a number of burns.

Now, a properly calibrated and updated SD-1, through a concatenation of infrared lights (similar to technology used in Gen-5 night vision) had been designed that would give a submersible pilot an eighty-seven percent ghost-free field of vision in up to thirty feet of dark water without support light. I was banking on it. No lights at night, no detection from the surface.

The second multifunction SD was a collision avoidance system—a nifty 360-degree CA technology that kept the pilot informed with a heads-up display in the helmet's face mask. When you're down there groping around in the dark, nothing is more reassuring than a parade of silent, informative, and unobtrusive environmental icons. Especially when they are confirming that you are on the right track. If I had taken the time to install the SD-

CA that first day when the man with the speargun appeared on the scene, I might have spotted him in time to avoid one ear-splitting, headache-inducing whack on the head.

At 2330 hours, Poker and I went over the plan one final time. Launch at midnight. As soon as feasible, submerge to a running depth of five fathoms to avoid as much of the effects of the surface agitation as possible. Then I begin working my way south in the channel to where Poker had discovered the hole in the *Shanchu Fhin*'s security net.

Poker Palmer is and always has been a thorough test jockey. That's one of the reasons I hold him in such high regard. Now he was giving me my final briefing. "You've got enough air for two hours, but that means you'll have to incorporate the life support bottle off of the sled. Carry it or know where it is. Got that? Start frequent monitoring of your LSS and MDT at the ninety-minute mark. Set your pulse alarm. Make certain you are where you can switch over to the sled air at MDT-90. I checked the bottle; you have forty minutes of sled air. That means you better be pushing that sled of yours back up on the beach at ten minutes after two. Got it?"

I continued suiting up while Poker lit up. Always a little nervous before a test, he exhaled a cloud of thin blue-gray smoke, stood up, and tried to inhale it a second time. He checked my harness, connections on my helmet, patted me on the back, and gave me a five count to test the audio. Then we pushed the sled and dolly down to the water's edge, fought the wind while I crawled into the cockpit, pushed forward until I was in three or four foot of water, and started throwing thruster switches.

I began working my way toward the wreckage of the *Baja Lady*. I was aware that just a few feet above me the surface was in turmoil. When I took the Pony I down, wave height in the channel still hadn't maximized; it was running at seven to nine foot.

On the bottom of the channel, it was for the most part a world of permanent impermanence. A world where nothing changes and everything changes. What is there now and will be there a century from now is gone in the wink of an eye. It can be a world of spellbinding color or, by night, a universe void of hue, tint, and tinge. At night, with your sight occluded by technology, confined to what a situation display wants you to see, it can be a surrealistic monocolored landscape populated by nightmare images.

Progress is slow. Mission time is devoured by the sheer task of simply getting where you are going. Then, just when I begin to think I am trying to accomplish the absurd or preposterous, the goal is attained, and I win one.

In this case, there it was, right in front of me, just like Poker said it would be—a big, gaping hole in the *Shanchu Fhin*'s security net. It was big enough to take the sled through, but that is when I made my first mistake, I decided against it—too much chance, I figured, of me bumping something with the sled or the Chinese picking up the sled's cavitation.

I parked the sled, activated the infrared vision processor in my face mask, made certain the collision avoidance relay display in my helmet was available if I needed it, and swam through the net.

Elapsed dive time: 37min 31sec.

If Poker was as right about this as he had been about everything else in our dive prep, I probably wasn't much more than 250 to 300 yards from the wreckage of the deckhouse. Concerned that the folks aboard the *Shanchu Fhin* might have deciphered the set of signals from the previous dive, Poker had insisted we change signals for the second. I was instructed to press the transmit button once—but only after I was inside the net, and after that only to indicate that all systems were functioning. I would press the same button twice if I encountered some sort of delay or difficulty. Followed, of course, by again hitting the transmit button one time to show that the situation had been corrected or the obstacle had been eliminated.

I was inside the net and more than halfway to the wreckage when I suddenly encountered a couple of curious four-foot-long blacktip reef sharks. They circled around me a couple of times and then decided it was in their best interests to avoid me. Whether it was the hour, the conditions, or the environment, after the blacktips departed for less populated waters, I realized my mind was occasionally straying. I had momentarily lost my focus and

caught myself wondering what else I could encounter in a net where there was only one way out.

I stopped to get my bearings and check my gear.
EDT: 43 min 21 sec.

The deckhouse of the *Baja Lady* first appeared on
the UNV unit as a hazy half image. Then, when I
was less than thirty yards from the wreck, what was
left of the deckhouse began to crystallize and take
shape. I was approaching it from the direction
where the bow had once been. That meant I had
to work my way through the debris of the helm,
through and past the galley, and finally to the deckhouse and salon area. After I had made it that far,
it didn't take long to identify the eight panels that
were going to get most of my attention. I had
strapped Poker's utility belt around my waist when
I left the sled. The eight panels that were still intact
had been installed with painted screws to match
the woodgrain, and I used Poker's handy-dandy underwater electric drill. The lad had all the toys.

I started with the panel closest to the food lift that
delivered food from the galley. Surprisingly, it came
off with a minimum of fuss, but the narrow bulkhead area behind it was empty. I shoved the panel
aside, checked my chrono, and hit the transmit button one time. At EDT 51min 56sec, Poker knew I
was in and on.

The second panel came off even easier than the
first, but the results were the same. When I succeeded in prying the third panel off of the bulkhead

frame, I hit pay dirt. A small area had been torched out of one of the welded horizontal stanchions, and good old mistrusting Tyler had installed a small combination safe.

I once had a convicted safecracker tell me that combination safes were easier to crack than any other kind of security device. He had logged thirty years in two different federal prisons, so I figured he knew what he was talking about. On the other hand, I have a whole different attitude toward safes. Either a person knows the combination or he doesn't. If he doesn't, he comes to another fork in the road. Either he finds a way to open it or he walks away from it. I hadn't come all this way to walk away from it.

I twisted the combination dial back and forth a couple of times hoping maybe Rowland had figured that whatever was in the safe was concealed well enough that locking it wasn't necessary. No such luck. If I wanted to know what was in the safe, I would have to torch it open. Thanks to Poker's tutelage and special Navy training, I was familiar with the Belton type UW acetylene torch in Poker's tool belt. Built primarily for use under water, they are small and dependable. In addition, they have illuminated gauges to indicate the remaining volume of the unsaturated compound of carbon and hydrogen.

I pulled the torch out of the tool belt, triggered the igniter, watched it flash and develop an intense blue flame, and crossed my fingers. Wasted concern. I cut through the steel like a pro, and the safe opened up like a hooker in night court.

Elizabeth Carter had claimed she and Rowland had put the CARTO Project's code keys behind a bulkhead panel in the ship's salon. She had revealed how the code keys were incorporated in gelatin discs for insulation from temperature variation, but she had not said what those keys looked like. Why not? I was willing to concede that maybe, just maybe, she hadn't actually seen them.

The part that was even harder to understand was why she had indicated she helped Rowland hide the code keys but she was either unable or unwilling to tell me which panel. Again, why not? Elizabeth Carter was asking for help, but she seemed to be holding back information. For whatever reason, other than revealing that she and Rowland had hidden the code keys behind a bulkhead panel in the ship's salon, she hadn't given me much to go on.

With the safe now open, I was even more perplexed. The only thing in the safe was a small, hermetically sealed, six-inch-long brass container. It looked like a cigar case. I studied it for a moment or two and looked at my watch. EDT 69min 57sec.

I had something hot in my little hand. More important, that something had been hidden in a safe behind a bulkhead panel. It would have been easy to assume I had the code keys, but I wasn't sure I did.

Like acetylene torches, gelatin discs are tricky. They have to be handled with care, and if they are

261

exposed to the wrong combination of environmental conditions, they distort. Value of the data on a gelatin disc when that happens is absolute zero. I had no way of knowing, but it did not seem likely that saltwater was on the list of acceptable environmental conditions.

I placed the container in my catch bag and zipped it shut, refusing to risk exposing and damaging the contents. That was the safe part. The gamble was, if the brass case didn't contain the code keys, I would have to return to the wreck for still another dive. Not something I would be looking forward to.

At EDT 80min 13sec I gave Poker a one-tap message and made ready to return to the sled. Big mistake. Instead of celebrating what I believed was a victory, I should have taken time to scan the parade of icons on my IA display. If I had, it's only reasonable to assume I would have seen them coming. If I had seen them coming, I might have had a chance.

There were two of them and they were all over me. It happened quickly. One of them grabbed me and the other launched something. Whatever he set in motion terminated in my left shoulder.

The pain was one thing. But I quickly discovered I had another problem. The obviously tainted concoction my assailants had applied to whatever it was that penetrated my shoulder was proving to be even more of a handicap. Slowly, and definitely surely, I was beginning a helpless spiral into a very ugly world where there was little to record but pain and confusion.

Clawing my way out of wherever I had been was far more difficult than I anticipated. I had no idea where I was. Parts of me wanted nothing to do with consciousness, and parts of me were complaining that the lights were too bright. The unpleasant journey from total darkness to dazzling light should take longer than a nanosecond. It should be a gradual thing. It wasn't. Also, a person should also be allowed an adjustment period between the prone position and "sit up and pay attention." I wasn't.

Things were happening fast, but one by one the fragments of my nightmare were beginning to mean something. I was slowly gaining control of my brain. Whatever I was lying on was hard. Whatever I could feel, hurt. I had a nasty headache, a touch of double vision, and a whole lot of questions. Without wishing to be one, I was one of the main characters in a slightly out-of-sync James Bond movie. The only real difference was the setting. 007 always regains consciousness in some high-tech sub or missile-launching facility with a long-legged, gorgeous redhead tied up next to him.

It didn't take long for me to figure out I hadn't fared as well as Sean Connery usually does. From what I could see, smell, and hear, there was sufficient reason to believe I was in the wheelhouse of the *Schanchu Fhin*, and there was a numb, anesthetized sensation in my left shoulder. I was surrounded by several obviously Asian and obviously hostile young men. In their midst was a Chinese gentleman wearing a blue and white seersucker suit. He was heavy, bald, and he wore glasses. From my place on the floor he looked big. Later, on my feet, he wasn't all that imposing.

"Will someone tell me what this is all about?" I complained.

My hosts had stripped me to the waist, but I was still wearing the bottom of my hot water suit and boots. My tanks, dive harness, gloves, head cushion, neck collar, and helmet were all stacked in a pile next to me. Someone or something had systematically reduced my dive gear to rubble.

"I confess that I am surprised to discover you are an American," the man in the suit admitted. He spoke better English than several girls I dated. "Until you were brought aboard several minutes ago, I was convinced we were dealing with local fishermen. Admittedly, overly ambitious and inquisitive local fishermen." He glanced down at what was left of my dive gear and continued. "But I see that I was in error. I realize now that local fisherman could not afford the type of diving gear I see there."

"You mean what it used to be," I growled. "It doesn't look like you left much."

The man in the suit ignored my complaint and pointed to a straightback chair next to the helm. "Won't you have a seat?" he said. Considering tone and expression, it came across more like a command than an invitation.

I didn't tell him, but I was more than happy to accept the offer. Sitting down and nursing my bum shoulder made more sense than standing in the middle of a Chinese wheelhouse trying to figure out where I had gone wrong. Regardless of what kind of threats the man in the suit made, I was already resolving to put an end to the search for Tyler Rowland. I didn't have that much to prove to myself.

I sat down and tried to examine my shoulder. I was still poking and grousing about my lot in life when he informed me his name was Chow Wuhan. "Considering your situation, I assume you have questions," he said.

"Where do I go to complain about the hospitality?"

Chow wasn't amused. "And where do I go to protest the fact that even though my ship has deployed a security net around an area where we are conducting research, local fishermen and now you refuse to respect our designated and properly marked exploration area?"

I knew Chow didn't expect an answer. Instead he made an all but imperceptible nod in the direction of one of his men. The man left the wheelhouse and returned moments later with two glasses and a half-empty bottle of Jim Beam. He handed them to Chow, who casually splashed a couple of ounces in each glass and handed one to me.

"Actually, I am happy to learn you are an American," he said. "One of the things I enjoy most about conducting business with you Americans is your

265

penchant for good bourbon. I trust you do like bourbon, Mr. . . . ." The smile intensified. "I don't believe you told me your name."

I didn't answer Chow because thus far I hadn't found much about him to like. Shooting people with spearguns aside, Chow was complicating in rather unpleasant fashion the search for the code keys. I was willing to bet he was the one behind Rainbow's untimely demise. He may not have pulled the trigger, but there was a good chance he was the one who ordered it.

"Very well, then, may I ask what you were looking for?" Chow pushed.

I have never been very good at making up stories on the spur of the moment. But I have to admit, on this particular occasion I managed to author one of my better efforts. "The name of that vessel you are anchored over is the *Baja Lady*," I began. "It is, or rather was, owned by a man by the name Tyler Rowland. Tyler Rowland is a friend of mine. He left San Francisco some three weeks ago, telling everyone he was headed for Cabo San Lucas. I know his itinerary included a scheduled stopover at Bahia Magdalena for supplies."

Chow Wuhan was one of those finicky and excessive people who make a stage production of even the smallest gesture. As he listened he extracted an oval-shaped pastel cigarette. When he lit it, it was obvious he enjoyed his performance as much as he did the cigarette. When he finished lighting up, he urged me to continue.

"So—when Tyler failed to show up for our meeting in Cabo San Lucas, I started looking for him. I knew he had put in at Playa Tranquilo, and he told people we both knew that his next stop would still be Bahia Magdalena. When I got to Las Cuevas I heard about an American yacht that had sunk in the channel. It wasn't the *Baja Lady*, but it got me to thinking. When I started looking around I learned you had your nets deployed over the wreckage of another yacht, and the locals said you threatened them when they got too close to your net. I knew Tyler had something on board that meant a great deal to him. I just didn't know what . . . but he had boasted it wouldn't be long until he came into a large amount of money."

Chow studied the smoke from his cigarette. "Do you know why your associate was planning to stop in Bahia Magdalena?"

"No idea," I lied. I was losing track of just how many lies I had told Chow. "I do know Tyler doesn't even like Mexican food well enough to stay any longer than he had to."

Chow cleared his throat. "Let me tell you why your friend planned a stop in Bahia Magdalena," he said. "Your friend was delivering something of considerable value to me. We were—how do you Americans say it?—in the process of consummating a very important business deal."

Evidently, Chow wasn't the least bit concerned about how much he revealed about what had transpired between himself and Rowland. He was either telling me because he was buying my story about me being nothing more than a friend of Tyler Rowland, or he planned to see that I didn't leave the *Shanchu Fhin* alive. It was a safe bet he favored option number two.

"So what happened?" I asked.

Chow hesitated before he continued. "Your friend Mr. Rowland assured me he would have it with him when he arrived in Bahia Magdalena. But in the process, a most unfortunate thing happened. At the appointed time and place, his ship made radio contact with my deck officer. Then, quite suddenly, his vessel exploded. We raced to the scene, of course, to be of assistance. Later that day we recovered the bodies of two crewmen but not that of Mr. Rowland."

"What did you do with the bodies of the two crewmen?"

"We buried them," Chow said.

"Is there some reason why you didn't turn the bodies over to the Mexican authorities?"

Chow Wuhan played the game better than I did. He didn't hesitate. "The nature of the transaction between Mr. Rowland and me would best be served if as little as possible was known about our dealings."

"Why? Was it illegal?"

I thought I was pushing it, but Chow seemed to be amused. "You are sometimes amusing and sometimes perceptive, my nameless American friend. But you are not very convincing. A man casually looking for his friend does not come equipped with expensive submersible sleds to facilitate his search."

"What can I say—I just happened to have one in the trunk of my car," I tried. "Doesn't everyone?"

While Chow Wuhan went through the ritual of ridding himself of what was left of the first cigarette and preparing to light another, I was trying to see what had happened to the small metal canister. I knew I had tucked it in the catch of my wet suit, but I was equally aware that Chow and his crew had gone through my gear while they waited for me to regain consciousness. When I spotted it lying on the chart table, Chow saw me. He cocked his head to one side and picked the canister up. "Forgive me," he said, "I see you were carrying this pack of cigars when you were—how shall I say it— interrupted? Perhaps you would care for one now?"

I shook my head. My heart sank. The seal had been broken. If the gelatin discs were in there and Chow hadn't taken the proper precautions, they were ruined. While I watched, Chow removed the metal cap and showed me the cigars—a five-pack of Garcia y Vega. The pack had been opened, but no cigars were missing. Chow studied the case for several moments. "Clever way of keeping your cigars dry," he said. "However, I confess I am surprised to see someone who appears to be such an avid diver like you smoking. I am told most Americans look upon smoking as being bad for their health."

R. Karl Largent

"Each to his own," I grunted. "I'm more interested in why you think you have the authority to keep others away from the wreckage of Rowland's yacht."

Suddenly Chow's round and cherubic face seemed just a little less seraphic. "Because, Mr. American without a name, your friend Mr. Rowland sold me something—something for which my government paid a great deal of money. Mr. Rowland received half of the agreed-upon amount of money when he visited China. It was decided we would meet here at Bahia Magdalena, at which time he would turn over the merchandise." Chow paused to again savor his cigarette. "Then, after I had been given the opportunity to both assess and accept the merchandise, I was to see that Mr. Rowland received the rest of the money due him."

Our conversation had reached the point where I knew my survival depended largely on what kind of thespian talents I could drum up. I knew I had to give Chow the impression that I knew nothing of Rowland's dealings with the Chinese. I also had to convince Chow that what I was really concerned about was the whereabouts of my old buddy Tyler.

"Your people actually saw the *Baja Lady* go down?" I asked.

"The vessel was within five hundred yards of us when it exploded," Chow confirmed. "We, of course, suffered some minor damage as a result."

"You say you found two of Rowland's crew but you never found Rowland?"

"Perhaps I should clarify," Chow said. "The fact that we did not find your friend's body should not surprise you. The explosion aboard the *Baja Lady* was quite violent. When I say we recovered the bodies of the crewmen I am perhaps guilty of overstating. In actuality, we recovered only parts of two bodies."

"Are you certain one of them wasn't Rowland?"

Chow shook his head. "Quite certain. When you pay a man that much money and he owes you something in return, you do not forget what he looks like. No—neither of the two bodies we recovered was your friend Rowland."

I had the distinct feeling that Chow Wuhan was growing weary of the verbal sparring. I also had the feeling that patience wasn't his strong suit. If there was any hope of convincing him that I was more interested in finding Rowland than finding the code keys, I had to make him think I was taking his word that Tyler Rowland couldn't have survived the explosion.

How would I do that? By insinuating, of course, that I was ready to give up the search. If I could convince Chow of that, I figured there was at least a fifty-fifty chance he would send me packing. But he would do so only after giving me what he considered to be a good and proper warning never to show my face again anywhere in the vicinity of the *Shanchu Fhin*.

Suddenly there was a protracted period when neither of us was saying anything and I could hear the wind and waves pounding the hull of the bogus trawler. "So how do we resolve all of this?" I finally asked.

All of a sudden Chow's mien went from difficult to impossible to read. Early on, there had been times when he appeared to be vaguely amused and perhaps even smug. No longer. His expression was suddenly indecipherable.

I've often heard Occidentals use the word "inscrutable" when discussing the Chinese. That described Chow Wuhan. He appeared to be ruminating about his response, but he wasn't giving any clues as to which way he was leaning.

Once again I caught the nearly imperceptible communication between Chow and one of the members of his crew. Chow barely glanced at the man, nodded, furrowed his brow, extinguished his second cigarette, and lit a third. The man disappeared down the companionway. Same routine as before. "Tell me, my American friend, how good of a swimmer are you?"

"I manage. But," I tried to qualify, "I might not do so well with one of your darts in my shoulder. Over the years I've noticed that sort of thing tends to slow me down."

Chow wasn't the least bit commiserative. "Well, then, I am about to present you with a challenge. I have always heard how you Americans like a challenge. How far would you say it is to the coastline? And how far would you estimate it is to the reef?" The way he said it, I had a pretty good idea what was coming next. Chow Wuhan may have been in-scrutable, but his ego was getting in his way. He was too pleased with himself not to let his goon crew know what he was thinking.

"If that's the million-dollar question, Chow, you owe me. I looked at the charts. The channel is eight miles wide, and your would-be trawler is anchored less than five hundred yards from the reef."

Chow shook his head. "I like to think of myself as a magnanimous man. Therefore I have decided to give you a sporting chance, my American friend. You see, I do not believe you, but I have no way of knowing whether I am simply being overly suspi-cious or whether I am being perceptive. I confess I lean toward the latter, but when I am uncertain I try to be somewhat lenient.

"Our little conversation is over, and I have de-cided to permit you to swim to shore or to the reef. Whichever you prefer. It is up to you. However, I should point out that Captain Lee reports the inten-sity of the storm has still not abated. Making it, I believe it is safe to say, quite difficult for a swimmer to achieve either objective. Especially with what that swimmer believes to be a small infirmity.

"Swimming all the way to shore would be, I think, quite taxing. Swimming to the reef, while a much shorter distance, could be equally distressing. Have you ever had the misfortune of having the waves pitch you up against a jagged coral reef?"

Two of Chow's goons jerked me to my feet, shoved me toward the door of the wheelhouse, and out onto the deck. If I hadn't known better, I would have sworn that Chow and his people had thrown me into a Maytag. Maybe Celia was no longer a full-fledged hurricane out in the Pacific, but in the Bahia Magdalena channel she was creating more chaos than any of us were prepared to handle.

The *Shanchu Fhin*, despite her size, was floundering around like a drunken deckhand. Not that it mattered, but I knew the ship wasn't in any real danger of sinking. Still, seven-to-ten-foot waves were pounding Chow's would-be trawler and inundating the deck. The scuppers weren't keeping up with the wash, and I was standing in a good foot of water.

That may well have been my main concern if it hadn't been for the little guy Chow had sent scurrying out of the wheelhouse a few minutes earlier. He lunged at me, and I plummeted over the side. I hit the water, sank, clawed, and sputtered my way back to the surface, only to realize the son-of-a-bitch was shooting at me.

Journal No. 10

The guy had a repeating rifle, and the rain-whipped deck of the *Shanchu Fhin* was proving to be a poor attack platform. It was heaving up and down like a spinster's chest in a male strip club.

I knew that the likelihood of Chow's gun-toting goon hitting me was remote. Still, he was a concern; men operating under far more stringent conditions have gotten luckier.

If his situation wasn't the best, mine was a whole lot worse. One minute I was riding the crest of a fifteen-foot swell, and the next I was trying to stay afloat in the trough. Fortunately, Chow's skinny gunman and I never quite got into sync. He was shooting up when I was down and vice versa.

R. Karl Largent

Even with that, I was clearly the one in danger. The beach at Las Cuevas was slightly less than eight miles due east. The reef was fifteen hundred yards in the other direction. Under the best of conditions, an eight-mile swim would have been a monumental and near impossible achievement for me. I am not a distance swimmer, I am a sled tester.

The storm's intensity had abated only slightly since noon, but even with less storm to cope with, I figured my odds of making it to shore were no better than a hundred to one. Like Chow said, even though the reef was a lot closer, it was no more attractive. I picked up a severe case of coral poisoning in a cave off Jamaica one time, and I was more than eager to avoid having waves slap me up against the reef—even if I could make it. Once was enough.

Obviously, I hadn't mentioned it to Chow, but in my mind I had a third option. It wasn't exactly a good one, but it was far better than the reef and probably just as feasible as trying to make it all the way to shore. Option number three, succinctly stated, was the spare oxygen bottle on the Pony I. Poker had indicated he'd checked it and loaded it. That meant there was an additional forty minutes of air on the sled if I could get to it.

But getting to the sled and that life-saving bottle was going to be the challenge. I had one good arm, and Chow had sorely crippled my diving capabilities by cutting up and trashing most of my dive gear. I still had my wrist gauges, my buoyancy belt, a

276

watch, and the bottom half of the wet suit along with a pair of boots—but that was it. Missing were niceties like a helmet, air tanks, a good knife, and some other gear I had come to regard as essential.

Getting to the sled was going to be difficult, maybe impossible—but until it proved otherwise, it seemed like the most achievable option of the three.

I had already checked twice to make certain I still had the little brass case containing the cigars. At some point during the confusion and posturing in the *Shanchu Fhin*'s wheelhouse, I had tucked it under my belt, between the wet-suit pants and my swimsuit.

The real surprise was that Chow had let me get away with it. I have no idea what he thought code keys looked like, but if it had been me and I found something with the lid sealed, I would have been suspicious.

Of course, if I did make it back to shore, I was going to look pretty silly if the only thing I had to show for my ordeal was a brass cigar case. Whether or not the code keys were somehow tucked away in there was the mystery of the day. And under the circumstances, it didn't look like I was going to know the answer to that one for a while.

It is not advisable to take the time to estimate distances when you are preoccupied with trying to avoid getting shot and keeping your head above water at the same time. There was enough salt water in my eyes that I was having trouble seeing. I had lost sight of the ship, and I had no idea whether Chow's man was still shooting at me or if they could even see me. The combination of howling wind and wave action was drowning out any possibility of me hearing rifle fire. The roller coaster ride, swell to trough and back again, was making it doubly difficult to get a handle on just how far away from the *Shanchu Fhin* I had managed to get.

I did know I hadn't progressed quite as far as the security net . . . that was still a couple of hundred yards up ahead of me. When and if I did make it to the net, the Pony I had to be somewhere along the perimeter and no more than ten or twenty feet from the hole Poker had found in the net.

I wasn't the least bit concerned about whether or not I would trigger the sensors in the *Shanchu Fhin*'s security net. The wave action had to be doing plenty of that already. I had a fleeting vision of the monitors in the *Shanchu*'s op room looking a whole lot like the back panels on a tilted pinball machine.

I lost track of how many times I stopped, treaded water, caught my breath, and tried to get my bearings. I was also becoming concerned that my mind had started playing a few tricks on me. There was no way for me to tell whether I was seeing something because I wanted to see it or if that's the way it actually was. Whatever the reason, it did appear as though I was swimming away from the reef and the reef was now twice as far away from me as the ship. If I was right, that meant I had to be getting close to the eastern perimeter of the security net.

Each time I went through my reconnoitering routine I finished it off by turning back and facing the direction of the Las Cuevas coastline before I began swimming again. Finally, it paid off. I caught a glimpse of one of the net's blinking warning lights and let out a whoop, swam to the net, and implemented my plan. It wasn't exactly what anyone would call convoluted, but the thing that made it attractive was I figured it would work. Both Poker and I had estimated the security net to have a drop curtain of thirty to perhaps thirty-five feet—close to the same depth in the channel where the *Baja Lady* had gone down. That simplified the plan: Dive to the bottom, holding on to the net at all times with my left hand to make certain I didn't become disoriented, swim as far as I could along the bottom of the curtain, use my right hand and arm as a probe, and come up when I needed more air. Like I said, simple.

There appeared to be only one flaw in my plan: If I began working the bottom the wrong way along the curtain, I would on each successive dive be working myself farther and father away from the sled. Since departing Chow's company I had been trying to swim in the general direction of where I had parked the sled, but there was no assurance I was even close. Every time a giant swell picked me up and slapped me down in a trough, there was a good possibility it was throwing me farther off course.

I gave myself several moments to purge the effects of the salt water and tried to visualize each step of the dive sequence. In my mind, everything was there, every possible precaution was being taken. In truth, there weren't a whole lot of precautions I could take, because I didn't have all that much to work with. For the most part, I was working with a plan based on hunches, maybes, and long shots. If my plan was going to work, I knew I would need mucho luck to go along with it.

I took a deep breath and started down. Using the net as an aid, I crawled my way hand over hand to the bottom. Then I began working my way along the bottom of the net, pulling myself along with one hand and groping with the other. Every time I opened my eyes, it took only a matter of seconds for them to start burning bad enough that they closed involuntarily.

Despite my vision problems, I came up after the first dive feeling slightly more confident. I knew I could do it, and I knew the procedure worked. What I didn't know was how much ground I had covered, or even if I had been working the net in the right direction.

I went down a second time and then a third. By the time I surfaced from my sixth dive, I realized I was beginning to feel the first real pangs of uncertainty and discouragement. The ebullience I felt after that first dive was wearing off fast.

After that I lost track of the number of dives and how far I had progressed. I had no idea how long I had been out there, and despite the fact that I was in what most people would have referred to as sub-tropical waters, each time I surfaced I became more aware of a chill. I was fast running out of gas and hope. There was a dull ache in my chest, and my fingers were thick, clumsy, and getting numb.

On the other hand, the weather seemed to be changing. Wave action was less pronounced. The winds were diminishing. The rains had slackened. Even so, the day had somehow managed to become even darker.

I was beginning to have real doubts. I remember thinking for the third, fourth, maybe even the fifth time how I might be pulling myself in the wrong direction. Maybe, I was thinking, I should have headed south instead of north around the perimeter.

I don't know what it was, the thirtieth, maybe even the fiftieth time I had gone down, but I reached the bottom, started clawing my way along, and suddenly made contact with something. The aquatic gods had decided to smile on me. There was no mistaking what it was. My right hand caressed the bullet-nosed configuration at the front of the sled, and then I ran my hand over the acrylic windshield and finally down to the instrument panel. I fumbled along until I pressed my index finger on the ignition button and felt the subtle vibration of the battery feedback.

By then I was out of air, and I knew I would have to claw my way back to the surface. But now that I knew where I was and, more importantly, where the sled was, I treated myself to the luxury of a few extra moments on the surface. I knew it wasn't the case, but it continued to seem a little warmer, a little less choppy, a tad less windy, and the waves less threatening.

When I figured my restrained celebration had lasted long enough, I went down for the spare oxygen bottle on the sled. It didn't occur to me until days later, but if I had followed the standard FSORC test procedure for the shallow-water abandonment of a submersible, I would have taken both on-board oxygen bottles with me when I went to explore the wreckage of the *Baja Lady*. In this case, not doing what I was supposed to do may well have saved my life.

It took a little coaxing and tugging, but I managed to get the number two oxygen bottle out of the bottle bracket, rotated the valve, plugged in the auxiliary mouthpiece, made an adjustment, and took my first gulp of bottled air. When that happened, life suddenly started looking a whole lot more promising. I took three or four more modest hits just to make certain everything was in working order, returned to the console, hit the start button, fumbled around until I found the console's "ballast purge" switch, and settled back to wait for the port and starboard buoyancy cylinders to do their job. All the while I was mentally awarding cash bonuses when I got back to FSORC.

I knew that when I broke through to the surface I'd be home free. All I had to do was activate the homing beacon, put her on AP, and live to tell my grandkids about it.

I'll never know what made me open my salt-water-tormented eyes just when I did. Premonition, gut feeling, or some kind of an ominous omen. But open my eyes I did . . . and just in time to see it coming straight at me. It was a tiger shark, a big one—eighteen, maybe nineteen foot. Maybe bigger than that. Sharks all look the same to me—dangerous, mean, and ugly. Despite that, I would have bet my last dollar this was the same one I'd spotted the first day Carlos motored me out into the channel. And probably the same one that conducted a feeding frenzy on the Admiral's friend Rainbow.

The minute I saw the shark I instinctively rolled the Pony I over on the starboard side. I don't know what most folks would have termed it, but I regarded it as one hell of a collision between beast, man, and machine. If he was going to take a chunk out of something I wanted it to be the port and starboard skids and maybe even the battery shield. I did not want it to be any part of Abraham Joseph Furnace. FSORC has all the resources it needs to build another Pony I sled. Another A. J. would be a stretch.

I closed my eyes, waited for them to quit burning, opened them again, started checking for damage, and caught a glimpse of the hydraulic manipulator. The force of the blow had doubled it back on itself. It wasn't supposed to be. That was all it took to convince me I would be a lot better off if I dismounted and tried to keep the sled between me and trouble.

I let the sled settle to the bottom. My eyes were burning, but I had already worked that one out. Better to have the eyes burning than have an oversized tiger shark get into position to take a bite out of my hide.

The shark continued to make passes, each one a little closer. Finally, one of the passes was close enough to knock the sled back over on its side. The minute that happened, my mind was thrown into a full-throttle run-away mode.

If you read much about sharks, you know that tiger sharks are supposed to spend their summer days lounging around on the ocean side of the reef. This one was in the wrong place at the wrong time with wrong intentions. He was aggressive and seemed to prefer hanging around in the channel, probably because tasty morsels like Rainbow occasionally popped up. They say that sharks don't like the taste of human flesh. I wonder if Rainbow knows that.

I had decided my best defense until I could think of something better was to curl up in a ball, make myself as small as possible, and crouch down beside the Pony I for safety. I did just that and waited. At that point I had decided all I had to do was survive the shark's next pass, because I had determined what my next move was going to be. The same nitrogen-fueled dart gun that had sent one of Chow's men back to the *Shanchu Fhin* with a six-inch stainless steel dart in his thigh was going to make life a little less pleasant for one tiger shark. I pulled the four-foot dart gun out of the sled's metal scabbard, dug blindly around through the equipment bay until I found the stainless steel darts, loaded, spun the nitrogen cartridge into the lock position behind the trigger, and released the safety.

If it worked a second time, when I got back to SFO there was going to be an even bigger bonus.

I crouched, squinted, and brought the dart gun up into firing position. The shark veered back toward the sled, made his pass, came close enough that I found myself looking him straight in the eye, circled out, away from me, and back again. He was sizing me up for the kill. I reached for the dart gun, coiled one very numb index finger around the trigger, and waited.

I still don't know exactly where a shark's brain is located, but I figured one six-inch stainless steel dart with a nitrogen kicker, buried a good six or seven inches in the middle of that deadly, silver-gray snout of his would do about as much damage as anywhere I could aim. All I had to do now was prove it.

He was circling for the kill, and I was still struggling to get the dart gun out of the sled holster. But while that was one problem, there was another equally vexing situation materializing. Salt water was winning. Eyes were losing. I was long since past the stage of being able to keep them open. Unless I could come up with something real quick, cloudy vision and salt-water-saturated eyes were about to keep me from getting a clear shot at the shark.

I knew he was coming at me. You don't have to see it—you can feel it, sense it. The best I could do was squint hard, eyes little more than slits when I finally pulled the trigger. Squinting is a prologue to mischance, to thinking you have the shark in your line of fire.

I didn't.

The stainless steel dart hit at an awkward angle, seemed to explode, took out one of the creature's eyes and a chunk of flesh about the size of a bowling ball. Whatever it hit, it did not hit that critical area that sends a message to the brain that says you are supposed to die. Instead he veered away leaving a trail of blood, circled, and headed back for a second try. There wasn't enough time to reload, and all I was seeing at that moment was one very blurry, double ugly, wounded nightmare coming straight for me.

In situations like this, you can only react. I shoved the steel shank of the dart gun at him hoping I could fend him off. I didn't expect the gesture to do much, but it ended up doing even less than I anticipated. The dart gun twisted out of my hands, swirled away from me, and I had to hit the floor of the channel to get out of the way of the shark.

His third pass was the one that got me. I saw him coming, I tried to get out of the way again, but he had ten million or more years of shark-perfected radar working for him and he got what he was after.

He chomped down on the only thing he could get to, a dive boot and my left foot. There was the sudden sensation of wetness and a prickly intimation of heat where moments earlier there had been a kind of numb and gelid sensation.

In some sort of detached and clinical way I knew exactly what was happening. I knew he had me by the foot, and he seemed to be standing on his head doing some kind of frenzied and primitive dance. I could feel myself being yanked back and forth, dragged through the water like a double-jointed doll. I couldn't see anything clearly, but I could feel. There was pain, but not at all like the kind of pain I would have anticipated if I had been told I was being attacked by a shark. There was fear, but there was just as much denial . . . none of this was really happening.

Through it all I felt like I was looking obliquely at a monochrome world of variations on gray that was suddenly tinted with a garish pinkish color. Then I realized the shark had let go. He was through shaking me. But now he seemed to be engrossed in another kind of grotesque devil dance. He was spinning, thrashing, and gyrating while he enveloped himself in a cloud of smoky crimson. I couldn't see well enough to determine what was happening, but I could feel myself being encircled by someone or something, an oxygen mask being clasped to my face, and the sensation of being jerked up and spun away. After that I quit recording.

R. Karl Largent

* * *

It was a gauzy world—amorphous, indeterminate, chaotic, shapeless. Its only definition was pain. I was coming back, returning, making my grand entrance. The only thing that was missing was the band.

"Can you hear me?" a voice was asking. It was feminine. The word clinical came to mind.

"I think he's starting to come around," someone else ventured. Not feminine.

"He may be confused," another offered. "He's pretty well loaded up on morphine."

"Not yet," someone else said. "It's too soon."

"Morphine?" Poker sputtered. "How much?"

I recognized Carlos's voice. He admitted he didn't know how much he had given me or how long he had it. "I've been keeping it on the boat since the Centas boy ran a marlin hook through his hand two years ago."

At first I couldn't even be certain I was part of their conversation . . . or even that the voices were talking about me. My head was pounding, my tongue was as thick as a summer sausage, and my eyes felt as if someone had been poking at them with a blunt stick. At the other end, I had a throbbing sensation in my left foot and leg. I felt like one of those rodeo clowns who wasn't agile enough to get away from the bull.

When I was finally able to get my eyes open and at least partially focused, I first made note of the fact that I was spread-eagled out on a table in the hotel dining room, and then I managed to lift my head up so I could get a look at my leg and foot. It was bundled up in swaths of what appeared to be the hotel's finest table linen. Marie was standing next to the table and was wearing a half smile. The other half was an expression of concern.

"You can thank Marie," Carlos informed me. "She's the one that stitched you up. She's good at it. She gets lots of practice."

Marie was grinning. "I learn to sew one time when I fix Captain Martinenez a holiday turkey for some of his friends."

Poker had taken up his post on the other side of the table from the woman. He was confirming what Carlos and Marie had already said. "It don't look to me like there's permanent damage," he said. "But you'll probably be hobblin' around for a while. That shark did a number on you."

Unfortunately, my head was clearing faster than the morphine could work on my pain. My foot was throbbing, and if I thought a little profanity would have helped I would have unleashed a tirade or two. At the moment, though, I was looking around the room at a sea of faces and realizing I was lucky to be alive. "I owe you," I said, looking at Poker.

Poker has heard that one before. Over the years, Poker Palmer had saved my bacon on more than one occasion. I've often said, when it comes to A. J. Furnace, Poker should have the word "lifeguard" tattooed on his chest. He told me what happened.

"When we lost radio contact, I figured it could

be due to anything from the storm to some sort of malfunction on the sled. So I decided to wait awhile and give you time to get back on the surface and make contact. When that didn't happen, I figured I better go see what happened to you."

"How did you know where to find me?"

Poker was still grinning. "You said you intended to work your way into the *Lady*'s debris field by passin' through that hole we found in the net the other day. The rest of it was just knowin' how you think. I figured you'd leave the sled outside the net so that you'd be less likely to set off the security alarms. I guessed right. You know the rest. You and the shark looked like you were goin' for the best two out of three falls when I spotted you . . . and I hate to tell you this, but that shark looked like he was winnin'."

"One more time, I owe you," I said. But before I could add anything to that, Amy was bending over me asking what I had found. Carlos and Marie had removed what was left of my dive suit, and I fumbled around the top of my trunks looking for the cigar case.

"Is this what you're looking for?" Carlos asked. He handed me the cigar case. "It fell out of your dive gear when we cut the suit off," he said.

I gave it to Amy and she started frowning. "What's this?"

"Believe it or not," I said, "I think this is what we've been looking for. Elizabeth Carter said the code keys were embedded in gelatin discs. This cigar case was hidden behind a bulkhead panel. If my hunch is right, the discs are hidden in that little brass case."

Amy Reed looked disappointed. She studied the case for several moments, and I watched while she pried the top off and looked at the cigars. When she saw the cigars, each wrapped in cellophane, she managed to look even more disillusioned. "If the code keys are here, where are they?"

"That's the sixty-four-dollar question. I don't know where they are, and that's why we have to be very careful. If Rowland is the one who put them in the case and concealed them, we have to hope Elizabeth Carter helped him. At this point, it's beginning to look like she may be the only one who knows how to retrieve them."

Amy was still frowning. "Are you saying you're convinced Tyler Rowland is dead?"

"I think it's a strong possibility," I said. "In the last few hours I've been twisted more ways than a cheap girdle. But I pretty much believe what Chow Wuhan was telling me, for the simple reason there was no need for him to lie. At the time I think he thought he was in the driver's seat big time . . . that the truth wouldn't come back to haunt him. In other words, I think he was telling the truth when he said the *Baja Lady* exploded like a bargain-basement rocket. He also said he found parts of two of Rowland's crewmen—but he was equally adamant that he hadn't found Rowland's body."

"What are you driving at?" Poker said.

I knew what I wanted to explain, but it was becoming increasingly difficult to keep my focus. I was beginning to slur my words, and my mind was wandering. My vision was still blurry, and I noted with some relief that the pain in my leg and foot seemed to have subsided somewhat.

I saw the faces closing in around me, looking at me like they knew exactly what was happening. Then, somewhere off in another universe I heard a strangely familiar voice—but this time it was distant, fuzzy, and garbled. That's when I heard the voice say, "Good. I think the morphine is starting to take hold. He should sleep for a while now."

They say most familiar and pleasant recollections are triggered by odors and scents. Perhaps that was what flagged me back into the conscious world. There was something enticing and inviting about my return to awareness. And there was an instant mindfulness of the fact that I was not, as yet, a whole person. I still had a tender shoulder thanks to one of Chow's goons, a wholly indistinct way of viewing the world thanks to the salt water and the morphine, and one very sore leg, ankle, and left foot. From the knee down, even with the painkillers Amy and Carlos had been pumping into me, it felt like hamburger looks.

I expected to be a whole lot more difficult to get along with when the morphine wore off.

Still, the thing that appeared to be bringing me out of my drug-induced stupor, at least temporarily, was the aroma of perfume. Not one perfume, but two. Two perfumes meant two women. If I hadn't known better, I might have believed there was something to aromatherapy. I still hadn't opened my eyes, but there was no lack of anticipation.

When I finally succeeded in forcing the orbs open, made an honest effort to clear them, and enjoyed a reasonable degree of success, I was rewarded. There were two of them. Enticing Elizabeth. Alluring Amy. Elizabeth was smiling. Amy looked relieved. They both looked good. Silent prayer. Morphine, don't fail me now.

Normally I'm not the kind who reads a great deal into the way a woman looks at a man, particularly me. But this time there was no mistaking the looks I was getting. Both of them, I was convinced, were encouraging me to come out and play boy-girl games. I wanted to cooperate. I even tried propping myself up on my elbows to extend a proper welcome to the charming Ms. Carter. It seemed the gentlemanly thing to do. After all, she had obviously made the long and arduous journey from San Fran to Las Cuevas while I, unseemly laggard that I am, was seeking solace in the arms of Morpheus.

Anytime anyone goes from a drug-induced, mostly insentient universe to one where there is at least a modicum of awareness, there is bound to be confusion. I was A-1, blue-ribbon confused.

There was a definite mental fuzziness to my world. I recognized Amy Reed. I recognized Elizabeth Carter. I did not recognize the man who stood in the shadows near the back of the room.

"Welcome back," Elizabeth Carter was saying. "I was hoping we wouldn't have to leave without an opportunity to thank you."

The words *thank you* and *leave* were still rattling around in the back of my head when I heard the man standing toward the back of the room speak up. "Come, come, Elizabeth, don't burden Mr. Furnace with too may accolades. I feel certain he would tell you he only did what was expected of him."

It took me several moments to put the pieces together and realize that I was looking at none other than Tyler Rowland.

For the record, up to that very moment the only image I had of T. Rowland was one of those corporate mug shots in the Unitrieve annual report—the standard pinstripe suit and button-down collar. But now I could see he was a relatively tall man with a symmetrical face, more gray in his hair than mine, chestnut eyes, and a ready, likable smile shadowed by a small, neatly trimmed moustache. Clark Gable came to mind. I could see why he had woman trouble. He looked trim, and he was one of those people who move with effortless style and grace.

"You will forgive me, Mr. Furnace, for any discomfort and inconvenience we may have caused you by tying your hands. But I'm sure you realize it was necessary."

Spinning back into my own little universe after

enduring a prolonged bout with exploding rockets, bodily outrage, and darkened oblivion doesn't guarantee that someone is going to recognize their surroundings. I was groping through the fog and trying to reidentify all the little warts on my life plan. I knew what was wrong. I was still suffering from sharkitis. I was still trying to identify good guys and bad guys, and there was a painful awareness that I was in no condition to do anything about life's inequities.

Up until Rowland had mentioned it, I hadn't realized my hands were tied to the sides of the four-by-eight-foot piece of plywood that was serving as my bed. I could and already had propped myself up on my elbows, but that was as far as I was going to get.

"I can see you haven't quite sorted this all out. Am I correct in that assumption, Mr. Furnace?" Rowland was talking to me, and while everything else in my world seemed slightly garbled and a little twisted, Rowland, unfortunately, was coming through loud and clear. "I suppose Elizabeth and I do owe you some kind of explanation."

I could see Elizabeth Carter standing at the end of my bed. She looked slightly insouciant. Perhaps a better word would be giddy. "Tell him, Tyler. I believe Mr. Furnace is the type who can appreciate our little intrigue."

Rowland pulled up a chair and sat down beside the bed. He was, as my nine-year-old nephew would assess him, *way cool*. He lit a cigarette and paused momentarily as though he wasn't quite sure where to begin. Finally he cleared his throat, studied his cigarette for several seconds, and began. "Some of this I feel certain you already know, some you may have no doubt deduced, and some may prove to be rather enlightening. So, while some of what I am about to tell you may prove to be redundant, bear with me; other things I tell you may prove to be quite revealing.

"You are aware, of course, that Ms. Carter and I made a business trip to Beijing a few weeks ago," he began; "a rather lucrative little sojourn, I might add. But first a little background information. As you already know, I am president of Unitrieve, a firm that up until a year and a half ago had a rather bright future. Then—how shall I say it?—our fortunes changed, and, unfortunately, mine along with it. Despite the fact that we successfully completed work on a potentially lucrative DOD software package identified as the CARTO Project, we were losing a great deal of money. In case you are not familiar with it, it is software based on a revolutionary new computer language utilizing random numerical syllabification."

While Rowland plodded on, I was looking around trying to determine exactly who was in the room. The only other people besides Rowland and me appeared to be the two women. There was no sign of Carlos, Poker, or anyone else in the Las Cuevas crew.

"Unfortunately, when our president, George Tem-

pleton, and the less than brilliant contract administration department negotiated the parameters of
the CARTO contract, they did not cover us for—
how shall I phrase it?—certain cost contingencies.
It was a fixed-price contract. Not cost plus. Consequently, some admittedly excessive but quite necessary costs over and above original projections
could not be recovered. In the end, it took Unitrieve
eighteen months longer to wrap up the CARTO contract than anticipated. Resulting, Mr. Furnace, in
documented cost overruns of well over a half-
billion dollars.

"We appealed to the DOD for contract modifi-
cations. The DOD refused, and as a result, Unitrieve
was looking at possible financial ruin. If that had
happened, Mr. Furnace, I would have been out as
president, hundreds of production people and engineers would have lost their jobs, and—"

"I'll bet you were really concerned about those
other people," I jabbed. Every now and then I hear
myself say something and I think, Where the hell
did that come from?

Rowland ignored my little barb. "So when a business associate suggested that perhaps others might
be very much interested in the code keys, I contacted representatives of other governments, all of
whom were on somewhat less than amiable terms
with dear old Uncle Sam. Most knew of the CARTO
Project and were eager to hear what I had to say.
Some were even eager to do business. Ultimately,
the Chinese invited me to Beijing, a mutually satis-

factory sale price for the code keys was negotiated, and my financial future was enhanced. I received half the money, and Mr. Wuhan and I agreed to meet here in Bahia Magdalena to make the exchange."

"So what happened?" I pushed.

"My good fortune, as they say, got even better. When I returned to the States I was contacted by Iraqi officials who were willing to offer me even more money for the code keys than the Chinese. When that happened, a change in plans was necessitated. I had to figure out a way to sell the code keys to the Iraqis and make Mr. Wuhan believe I had every intention of delivering the code keys to him here in Bahia Magdalena just as we negotiated in Beijing. That's when Ms. Carter stepped in and wrote the rest of the script.

"As you well know, Ms. Carter helped me hide the code keys in a small brass container and conceal them behind a bulkhead panel in the deckhouse aboard the *Baja Lady*. Incidentally, I do appreciate your recovering them for us. Looking back, we now consider the concealment of the keys an unnecessary precaution. But at the time, we were concerned that someone might discover that the security of the code keys had been compromised and a search would be conducted. Since both my wife and her brother knew I was planning a little excursion, we thought it best to make certain the code keys were not discovered."

"So what went wrong?" My head was clearing

298

fast. Rowland was right, there were a number of details I hadn't noodled out yet.

"A small miscalculation. I had planned to rendezvous with Mr. Wuhan as originally planned. When Mr. Wuhan boarded the *Baja Lady* prepared to examine the merchandise, the ship would blow up, and regardless of who on Mr. Wuhan's staff survived the explosion, Chinese officials back in Beijing would be convinced that they had been the victims of enormous misfortune. Of course, the code keys and I would have escaped the inferno just prior to Mr. Wuhan's boarding."

"But something went wrong, right?"

"Very perceptive, Mr. Furnace, very perceptive. Once again I am reminded of that old adage, If you want something done correctly, hire a professional. You see, I was the one who devised the plan, planted the explosives in the engine room, and wired the timing device. Apparently, there was a small miscalculation. The switch was inadvertently activated, and the explosion occurred before Mr. Wuhan had an opportunity to board the yacht. I, of course, managed to escape, but in doing so, I was forced to escape without the code keys."

"And that's where I came in?"

"I am not a skilled diver, Mr. Furnace. My skills, in fact, compared to yours, are quite rudimentary. Furthermore, the combination of my former associate, Mr. Wuhan, anchoring over the wreckage and then deploying his considerable resources made it impossible for a novice like me to retrieve the code keys. I knew I would need someone more resourceful than myself. I contacted Ms. Carter, and she took care of the rest. Fortunately, the curiosity of Ms. Reed's superiors at Cal Maritime only hurried the situation along. In the end, all I had to do was wait. Rather clever, don't you think?"

"Why me, Rowland?"

"Who better? We knew of your considerable skills and resources because of your brother's involvement as a member of the board of directors at Unitrieve. One thing I learned early in my career, Mr. Furnace—in any convoluted situation there is usually a very simple if unpleasant solution."

"Well, I guess that answers one question," I sighed. "The code keys were in the brass cigar holder. Right?"

"Indeed they were," Rowland admitted. He turned away from the bed and beckoned to the Carter woman. She walked up to the makeshift bed and stood there. There was a glossy, complacent look on her face. Stepdaddy Galen would have termed it the look of a winner. If you are male and have managed to reach the age of sixteen without seeing that expression on some woman's face, you've either been living in a cave or you're a novitiate.

"Elizabeth, my dear," he said, "why don't you demonstrate for our friend Mr. Furnace how easy it would have been for him to verify that the code keys were in fact concealed in the cigar case."

Elizabeth Carter was wearing a feminine version

of what I have always thought of as a Jungle Jim type safari jacket. Khaki-colored. Buckle at the waist. Lots of pockets. The only thing missing was the pith helmet cocked at a rakish and somewhat stylish angle. I couldn't help but notice that she looked better in her outfit than Jungle Jim ever did, and slightly more comfortable in the Baja environment than Amy Reed.

She was a bit theatrical with the procedure as she opened the brass canister, reached in her pocket, took out a small knife, removed a cigar, laid it on a jury-rigged table, and sliced it open. There it was, a small gelatin disc about the size of a silver dollar, tightly rolled and compacted into an inch-plus-long column about the diameter of a soda straw. Then she repeated the procedure on a second cigar. When she finished, she stepped back, still smiling.

Rowland picked up one of the discs, dropped it on the floor, and ground it into a gummy residue with his heel. "Rather clever, wouldn't you say? You see, all the discs are the same. If one happened to get lost or destroyed, there was till a complete set of instructions in each of the remaining cigars. Unfortunately, I can't take credit for it. I'm afraid Ms. Carter should receive credit for that creative little wrinkle as well."

I looked at the Carter woman. I was beginning to get the feeling she was the one who had been the impetus behind Rowland's entire scheme. To her credit, if the scheme worked, Rita Rowland was out and Elizabeth Carter was in; not only would she have Rowland, she'd have her share of the money too. However much that was, it was certainly better than an administrative assistant's salary. I had to admit it wasn't a bad parlay.

The jury was still out, but if Rowland was actually successful in pulling off his nefarious scheme, it would be primarily because Liz Carter had played her role in this melodrama to the absolute hilt.

"Was it necessary to kill Templeton?" I asked.

Rowland shook his head, took out his handkerchief, and mopped his forehead. "I'm afraid we were just a bit too exuberant in the way we handled George. Everything was going well, and Jacob was playing right into our hand by insisting that no one in the company discuss my disappearance with anyone outside of the company. Unfortunately, George was never a team player, he was a rule follower. Accounting background, you know. As far as Templeton was concerned, we only meant to scare him."

"Elizabeth Carter?" I asked.

"As I've said so many times, I couldn't have done it without Elizabeth's help."

"So what happens now?" I asked. "You've still got the code keys and half of what Wuhan agreed to pay you. If I were in your shoes, I'd consider that the best of both worlds. If you'll pardon my saying so, though, it appears as though you haven't really thought the last part of this through."

Rowland scowled at me. I had caught him off guard. "I'm afraid I don't understand," he said.

"If you were so inclined, you could take the money and your friend here, run off to Brazil, Argentina, someplace like that, live the life of luxury, and I could take the code keys back to Unitrieve."

"And why would I be so foolish?"

"The feds would have a tough time ferreting you out, and since Wuhan never actually got his hands on the keys, it's like it never happened. No harm, no foul."

"Is that what you are suggesting, Mr. Furnace?" From the tone of Rowland's voice, I thought the suggestion just might have appealed to him. But before I could confirm that impression, he started to laugh. "You amuse me, Mr. Furnace. Do you take me for a fool? Why should I be satisfied with the money Wuhan was witless enough to pay me when I can become a very wealthy man by simply concluding arrangements with the government in Baghdad?"

It was becoming apparent that appeals to Rowland's common sense weren't working, so I decided to try threats. "You know I'm going to do whatever it takes to stop you," I said.

Rowland was shaking his head. At the same time, he was smiling. "And that is the unfortunate part of all of this," he said. "Up until now, with the exception of George Templeton and two rather wretched and quite expendable crew members, very few people have actually been inconvenienced as the result of our little effort at duplicity. However, now I am afraid all of that has to change. You see, Eliza-

beth and I have a rather important engagement
elsewhere . . . and we must be absolutely certain
that neither you nor any of your associates interfere
with those plans."

Rowland paused, rubbed his hands together as
though he was crystallizing his thinking, and lit another cigarette. He considered what he was about
to say for several moments before he continued.

"No, unfortunately, Mr. Furnace, I don't believe I
dare take the chance of letting you live. If I were
foolish enough to do that, you would have the opportunity to let others know not only what Elizabeth
and I have done but what we are planning to do as
well."

I decided to try one more time. "Give me the
code keys, Tyler. You take the money. You have my
word," I said; "what you and Liz Carter do with Wuhan's money and where you go from here is no skin
off my nose."

As I mentioned earlier, I am not now and never
have been a good liar—or actor. For some reason,
I am simply not convincing. People see through me.
Folks read me like a supermarket rag. When I tell a
slight untruth, does my neck get red? Does my nose
grow appreciably longer? I don't know what gives
me away, but Stepmother Leslie, Stepfather Galen,
and a host of young ladies ranging from prep
school through college and beyond can attest to
the fact that the art of believable prevarication is
not one of my long suits.

When I finished, Rowland did more than just

laugh. I had whispered most of what I had been suggesting, and now he saw fit to repeat it aloud for Carter's benefit. Then he said, "Trust me, Mr. Furnace, we have an eminently more workable plan. As Elizabeth said, we are grateful to you. You were able to retrieve the code keys for us. Since you and your friends have been such a big help to us, I have decided to make your deaths as agreeable as possible."

Rowland hadn't missed a beat when he used the words "your deaths."

"I have instructed Ms. Carter to give you another injection of morphine. Admittedly, this one will perhaps be a little stronger than the ones you were administered prior to my arrival.

"Then you, along with your associates Mr. Palmer, Ms. Reed, and certain other members of the Las Cuevas fishing community, will be dispensed with accordingly. You and Ms. Reed will be locked in the storm cellar of the hotel here, some flammable liquid will be spread liberally throughout the structure, and the place will be set on fire. Those who don't actually burn to death will die of smoke inhalation. If and when the authorities find your bodies, they will assume a most unfortunate accident. Of course, a similar fate awaits your friends.

"I am not a heartless man, Mr. Furnace. Prior to the time you depart this vale of tears, you will have ample opportunity to try to figure out ways to avoid your untimely deaths. But I doubt that you will be able to do so. After all these years in the dry Baja

Sur climate, I rather imagine this old hotel will burn like kindling."

With my hands tied and the barrel of a snub-nosed revolver buried in my temple, I took my medicine like a good little sailor. The truth is, I didn't have a whole lot of strength to protest. Elizabeth Carter, as it turned out, was as handy with a syringe and needle as anyone in Carlos's camp. I fought the certainty of further incapacitation for as long as the onset of the morphine would allow. To no avail, though. It wasn't long before I fell off the edge of the earth.

When I regained consciousness or some semblance thereof, I discovered I was still in the dark. This time, I opened eyes and a clearer vision than I had enjoyed at any time in the last several hours weren't doing a thing for me. I was awake, but I was numb. I knew I had arms, legs, hands, and feet, but I couldn't feel them. The brain was broadcasting an alert, but nothing was responding. That's when I realized Amy was trying to get through to me.

"Wake up, A. J., wake up."

There was nothing dulcet, sexy, or charmingly feminine about the lady's efforts. Nor was there panic in her voice—but it was close to it. "Damn it, A. J.," she shouted, "wake up!"

In my mind I was doing exactly what Amy wanted me to do. I could hear her, see her, feel her. Everything was there except the ability to react. I tried to get up, but the body parts that I needed to accomplish that rather simple maneuver simply weren't willing to cooperate.

I tried shaking my head to see if it would help me clear away the cobwebs. It didn't. If anything, it hurt. But I had the feeling that if I could sit up, things would be a whole lot better. I knew I was still teetering on the verge of incoherence, but I was trying to make Amy understand that I wanted her to take my hand and help me get into a sitting position. When she finally understood what I wanted her to do, she grabbed my hand, pulled, and instead of setting up, I folded up like an accordion. Efforts to get off my makeshift bed, rejoin Las Cuevas's gay social whirl, and be constructive were falling far short of expectations.

All it had accomplished so far was a hammering sensation in my leg and foot, coupled with a waste of what little energy I had to offer.

"Where are we?" I finally managed.

"I think we're in the storm cellar under the hotel," Amy said. "Before they stuck that damned needle in me, Rowland and Carter were talking like that was where they were going to leave us."

"How long have we been here?" I was proud of myself—I had asked two questions in a row. Both of them had come out sounding pretty much like I hoped they would. The words came out in the right sequence, and most of them made sense.

"I'm—I'm not certain," Amy said, "I know it's been a while, but there aren't any windows and I don't know how much longer this flashlight I found is going to hold out. The batteries are getting weak."

"Any idea what happened to the rest of the people—Poker, Carlos, Viktor, Bo Bo?"

Amy was shaking her head. "I don't know. I saw the Carter woman give you the injection; then Rowland grabbed me. He held me while she did a number on me."

"Morphine?"

Amy shook her head. "I don't know what it was. But whatever it was, it hit me hard. I felt myself getting groggy almost immediately. After that, I don't know what happened, and I don't know how they got us down here."

The third time was the charm, I finally managed to get all the component parts synchronized and working in unison. It wasn't exactly a ballet, but I made it. I shoved my legs over the edge of whatever it was I was lying on and sat up. The moment I did, I felt my leg start throbbing. I winced, but in the dark I couldn't tell whether I had elicited any sympathy.

The next test was going to be whether I was able to stand on my leg after I put weight on it. From where I was at that moment, actually walking seemed like a bit more than I was ready to tackle.

It was too dark to see Amy, but I knew she was there. There was an Amy heat and an Amy scent in the room. The rest of my sensory bombardments weren't all that pleasant. There was a parched, desiccated odor in the room that was almost as hard to take as if it had been mildew or fungus. Amy had turned the flashlight off to save what little energy she could. "I'm going to try standing up," I announced.

"I found the stairs earlier," she said. "I checked the door at the top. It's locked. I tried bumping it with my shoulder, but I couldn't get it to budge."

No surprise. I figured that a soaking wet, five-foot-six-inch-tall Amy Reed wearing nothing more than a pair of ultrafeminine skivvies might tip the scale at one hundred and twenty pounds. But that, fortunately or unfortunately, depending on your perspective, was about all she had to throw at the door. She clearly didn't have the bulk of a body builder on her side, and most of the curves weren't muscle.

"Think I might have any luck if I tried?" I asked.

"With that leg and foot of yours, I doubt it," she said, "but maybe it's worth the effort. We can't just sit here hoping someone will find us."

I took the flashlight, turned it on, and poked the beam up the stairs. The steps were made of stone. They were narrow and they were steep. Whoever built them had designed them for one purpose only: to offer an escape from something menacing on the surface. I am and always have been a proponent of the pragmatic approach; when you are seeking shelter from a hurricane, your last concern should be aesthetics. As Stepfather Galen once said, "You want whatever separates you from the fury of whatever it is you are trying to get away from to be as strong as whatever it is you are trying to get away from." (You won't find that one in any book of famous quotes.)

I limped over to the bottom of the stairs, putting as much pressure on the leg and foot as I thought I could handle. It was tougher than I anticipated. Moreover, when I started up the steps, I had to go one step at a time, right leg first, up one step, drag the left.

When I arrived at the top of the stairs, it was easy to understand why Amy had been unable to budge it. It was constructed of heavy planking, in all probability utilizing the timbers of one of Las Cuevas's shipwrecks. The gap between the door and the frame was wide enough for me to get my fingers through. But at that particular moment, it wasn't the massiveness of the door that bothered me, it was the smell of smoke.

Rowland was a damn fool, but he had kept his word. He had set the hotel on fire.

Journal No. 11

Sunday, June 14

Four things happened in rapid succession. First, I started shouting at Amy to let her know I could smell smoke and tell her it looked like Rowland had carried through with his threat. There was no subtle way to tell her the hotel was on fire.

Second, Amy somehow managed to stumble her way in the inky darkness to the top of the steps.

Third, we both began pounding on the storm cellar door, hoping someone was out there who could hear us.

Fourth, when things were looking their darkest, they managed to get just a little darker. In the confusion and pounding, I dropped the flashlight and we were plunged into an inside-the-coffin kind of blackness.

Amy's pleas for help were punctuated with a string of profanity, and I made a mental note that if we somehow found a way out of Rowland's devious little deathtrap, I wanted to compliment Amy on her imaginative approach to expletives and a smutty vocabulary.

"How the hell are we going to get out of here?" she cried.

"Any way we can," I said. "Keep pounding on the door and hope and pray someone hears us."

At last I heard what I thought was a voice outside. I told Amy to cool it, and we waited. Then, just as I was about to start pounding again, I heard an encore. There was no way of knowing who it was, but unless it was Tyler Rowland or Elizabeth Carter, it didn't matter. The person on the other side of that storm cellar door was a potential lifesaver.

"Keep pounding," I shouted. "Whistle, scream, shout, anything to make noise. Let 'em know we're in here."

Amy and I were still going at it with both hands when I finally saw the door open a crack and caught a smoke-clouded view of the Admiral's hollow-eyed and shriveled face. He was straining with the weight of the door, and I threw my shoulder against it and got it open partway. I told Amy to get her pretty frame out of there. She scampered up and through, turned around, and helped the Admiral hold the door open while I squeezed my way

312

out into the night air. I was coughing and praying at the same time.

Initial assessment? We had made it out just in time. The worst of the storm had passed. The wind had died off, and all that was left of the rain was an irritating drizzle. I gulped in as much fresh air as my lungs could handle and began clawing and crawling my way across the hardpan, away from the fire. When I thought I had crawled far enough, I rolled over on my back and looked up at an angry, out-of-control, red-orange firestorm. The biggest building in Las Cuevas was a roaring conflagration, and the only thing that saved us was the fact that we were in the cellar below the west wing. The fire simply hadn't progressed that far yet.

Tyler Rowland had kept his promise. He had put the torch to the building on the east side near the ice maker, and it was an inferno.

Down the street toward the dock area, I could see a gathering of stunned villagers, They appeared to be mesmerized, obviously too overawed by the immensity of the fire to do anything about it. When I finally quit coughing, I got around to asking Amy if she was all right. She managed some sort of affirmative answer and indicated all she needed was a little time. When I looked at the Admiral, his eyes were glassy and he was trembling. "I owe you one," I told the little man.

The Admiral had finished his heroics and already slipped back into his gossamer world where two and two doesn't equal the obvious and no one seems to care that it doesn't. He was sitting on the ground beside me. His eyelids fluttered like nervous birds and he was mumbling some kind of oblique orison only he understood. It was that world where the distraught and disturbed pay homage to their apparitions—the ones they are either unable or unwilling to elevate to obeisance.

Beyond the Admiral and his confused litany, I could hear other sounds—terrible sounds like the moaning of dried wood being consumed by fire and the wails of helpless varmints that had inhabited the voids in the walls of the old building.

Finally the Admiral collected himself, turned, and pointed at a somewhat misshapen, elongated bundle laying in the puddled street in front of what was left of the hotel.

I thought about trying to get to my feet, made the effort, and was punished by the residue of shark bites. The remnants of the attack were acting as if they thought I had forgotten to acknowledge them. Somewhere I found the strength to push myself up until I was supporting my weight by kneeling on one knee and waiting for the Admiral and Amy to help me through the rest of the exercise. They half pulled, half dragged me to where I could get a better look at the bundle. I was fairly certain I knew what it was, I just didn't know who it was. Someone had thoughtfully thrown a worn-out, threadbare blanket over the body.

Amy stooped and pulled the blanket off. The Admiral knelt down in the wet dirt and rolled the body over on its back. I was prepared for it to be bad. I just wasn't prepared for who it turned out to be or how bad it actually was. The body under the rain-soaked blanket lying in the middle of the rutted main *calle of Las Cuevas* was Elizabeth Carter.

When the villagers realized what we were looking at, they moved in closer and began milling around the body. I could hear them muttering.

There was one very nasty oversized bullet hole in her right temple. Someone had been pressing the muzzle of the gun against the woman's temple when they pulled the trigger. A sizable portion of the left side of her head where the bullet had exited was missing. There were pieces of what had once been a very pretty woman's face scattered around in the mud.

I've seen dead people before and I've seen people who were ushered into that unfortunate condition by a gun, but none quite as violently as Liz Carter. Maybe it was because it had been a very pretty face. The force of the slug had twisted and gouged what was left of her head into a caricature—a very unflattering death mask. When Amy realized what she was looking at, she recoiled and began to cry. It came out sounding more of a whining sound, reminding me of a wounded puppy.

With the Admiral's help I managed to get down on one knee and close the Carter woman's eyes. Then I used my index finger to trace around the bullet hole in her temple. I'm a long way from being an expert on bullet holes, but the blood on Eliza-

315

beth Carter's forehead was dry and the wound had long since stopped bleeding. Since there was no way of knowing how long Amy and I had been locked in the storm cellar, there was no way to determine how long it had been since someone had put a gun to Elizabeth Carter's head and pulled the trigger. Not that it mattered. Dead is dead.

Joyce Kilmer once wrote, "Things have a terrible permanence when people die." Knowing the details of Elizabeth Carter's final few moments on this earth wasn't going to change the outcome.

"Who did this?" I finally heard Amy mutter.

"I make it a practice never to give long odds," I said, "but I'll give you ten to one on this one: Tyler Rowland."

Amy scowled at me. Then she protested, "But she was the one who helped him. She even told me that stealing the code keys and selling them to a foreign government was her idea. They were going away together."

I shook my head. "I don't think that mattered a whole lot to Rowland. It seems fairly obvious now that Rowland's real motivation for all of this wasn't the charming Ms. Carter. His turn-on appears to be money." I managed to get to my feet, winced a couple of times in the process, and looked at the circle of villagers. Most were women. There were two or three old men and a like number of children. "Did anyone see how this happened?" I shouted.

No one stepped forward. If anything, two or three of the women appeared to back away. With the exception of the trauma to her head and face, Liz Carter could have been sleeping. The body was still warm. Damp, not wet. Conclusion: She had been killed sometime after the rain slacked off. I looked at the Admiral and asked him how long it had been since it quit raining.

No answer. In all probability, the Admiral had already had his brief period of lucidity for the day. He was staring off into space, oblivious to what was going on around him.

"Senor, I saw what happened," a small voice said. The English was barely understandable. I looked up and saw a frail girl. No more then ten, probably younger. She was standing next to the kneeling Amy.

"You speak *inglés*?"

"She does," an older woman spoke up, "but she is frightened." She had moved in beside the girl and put her arm around her shoulder. "I am her *madre*. She saw what happened. She came in the house and told me she saw a man shoot a woman."

"Did your daughter recognize the man?" I pressed.

The girl's mother shook her head. "She said the man was not from the village."

Only then did it dawn on me that I hadn't seen any of the fishermen in the village. No Carlos. No Viktor. No Bo Bo. And no sign of Poker either. With the realization came a very ugly sensation in the pit of my stomach. It turned over a couple of times, and there was a twisting, tightening feeling. I only had one good leg, and the knee in that one went weak. Amy looked at the little girl's mother and asked her if she had seen the men. Apparently, she had run out of English. She answered in the peculiar kind of Castilian Spanish and Cal Mex spoken in Las Cuevas.

Amy did the interpreting. "She said not since she saw the man and the dead woman march several of them down to the dock area when the storm started to back off."

Less then a hundred yards back up the *calle*, the fire in the old hotel was continuing to ravage what was left of the two-story building. The pyrotechnics were over. All that was left now was the systematic devouring of the minute details and treasures that survived the initial inferno. Some of the women were crying, and I heard one child ask if the fire had destroyed the Coke machine.

I knew I couldn't make it on one leg, so I helped Amy to her feet and asked her to take anyone that was willing down to the docks to look for Poker and the others. Then I turned to the girl's mother and asked her to inform the authorities.

Now we had two bodies, the Carter woman and the Admiral's friend Rainbow. I didn't like having those kind of thoughts, but I knew it was entirely possible that we could have a lot more when we located the men Rowland and Carter had taken down to the dock. From the looks of things, the Mexican *policía* could be in for a long night when they got here.

318

It wasn't until I turned to watch the flames again that I saw what appeared to be another body near the burned-out ruins of the hotel's long porch. When I saw it, I had that nightmarish sensation a person gets when they realize the unfolding tragedy had just claimed someone special. It was Marie.

It was nearly ten o'clock in the morning by the time *la policía* arrived and took control. By that time a few rays of good news had managed to filter through the post-storm aftermath. Amy and a handful of villagers had located and released the quartet of Carlos, Bo Bo, Poker, and Viktor. Rowland and Carter had marched them down to the pier at gunpoint, tied them up, and locked them in the fishhold of one of Carlos's fishing trawlers. If Amy hadn't found them, they might very well have died there. Why Rowland had decided not to lock them in the basement of the hotel along with Amy and me was another puzzle. Maybe he figured that between the six of us we were more likely to find a way out. Since none of the men had been harmed beyond a few cuts and bruises, I had the feeling that Elizabeth Carter had talked Rowland out of doing anything beyond locking them up.

Apparently, that was where her powers of persuasion had ended. Unfortunately, she hadn't been able to talk him out of shooting her.

Despite having spent a number of hours bound, gagged, and left to die in the fishhold of a nearly fifty-year-old fishing trawler, the men were in surprisingly good physical and mental shape. One by one the Mexican authorities took their statements, and by the noon hour, the magnitude of what had happened to the tiny village had started to sink in. One of the village favorites had been murdered, the hotel was in ruins, and the buildings on each side of it showed the effects of the fire as well. Both Carlos and Bo Bo had tears in their eyes as they surveyed the damage. I suspect some of those tears were for Marie. Jean Jean did what she could to console the Admiral, and Viktor, refusing to look anywhere but straight ahead, reverted to being the stoic Bolshevik.

By one o'clock in the afternoon an ambulance, or the closest thing the Mexican authorities could find to one, arrived from La Paz, and I was packaged, along with the bodies of Rainbow, Marie, and Elizabeth Carter, for the trip back to the Baja Sur's version of a busy city. I was informed I was being taken to the central clinic in La Paz where I would be treated for shark bites and held for further questioning. Amy and Poker, seemingly of little interest to *la policía* and relatively unscathed by what had happened, indicated they would secure the remaining submersible and follow in the rental car.

Six hours after I arrived in La Paz, the doctors were through with me. My leg and foot had been cleaned and stitched up. It looked like a multicolored patchwork quilt. I had been injected with enough painkillers that I was semisociable even to the doctor who insisted I try to stand up and walk on it. Devout coward that I am, when it comes to pain, I am and was able to complain, bewail, and fret just enough to have the doctor double the dosage of the painkiller and authorize a walking stick. While I may not be up to snuff at lying, I am more then sufficiently adroit at whimpering.

It was nearly ten o'clock that Sunday night when I walked out of the clinic and into the arms of *la policía*. They saw fit to question me until somewhere around midnight and finally released me with that old admonition, "Don't leave town until we're through with you." (Maybe that wasn't precisely what they said, but that pretty much captures the flavor of it.)

Meanwhile, Poker and Amy had been busy. They had rounded up three rooms at the Hotel Perla and made the necessary phone calls back to the States. Amy reported that she had called her boss at Cal Maritime, and Poker, known only as Poker to my brother, had called Bro Roger to let him know what was happening.

"Did he offer to send one of the company planes down to retrieve us?" I wanted to know.

"Not that I recall," Poker said. "I think we're on our own."

Despite the doctor's orders to refrain from using alcohol while I was under the influence of heavy doses of Ligeral, I was able to coax Amy into the hotel's bar for a nightcap. As a rule, I avoid what the boys in my fraternity back at Stanford used to refer to as sissy drinks. But Amy was buying and we presided over a couple of cold something or others made of tequila, assorted other goodies, and cream.

"So what do we do now?" Amy asked.

"We call ourselves losers and go home to a deafening chorus of boos," I said.

The lights in La Terraza were low, the fans created a cooling breeze, Amy was wearing a pale blue, slightly off-the-shoulder ensemble, and her drink was cupped between her hands. She was assessing me over the rim of her glass. For the first time in days, she was wearing something other than one of those blasted designer survival outfits. Not that she didn't look great in the latter, but somehow she managed to look even better in the former.

While I tried to capitalize on the situation, a young guitarist meandered around the room doing what he could to set the mood and keep the people drinking. It wasn't working. For the most part, the storm had missed La Paz, but the patrons had been without power and sunshine for most of the day and did not appear in the mood to cuddle. Maybe they had worn themselves out already.

I listened to Amy hum along with every song and finally had to admit I wasn't familiar with anything the young man was playing. I may have been the only one. The young couple at the next table (I would have tagged them as honeymooners) danced every dance.

"Seriously," she said, "what now?"

"Well, first I go back to FSORC, admit to one and

all that while I was traipsing around the Baja and playing amateur sleuth I lost track of one half of a one-hundred-and-thirty-five-million-dollar development program, take my lumps along with assorted verbal chastisements, and ultimately return to Las Cuevas with a salvage team to retrieve the two sleds." I paused before I said, "What about you?"

Amy shrugged. Then she said, "I mean with Unitrieve."

"One of two things. If Uncle Sam somehow fails to uncover the fact that the integrity of the code has been compromised, Unitrieve might survive."

"Think that's possible?"

"Consider this: Who actually knows that Rowland stole the code keys? Hake? I don't think he'll tell anyone. Ruth Rowland is in the dark. Tyler Rowland certainly isn't going to tell, and Elizabeth Carter and George Templeton can't. That leaves you and me, I and we only know what we've been told. Why should anyone listen to us? We can't prove or disprove anything."

"But what if the government finds out that the code keys were stolen?"

"Well," I said, "scenario number two goes something like this. Jacob Hake can kiss good-bye to any money he expected to make off the CARTO Project. Unitrieve will probably fold, and some judge may even decide that Hake is the one responsible for what has happened and send him off to prison. Either way, the life of the random numerical syllabification program is suspect."

"But if that's the case, what good will it be to anyone?"

"That's the old espionage market for you," I joked, "and the risk in dealing with some bonehead who is willing to sell their country down the river. Today the information is good. Tomorrow it may not be."

Amy continued to study me for several moments. I think she was trying to determine whether or not she agreed with me. Finally she said, "Think Rowland will get away with it?"

"What's to stop him? He has the gelatin discs, the only other person who might have known what his next move was going to be is dead, and we have no way of proving what he has done or any way of stopping him. On top of that, he already has half of the agreed-upon monies from the Chinese. If he pulls this deal with the Iraqis off, wherever he goes he is likely to end up a very wealthy man. For all we know, sanctuary and a new identity might even be part of the deal."

I was fast getting to the point that I was inclined to congratulate myself. Despite being over-medicated and prone to suffer periods resembling what I had heard Alzheimer's was like, I was managing to hold my own. I was surprised at how much sense I was making, and I was hoping Amy would not regard my temporary one-legged status as an impediment to deepening our relationship.

I held my hand up for the waiter and signaled for two more drinks. Amy put her hand on mine and moved closer. I was expecting one thing, I got another. "I don't know whether this is worth anything, A. J.," she said, "but when Liz Carter told me what she and Rowland had done, she may have said too much."

"I don't follow," I said. The second drink hadn't arrived yet, but I was already beginning to feel a little fuzzy. I wasn't certain whether it was my proximity to Amy or the painkillers. Either way, my grip on the here and now was becoming more and more tenuous.

"Liz Carter told me that she was originally supposed to meet Rowland at La Playita in San Jose del Cabo. But she claimed that was before she heard about the trouble aboard the *Baja Lady*."

"La Playita," I repeated. "I know where that is. Galen and Leslie used to take me to Puebla la Playa, a tiny village across the street from the hotel when I was a kid. We spent many a Christmas there when I was growing up."

Amy sighed. "It probably doesn't mean anything. After all, that was then. This is now. Maybe Rowland changed his plan. Who knows?"

"Wait a minute," I said, "why should he? More than likely he thinks Carter was the only one who knew where they were supposed to meet. If that's the case, he wouldn't see any reason to change it."

"Maybe we should check into it?"

Suddenly I was dealing with the reality of having to take action with an appendage that guaranteed limitations. Up until that very moment I had been ignoring the certainty of reduced performance parameters. There was a good chance I sounded less than convincing when I said, "We'll bail out of here first thing in the morning. After, that is, we get a good night's sleep and I'm a little more alert."

My room at the Perla looked out to the west. Which is another way of saying the early morning sun did not forge its way into my room quite as early as it did the rooms that faced the off-coast islands. I had slept hard. The painkillers worked just like the doctor said they would. To some extent, the effects of the drugs had worn off during the early morning hours and I was all too aware that certain parts of me were going to slow me down when we started south. Still, I managed to get life and limb propped up on the edge of the bed. That's when I noted that the call light on my telephone was blinking. I picked it up, called the desk, and was promptly put though to room 314. Poker Palmer answered. "What's up?" I asked.

Poker was his usual velvet-tongued self. "What the hell happened between you and the Reed woman last night?" he groused.

"Nothing," I assured him. "But even if something had happened, I wouldn't tell you."

"If something had happened," Poker snorted, "I'd know it. You'd be grinnin' from ear to ear. Are you grinnin'?"

I ignored him and started over. "The more we talked last night, the more it begins to look like our little Baja adventure isn't over—at least not just yet. Amy remembered that Liz Carter told her she and Rowland were supposed to meet at La Playita in San Jose del Cabo after he finished his dealings with Chow Wuhan. Our plan was to get together with you this morning and figure out what we wanted to do with that information."

Poker waited for me to finish before he started laughing. "Someday you'll learn not to believe everything some dame tells you. I gotta ask you, is Hake offering some kind of reward for the return of those code keys?"

"Not that I know of. Why?"

"Because if he is or there is some kind of reward in the offing, your friend Amy Reed is out to get it."

"What are you talking about?"

It was difficult to tell whether Poker Palmer was amused that he knew something about Amy Reed that I didn't or if he was just jerking my chain. It took him a while to quit laughing so he could elaborate. Finally he said, "Amy is gone."

"You're not making any sense," I said.

"I went down to the car when I got up this morning, A. J., because I left a carton of cigarettes in the trunk. When I got down to the parking lot, one of the bellhops told me Amy had already shown up in the lobby earlier this morning and had the attendant bring our car around. He said he helped her load her luggage and she pulled out shortly after five o'clock."

I didn't tell Poker, but I felt as if someone had

kicked me in my sore leg. "I don't suppose she told him she was just going out for breakfast, did she?"

"All he said was that she asked how to get to the highway. Said she was headed south." By the time Poker finished telling me about it, he sounded less amused and somewhat more concerned. "Think she went after those code keys all by herself?"

That was exactly what I thought. I knew how Tyler Rowland had handled Elizabeth Carter, and there was no reason to believe he would be any less inhumane with Amy Reed.

"Get down to the desk and get us checked out," I said. "Then rent a car. You and I are headed for San Jose del Cabo."

It took all of forty-five minutes, but we were able to get a great deal accomplished. I managed to get dressed (no small chore with my leg), Poker hustled up another rental car, and with my old friend half pulling, half carrying me, we bailed out of the hotel parking lot with tires squealing. If the parking lot attendant was anywhere near right about the time Amy departed, a good (or bad, depending how you looked at it) four hours had passed—more then enough time for Amy to get to San Jose del Cabo and get herself in a whole lot of trouble.

What made the situation even more sticky was that we weren't all that certain where Amy was headed when she pulled out. We knew she had said Rowland and Carter planned to rendezvous at La Playita but La Playita was more than just a hotel.

It was a full-scale resort, and it covered a lot of territory. Enough territory that if she made contact with Rowland, and he responded the way I expected him to, Amy Reed, or what was left of her, could be almost anywhere. Not only were we in danger of losing Amy, we were in danger of losing Rowland as well. Tyler Rowland had to be thinking that if Amy could find him, others could too. Ergo, the wise thing for him to do was make himself real scarce—and there were any number of ways he could do that.

San Jose del Cabo is 120 miles southeast of La Paz on Highway One, roughly a three-hour trip from the Baja Sur capital. With Poker driving and me keeping a throbbing foot elevated as much as possible, I had me plenty of time to figure out what we were going to do when we got there.

According to Amy, Elizabeth Carter and Tyler Rowland had planned from the outset of their little scheme to rendezvous at the La Playita resort. Obviously, that was before Rowland had a change of heart and put a bullet in his former administrative assistant and part-time lover's brain. The sum total of which only led to more questions.

One, did Rowland get greedy and decide he no longer needed Carter? Or two, was killing Carter an impulse on Rowland's part? Three, had he changed plans—or had he planned to dispose of Liz baby from the outset?

I had no answers, of course, and there was even a question as to whether any of the foregoing was relevant under the circumstances. There was, however, one question that I knew was germane. Thinking that only he and Carter knew where they planned to meet, would he believe that was still a safe place to bide his time while he planned and implemented his next move? I was banking on the idea that that was exactly what he would think. Why? Because it was far enough away from the glitter of Cabo San Lucas and the glitzy hotels along the corridor that he wasn't likely to run into anyone he knew. Plus, the kind of people who vacationed at La Playita were seldom the kind who arouse suspicion.

Conclusion? San Jose del Cabo was the perfect place to hide.

Having carried my chain of inductive reasoning as far as seemed pragmatic and practical, Poker and I began the task of dividing up the workload. Since I was the one picking up the tab for this wild goose chase and the one with the wobbly wheel who would find it difficult to get around, I got first choice. I chose to conduct my part of the search in San Jose del Cabo where the pace was just a bit slower and I was less likely to get run over by a rambunctious tourist.

Poker agreed to check out, in addition to the nooks and crannies in Cabo San Lucas, the fast-track locations like the Hotel Palmilla, the Casa del Mar, and Cabo Real along the corridor. He drove me to La Playita and dropped me off in front of the hotel. It was already three o'clock in the afternoon, and we agreed to check with each other at the same location two hours later. I hobbled into the lobby, looked around, and decided to try the restaurant next door. What I was looking for was one of those bright young American college dropouts who drift Bajaward between futile attempts at a conventional education. They get a job at one of the upscale resorts and when not working spend their spare time romancing sweet, young (I almost forgot *rich*) ladies who likewise found their way to the Baja for vacation.

Guys like that always need money.

I found what I was looking for. He was lolling around the poolside bar, sipping one of those orange-colored tropical drinks replete with pineapple chunks and a purple umbrella. He had the required "don't miss a thing" eyes—the kind that can scan, sort, and catalog the legion of lovelies hanging around the pool in one pass. He was young, blond, tanned, and looked as if he had spent half of his life in the weight room.

I headed straight for him. "Work here?" I asked.

"Yes, sir. I'm off duty right now, but if there is anything I can do to help you . . ." He was looking at my bent wheel when he made his offer.

"I'll make it simple," I said. "I want to hire you. Fifty dollars an hour. That is, if you can come up with one of those golf carts so you and I can get around a little better."

"Is what you want me to do legal?"

"Does it matter?"

331

"No, sir. For fifty bucks an hour I'd carry you anywhere you wanted to go." He grinned. "But I can and will find a golf cart and I'll be only to happy to chauffeur it for you."

His name was Chris (guys who work in resorts never have last names). He claimed he was from San Diego, went to school at San Diego State when he had the money, and spent his time surfing and chasing girls around San Jose del Cabo when he didn't. Ten minutes after we introduced ourselves, he was back with a golf cart. I crawled in and told him what I had in mind.

"I'm looking for a guy who looks like Clark Gable," I said.

Chris gave me one of those *I wish I knew what the hell you were talking about* looks and said, "Clark who?"

Which tends to lend credence to what I once told Bro Roger: Nothing worth anything comes easy and shortcuts seldom work—even if you are paying fifty bucks an hour. "He's tall, has dark wavy hair, a sorry excuse for a moustache, brown hound-dog eyes, and big ears. My guess is that if he is here, he probably checked in late last night or sometime earlier today."

Chris was shaking his head before I finished. "I was on duty last night from midnight till eight this morning. I drove the van to the airport to pick up guests. All of them came in at one time. Their planes were delayed because of the storm. But I didn't see anyone like you described."

"If he's here he drove down from the north," I countered. "His name is Rowland, Tyler Rowland."

"Would he have registered under that name?"

Chris was asking the right kind of questions. "Don't know. Probably not."

"So what did he do, hustle your wife?" My new-found friend had an attitude.

"Worse than that, a girl I know. Then he killed her."

Suddenly my new business partner and part-time golf cart guide looked a bit uncertain about how long he wanted to continue his new enterprise. "When you find him, you aren't going to shoot him, are you?"

I was shaking my head. "No," I said, "I don't intend to shoot him. I intend to turn him over to the Baja police. But before I do that, I intend to find out where he is hiding something."

Chris looked relieved. "Got any ideas about how we go about finding this guy?"

"I'll wait here while you check with your friends at the main desk. Ask them to identify anyone and everyone who checked into La Playita after six o'clock last night." Then, to make certain that Chris baby responded with the appropriate degree of alacrity, I took out my wallet, peeled off a fifty-dollar bill, tore it in half, and handed him half. "Get me name, rank, room number, and horsepower."

Search partner indicated his understanding and departed. I sat in the golf cart and waited: wondering how hard Poker was working. Chris returned

333

less than ten minutes later with a list of hastily scribbled guest names of all who had arrived in the last
twenty-four hours.

"It cost me ten dollars," he admitted. "I'm not supposed to have access to this kind of information."
He was cautious. He looked around to see if anyone was listening. "Between six o'clock last night
and now, two couples and five singles have
checked in—three men, two women." Without
waiting for me to ask, he confirmed that there was
no Tyler Rowland.

I scanned the list, interested primarily in the three
single men who had registered. There was a Mal-
colm Hemminger and a Gordon Huntington; both
had arrived on the flight Chris had met at the airport. The third had apparently arrived by some
other means. According to Chris's list, his name was
Thomas Ritter. I shook my head. Thomas—Tyler.
Ritter—Rowland. If Ritter was Rowland, Elizabeth
Carter's former love interest needed some lessons
in chicanery and deception.

"Let's check out Ritter," I said. "Find out if he left
anything with the concierge. If he didn't, get a room
number and a pass key."

Again I waited. Somewhere during that interval
(after perusing the assortment of attractive women
that appeared to frequent La Playita), I found myself contemplating a vacation from my strenuous
executive duties at FSORC. La Playita seemed like
an excellent choice.

"I got a pass key but it cost me another ten," Chris

complained. "The guy working the desk is gay. He claims that putting the moves on the salad chef is getting expensive."

Chris was somewhat mollified when I demonstrated my continuing faith in his talents by forking over the other half of the fifty. "Room number?"

"Room 113W. He didn't leave anything with the concierge, and he's not in his room. In fact, Chino, the one working the desk, says Ritter went down to the beach. Apparently, he is expecting a call and he wants it routed to the closest cabana."

That was all I needed. Tyler Rowland, if in fact he was Tyler Rowland, was exhibiting exactly the kind of behavior I was hoping he would display. Suddenly I was a great deal more confident that I could predict how he would react—sorta. Without letting Chris know I was carrying one, I made certain my Makarov was tucked securely in my belt and instructed my new partner to take me to 113W. He did as I bade, I used the key, went in, and began searching. Twenty minutes later, I emerged from the room sans the gelatin discs and tried to figure out what my next move would be.

"Did you find what you were after?" Chris asked.

"Negative. Why?"

"Your hour is up," he said. He held out his hand and I peeled off another portrait of Grant. At that point the thought must have occurred to him that I was a bit too cavalier in the manner I was passing out fifty-dollar bills. Why? He held it up to the light to determine whether it was counterfeit. It passed the test. "Where to now?" he asked.

"The beach. This just might be a good time to talk to Mr. Ritter or Rowland or whatever he chooses to call himself at the moment."

It was two miles on a sandy road from the hotel to the beach at La Playita. Along the way, Chris inquired about the source of my fifty-dollar bills, why I had a bum leg, and what I intended to do when I confronted Ritter/Rowland.

"First," I told him, "I have to make certain he's the man I'm looking for. If he is, you and I are going to pound the hell out of him until he tells us what I want to know."

Boy Chris had to look at me twice before he was able to convince himself I wasn't serious about the part where he was expected to help me rough up one of the hotel's guests.

When we got to the beach, I had no trouble picking out Thomas Ritter/Tyler Rowland. It was June, it was hot, and it wasn't exactly the height of the tourist season. The beach was a long way from being crowded. Most of the folks were the kind who take advantage of off-season rates. The man I believed was Ritter/Rowland did not appear to be one of that kind.

The first thing I noticed was that Ritter/Rowland had separated himself from the rest of the hotel's patrons. We were close enough for me to recognize him but not close enough for him to be suspicious about any newcomers to the beach.

"Is that the guy?" Chris wanted to know.

I looked away. If Tyler was watching us, my gesture was designed to make him think I was more interested in the water than in him. "That's our man," I confirmed. "Now we move in. I'm going to let you out of the cart, and you're going to walk up to him and tell him he has a phone call at the cabana. He's expecting a call, so he won't be suspicious. Then while you're keeping him occupied, I'll circle around behind him and move in."

At that point I thought it prudent to let Boy Chris know I was packing a 9X18mm Type 59 Makarov and that I intended to use it to bully Rowland into fits of cooperation. "So don't freak out when you see it," I warned.

At that point, cabana boy's eyes were about the size of five-dollar casino chips, and there was a momentary concern on my part as to whether he could carry off our little caper.

"Do you have sunglasses?" I asked.

Chris nodded.

"Then put them on. Your eyes look like a couple of lighthouse beacons." Finally I asked, "Do you understand what has to be done?"

Chris repeated the plan word for word, crawled out of the cart, put on his sunglasses, walked casually to the closest cabana, and picked up a handful of towels. Then he began his perfunctory stroll in Rowland's direction.

While all of that was happening, I circled back up the beach, came around, and was finally able to position myself less than one hundred feet from Rowland and directly behind him. So far it looked as though he wasn't suspicious.

I took out the Makarov, checked the ammo clip, and waited. Boy Chris was less than ten feet from where Rowland was sitting and had already started to engage Rowland in conversation. He was telling him about the phone call. I watched Rowland get up, reach for a towel, and start to take a step toward my new partner.

At that point two things occurred to me. First, I realized that Tyler Rowland was packing a gun. If he wasn't buying Chris's story, beach boy was in trouble. Big trouble. Second, I would have preferred waiting until Rowland was completely distracted, but it was too late for that. He was up and moving, and I had no choice but to move in. The only thought I had at that point was, *Special Project training, don't desert me now.*

Journal No. 12

Monday, June 15

Picture if you will a two-hundred-plus-pound, forty-year-old, wannabe spy smasher roaring into battle to rescue his partner in a resort-pink golf cart with a garish pink and white awning. The golf cart was a necessity. Heroes cannot nor should they be expected to hobble into battle.

If I was an unlikely hero, Rowland was an even less likely villain. He obviously hadn't read the villains' handbook. He heard me, wheeled, and went for his gun. In my mind, the situation had escalated no further than the level of a skirmish. To Rowland, the situation was obviously more serious. When that happened, my friend Chris came to an occupational crossroads. He had to make a decision and

he had to make it fast. Should he throw a body
block on Rowland, thus disarming him, and in the
process have resort management strip him of employee status? Or should he assume that the guy
who had hired him at fifty bucks an hour had more
of the jolly green giants to pass out?

Chris (I will eventually have to obtain his last
name for my expense report) made the right
choice. Rowland wheeled, aimed, and that was precisely the moment Chris made his decision. He hit
Rowland with a flying tackle that knocked the gun
out of his hand and buried his face in the hot sand.
Chris had played two years of varsity football for
the San Diego State Aztecs. I made a mental note
to call the school's football coach and tell him the
kid deserved a full-ride scholarship.

By the time I managed to get out of the golf cart
and over to where Chris had pinned Rowland in
the sand, my partner had rolled him over on his
back and was threatening to plant his hammer-
sized fist in the Unitrieve president's mouth.

"All right, Tyler, get to your feet," I growled. My
leg was throbbing, but I wasn't about to let young
Chris have all the fun. Brandishing the Makarov out
in plain sight where Rowland could see it, I barked
at him to get up. He started to do exactly that—and
without the oversized beach towel to conceal his
soft undercarriage, Tyler Rowland did not look
quite so imposing.

While Rowland struggled to his feet, Chris was
proving to be worth his weight in fifty-dollar bills.

He was talking to the crowd that had gleefully gathered to watch the festivities, telling them I was an undercover police officer and that the situation was well in hand. I couldn't help but wonder if they thought my heavily bandaged leg and foot were part of the act.

The crowd, apparently disappointed that the brief flurry of activity was over, started to disperse. I shoved Rowland into the golf cart, handed my automatic to Chris, instructed him to keep the muzzle buried in the back of Rowland's head, and we set sail for Rowland's suite at La Playita. Along the way I began to explain what was expected of him. Boiling it down to its most succinct form, it was "Hand over the discs or I'll open up the back of your head like a cantaloupe."

Rowland's lack of response gave me the impression he was not the least bit concerned about my intentions. To convince him otherwise, when we got to his room, I had Chris plant him in a straight-back chair and point the Makarov at him, and I began enumerating the list of charges I could file if he did not cooperate. Then, when I finished, I pointed out what I was willing to do if he did cooperate.

"It boils down to this. Scenario number one: You turn over those discs to me and you can probably avoid having charges of treason filed against you by the United States government. I return the discs to Jacob Hake at Unitrieve and I keep my mouth shut about that part of your plan. Best you can hope

341

for? You'll probably avoid being shot by a firing squad. On the other hand, you still have to face the music for what you did back in Las Cuevas."

Tyler Rowland may have been soft, but he never flinched. He stared back at me like he was convinced that, long before I finished my diatribe, someone would come riding to his rescue. I was still staring at him, waiting for some kind of reaction, when he started laughing.

"You should have stuck to your underwater toys, Furnace," he sneered. "This time you're in way over your head. Spin all the scenarios you want. The fact is, I have the discs and you don't. Before you go around threatening someone with charges of treason, you really should have some sort of evidence to support those charges. So why not be a good boy and satisfy my curiosity? Show me your evidence. That's fair enough, don't you think?" Rowland's sneer had evolved into a condescending smile. "If it is convincing enough, I just might hand over those gelatin discs." Rowland was thoroughly pleased with himself by the time he had finished.

I hated to admit it, but Rowland had me on the evidence angle. Elizabeth Carter was the only one I knew who knew the whole story. But there was this rather significant problem: Dead people can't testify. True, she had confided in Amy Reed, but Reed was gone too, in all probability, out spinning her wheels somewhere along the strip between Cabo San Lucas and San Jose del Cabo looking for Rowland. Finally, there was me—and all I had was third-hand information—just a whole lot of hearsay. Rowland was right, there was no one who could corroborate my story.

Rowland laughed, stood up, lit a cigarette, went to the window, pulled the drapes back, and looked out. When he looked back at me, he was still smiling. "Suppose I just up and tried to walk out of here, Furnace. What would you do? Try to stop me? With that bum leg of yours? Of course you could shoot me. But you know what? I don't think you will. After all, I am a registered guest here. Even with your muscle-bound playmate here to support your version of what has happened, I believe the authorities are much more likely to believe me than they are you."

Rowland was winning, two falls to one. If I was going to come out of this thing with my credibility intact, I needed a rally. A former inamorata of mine (before she gathered her belongings and walked out on me) once accused me of being pigheadedly obstinate. I, on the other hand, choose to think of myself as little more than mildly tenacious, or at the very worst, a bit obdurate. It was that perspective that dominated my response.

"For all I know, you've already turned the code keys over to someone," I said. "That makes you a traitor."

Rowland was becoming more and more brazen. He walked from the window to his bureau and opened the second drawer. He took out a set of binoculars, took off the lens covers, unscrewed the lens, and carefully removed the gelatin discs. "You know something, Furnace, you are very close to being right," he said. "The truth is, I have been expecting a call from my new associates for several hours now. When that call comes through, negotiations will begin. Knowing the nature and value of what I have to sell, I see no folly in assuming that those negotiations will be both brief and lucrative. Do I need to remind you that there are several governments that are willing to pay a very handsome price for what I have to offer?"

Rowland was gloating. Instead of putting the discs back in the binoculars, he put them in the now familiar brass canister and put the canister in a briefcase.

Then he continued, "Unfortunately, your untimely arrival has complicated things somewhat. Now it will be necessary for me to move on before my associates get through to me. That, of course, will delay negotiations—but only briefly." Rowland shrugged to show that it was of little concern to him.

It was my turn to laugh. "What makes you think we are going to stand here and let you waltz out of here with those discs?" I said.

"That is exactly what you will do, because you and your muscle-bound friend are not quite as clever as you think you are. When you found me this afternoon I was relaxing on the beach, correct? Did it not occur to you that that was a rather curious place for me to be?"

"My stepfather used to say you can always count on a fool to do something foolish," I said.

"You would do well not to test my patience," Rowland said. "I do not suffer fools well."

I reached around and started to pull the Makarov out of my belt again when I heard a voice say, "What is it they say in the movies, A. J.? Something like 'I wouldn't do that if I were you.'"

Unfortunately, I recognized the voice. It was Amy. When I turned around, she was standing in the doorway to the bedroom and holding a small automatic. It was easy to conjure up visions of Amy doing all kinds of things, but using a gun wasn't one of them.

I turned to Chris. "Didn't you check the bedroom when I told you to search Rowland's suite?"

My partner was wearing the expression of someone who still had a great deal to learn about being a bird dog. "I couldn't check it out," he said. "The door was locked."

I was still castigating myself for hooking up with Chris whateverhisnamewas when Amy began to explain. "Let's face it, A. J., you are just plain not very good at picking people you can trust. When I stop to think about it, I find it hard to believe how easy it was for me to rope you into all of this."

Rowland couldn't contain himself. "I wish you could see the expression on your face, Furnace. You look like the kid who has just discovered there isn't an Easter bunny. It's real simple. I drove down here, checked into the La Playita, and just about

345

the time I was ready to crawl between the sheets, I get a phone call. It's your friend Amy. She tells me she is in the lobby and she has a cop standing just outside the phone booth. Then she tells me she is prepared to shout rape in the event I choose not to cooperate. I tell her to talk fast. She says she wants to make me an offer. For twenty-five percent of the deal I'm putting together, she goes along, keeps quiet, and after the payoff, she takes her share and disappears into the sunset. I know she can't make the rape charge stick, but while I'm fighting a rear-guard action with the local police, my deal could go sour. So I agree. In return, she guarantees me she says nothing to anyone. What else can I say? Those are the cards I was dealt."

I couldn't believe what I was hearing. Neither Rowland nor Reed could be trusted any farther then I could throw them, and here they were, cutting a deal with each other. I was looking at a ship crewed by crooks and fools.

Finally I turned to Amy. "You can't be serious about this," I said. "Think. You're cutting a deal with a guy who is selling his country down the river. On top of that, he shot his last partner in the head and left her to die in the middle of the street in Las Cuevas. What makes you think he's going to treat you any differently?"

Amy was smiling. It was as if she didn't hear me.

"Aren't you forgetting he is the same one who locked you in the storm cellar of a burning building in the middle of nowhere and left you to die? What makes you think he's going to treat you any differently than he did Liz Carter?"

Amy Reed gave me what I now recognized as a patented, saccharine-sweet, and very insincere smile. "I like you, A. J. You're a nice guy," she said. "But you are wasting your time. For the kind of money we're talking about, I think I can forgive a man a few transgressions. Bottom line, the money is good enough that I'm willing to take a few chances. I like the idea of being rich for a change."

I don't know what my comeback would have been because I never really had the opportunity to articulate it. The phone rang and Rowland snatched up the receiver. There was a whole lot of mumbling and head nodding on Rowland's end of the line, and then he hung up. He winked at Amy. "That, my dear, was the call I have been waiting for. We are on our way. All that is left to do now is make certain these friends of yours are unable to follow us. Normally I would suggest we shoot them, but that would be rather risky, don't you think? Someone might hear the shots. So under the circumstances, I can think of only one feasible alternative."

Tyler Rowland may have been a little soft around the edges when it came to flexing muscles, but he demonstrated the ability to move surprisingly fast. He produced an automatic of some kind, caliber, type, and nomenclature unknown; he was holding it by the barrel, and he brought the butt handle of the weapon down hard on my skull.

Things exploded. Pain, instantaneous and ugly,

347

was suddenly the dominant sensation. With one bad leg already in the books, it didn't take much to make the knee in my good leg buckle. I pitched forward with pyrotechnics occupying center stage. I know I hit the floor, because that's what happens when someone turns out your lights very suddenly. But I was already out—very, very unconscious—and I didn't feel it.

A friend of mine back in my fraternity days used to wake up each morning by opening one eye at a time. When you think about it, that little ritual makes a lot of sense. The one-eye routine avoids dumping ugly reality on a person all at one time.

It doesn't work quite like that. My one-eye survey revealed that Chris had fared no better. He had a large, marble-sized lump on the side of his head, his eyes were glazed, and from the expression on his face, he was somewhere between dead and wishing he could die.

"Are you all right?" I mumbled.

"I—I think—think so," he said. He vaulted from the question of health to one of economics. "Am I still employed? Do I get paid for the time I was unconscious?"

"Why?"

"Because if I'm not, I plan to sue you for whatever charges some lawyer can help me dream up. There must be some law against letting your employee get the daylights pounded out of him."

I ignored the threat, rolled over on my back, managed to work myself into sitting position, rubbed my eyes, and heard another voice. It was scratchy, distant, and slightly muted.

"Over here, A. J.," the voice said.

Before I could sort it all out, the voice was pecking away again. "Why is it I think some female had something to do with this?"

It wouldn't have mattered how much my head hurt, how long I had been unconscious, or what kind of condition I was in—I recognized Poker's voice. Too many cigars, too many cigarettes, and too much cheap whiskey make the man from Massachusetts sound like he has been drinking Sterno. Poker Palmer is the only person I know who actually received credit for not auditioning for his high school choir.

I looked around and saw him slumped down in a chair on the far side of the room. He was grinning, obviously way too amused by my situation. The more he grinned, the more I was determined to inform him that he had just been scratched from my will. The sorry excuse for a friend must have known what I was thinking, because he finally saw fit to exhibit some concern. "You gonna make it?" he asked.

I was overwhelmed with his display of compassion. I managed to nod my head, wished I hadn't when I realized how much it hurt, mumbled something about being glad he was there, and watched my world quadrille around like a fraternity pledge attending his first cotillion. Then I added, "even if you are a little late."

A long time ago I learned that Poker Palmer was not one to let verbal barbs dissuade or deter him. Instead of being offended, he looked at Chris. Chris was wearing a shirt with the words "La Playita" over his pocket. "Who's the kid?" Poker wanted to know.

"An engineer I recruited for FSORC," I lied. By the time I was able to get things sorted out and make my first attempt at standing up, I was asking Poker how he found us.

"It wasn't exactly brain surgery," he said. "I started out by describing you to the girl at the front desk. I said I was looking for a middle-aged gringo who looked like he was lost and had his leg bandaged halfway up to his hip. You must have been the only one around that fit that description. Right away she knew who I was talking about. She told me you were inquiring about one of the hotel's guests, a man by the name of Thomas Ritter. I put two and two together, bribed the desk clerk to give me a room number, and spent another sawbuck to get hotel security to open the door for me. You and the blond kid were lying on the floor. Didn't exactly catch our boy Rowland off guard, did you?"

I was trying hard to ignore Poker. I hobbled across the room to a chair, sat down, and looked for my Makarov. Poker had already picked it up and checked the clip when he handed it to me. Once again Rowland had provided us with proof he was a rank amateur. One, he left the Makarov behind. Two, it still had the clip in it.

"So where is Rowland now?" Poker pushed.

"I wish I knew," I said. "Somewhere along the line I overheard him tell Amy he was waiting for someone to contact him. From everything he said, I got the impression the contact was the one who was interested in the gelatin discs."

"Amy was here?"

"She's working with him now. Apparently, they cut a deal."

Poker looked disappointed—the kind of expression a man has on his face when he discovers the girl he has just asked to marry him is a former hooker. "They're working together now?"

I didn't answer Poker because I didn't have to. Instead I watched Chris try to clear his head. He was struggling to get the task accomplished. "If you wanted to get away from here and go somewhere else," I asked him, "how would you do it?"

The lad was cradling his head in his hands. His eyes were glazed, and he hadn't bothered to look at either one of us up to that point. Without looking up, he said, "Fly."

"Fly where? On what?"

"On Mexicana. Mexicana flies about anywhere you want to go—Mexico City, Guadalajara, Puerto Vallarta, Mazatlan. If the two of them are on the run and want to get lost, I can't think of a better place than Mexico City."

I winced. Ten, maybe twelve million people in

Mexico City, and that was only the ones the Mexican government was able to count.

"On the other hand, there are a couple of small airstrips where the two of them could charter someone to fly them to the mainland," Chris volunteered.

I still wasn't thinking clearly enough to try to put some kind of rational "find Rowland" plan together. To get things rolling, Poker hustled, pulled, and tugged Chris and me out into the fresh air where we could feel and smell the breeze off of the Bahia San Jose del Cabo. Eventually, the cobwebs and fuzzy images started to fade. I was still nursing a mild headache, but the bottom line was I was beginning to feel at least halfway capable.

Fifteen minutes later we were back in the lobby of the hotel and the young woman behind the desk was struggling to relay a message. Her English wasn't that much better than my ability to handle the combination of Cal Mex and Baja Spanish. She rolled the message by me twice, and when Chris realized I was still struggling, he interpreted.

"Rosa says there was a phone call for you from some man out at the little airfield on the road to Pueblo la Playa."

"Pueblo la Playa?" I repeated.

Chris nodded, "Loosely translated, it means the San Jose del Cabo beach east of here."

"What's the message?"

Chris shrugged. "No message. He says someone left something for you at the airport."

* * *

By the time Poker retrieved our Avis rental car, picked Chris and me up, and drove to the airfield, it was pushing eight-thirty. There was still plenty of sunlight, but the world consisted of long shadows and the day had finally started to cool.

We parked in front of a single-story, sun-baked building that looked as if it had been periodically sandblasted by the *caliente* Baja winds. A sign over the entrance to the building read *aerodromo,* and the building was fronted by two premodern Pemex gas pumps. One was for aviation fuel, the other for automobiles. The runway was hardpan, and there were two outbuildings, both rusty Quonset huts sadly in need of repair. From the looks of the place, business was either slow or nonexistent. I had never seen an airfield before that didn't have airplanes.

With the exception of two large dogs sleeping on the porch in front of the building, the place looked deserted. I hobbled in and found an old man sitting behind the counter. He was listening to a Mexican League baseball game.

"My name's Furnace," I said. "The people at La Playita said someone left something here for me."

The old man studied me for several moments, squinting, blinking, probably trying to determine if I fit the description of whoever left whatever it was. When he decided I passed inspection, he motioned for me to follow him. He limped, and I hobbled the hundred feet or so to the larger of the two Quonset huts. The garage-type door was padlocked, and the old man fumbled around for several moments try-

ing to find the right key. When he finally managed
to get the door open, I realized what my package
was. The building contained one dusty, dark blue
Chevrolet Cavalier. It was the one I had rented at
the La Paz airport a few days earlier—and the one
Amy had driven from La Paz to San Jose del Cabo
earlier that day.

I really can't tell you what I was expecting, but a
dirty two year-old rental Chevrolet was a bit of a
disappointment. Amy had left the car window
down, and a giant gray-black tarantula was dozing
on the driver's seat, oblivious to the heat. I walked
slowly around the car trying to figure out why Amy,
with major-league larceny on her mind, would
bother with making certain a rental car was returned. I was still trying to work my way through
that question when I realized there was a brown
business envelope lying on the car's dash. My ini-
tials were on the envelope. I opened it and found
two keys—one for the ignition, one for the trunk.
When I opened the trunk, I recoiled.

Tyler Rowland was curled up in the fetal position.
His eyes were open, but the bullet had entered his
skull under his chin and exited through the top of
his head. There was a very large and very messy
hole where the top of his head had once been, and
the crop of dense, wavy dark hair was matted with
a thick crust of red-black blood.

I am not now nor have I ever been the kind who
vows to get even. I would not have made a good
vigilante. I've learned that life has a way of getting

even with wrongdoers without my determination to intervene. Nor do I like to think of myself as someone who enjoys seeing someone who has parceled out his own special brand of misery get what's coming to him. But for some reason, this time it was different.

I wasn't gloating, and I wasn't particularly overjoyed to see how someone had decided to reward Tyler Rowland for all his transgressions. But I had to admit they had done an excellent job of it. When you bury the muzzle of a revolver in the soft flesh under someone's chin and pull the trigger, the outcome is seldom in doubt.

Rowland was clutching a brass canister. I took it out of his hand and opened it. The gelatin discs containing the code keys for the random numerical syllabification CARTO Project were intact.

But there was one more surprise—there was a note in the canister as well. Keep in mind I usually only get notes from my paper boy reminding me I owe him for three back weeks of the *Chronicle*.

A. J.
I suppose you can tell. This is the first time I shot someone. In all honesty, though, it was easier than I thought it would be.
By now you've found the discs. Thought everything would go down better if I returned them. I really don't need them.
I hope the car rental people aren't too upset about the mess I made in their trunk.

As it turned out, Rowland was an even bigger fool than I thought he was. What an ego. He actually thought I was more interested in him than I was the money.

Can you believe it, he even told me where the money was—the partial payment Wuhan paid him.

It didn't quite turn out like I thought it would. I suppose when you tell the people at Cal Maritime what happened they'll figure out that I'm not coming back.

Well, it's off to wherever. Look me up if you ever get there. After all, I'm a rich girl now. It always has been a money thing with me. This time it was just too much to resist.

Affectionately,
Amy

We had to wait until the following morning to catch a flight back to San Francisco. The police investigation at that little airport didn't take all that long. I removed the canister long before the police arrived, paid off Chris whateverhislastnamewas, and concocted a very believable story for the police. I wasn't the one who informed them about Rowland's killer, and neither did Poker. We didn't have to. The old man at the airport did that. The only time he was coherent throughout the entire police interrogation was when he talked about Amy. I understood. Amy Reed could do that to a man.

The Baja Conspiracy

We caught a flight to San Diego and changed planes for SFO. While we waited for our flight, I bought a copy of the *Los Angeles Times*. On the third or fourth page, down in the corner, I found a news item with the dateline Los Mechis, Mexico. It reported the crash of a small aircraft in the Gulf of California. According to the article, the plane was en route from San Jose del Cabo to Los Mechis. The plane's occupants, a pilot and one passenger, were reported missing.

I didn't say anything to Poker, but do you suppose . . . ?

THE
JAKARTA
PLOT
R. KARL LARGENT

The heads of state of the world's most powerful nations—the United States, Russia, Japan, Great Britain, Germany, and France—are meeting in Jakarta, on the island of Java, to issue a joint declaration to the Chinese government. China must stop its nuclear testing or face the strictest sanctions of the World Economic Council. But a powerful group of Communist terrorists—with the backing of the Chinese government—attack the hotel in which the meeting is taking place and hold the world leaders—including the Vice President of the United States—hostage. The terrorists have an ultimatum: The WEC must abandon its policy of interference in the Third World . . . or one by one the hostages will die.

____4568-0 $5.99 US/$6.99 CAN

R. KARL LARGENT

RED WIND

When a military jet goes down off the California coast, killing the Secretary of the Air Force, it is a tragedy. When another jet crashes with the Undersecretary of State on board, it becomes cause for investigation. When a member of the State Department is found shot in the back of the head, his top-secret files missing, it becomes a national crisis. The frantic President turns to Commander T. C. Bogner, the only man he can trust to uncover the mole and pull the country back from the brink before the delicate balance of power is blown away in a red wind.

___4361-0 $5.99 US/$6.99 CAN

Dorchester Publishing Co., Inc.
P.O. Box 6640
Wayne, PA 19087-8640

Please add $1.75 for shipping and handling for the first book and $.50 for each book thereafter. NY, NYC, and PA residents, please add appropriate sales tax. No cash, stamps, or C.O.D.s. All orders shipped within 6 weeks via postal service book rate. Canadian orders require $2.00 extra postage and must be paid in U.S. dollars through a U.S. banking facility.

Name_____
Address_____
City_____State_____Zip_____
I have enclosed $_____ in payment for the checked book(s).
Payment <u>must</u> accompany all orders. ❑ Please send a free catalog.